CHARES _AND THE_ COLOSSUS

XENOS ODIOUS

"Shall we perish from all annals of history, or shall we forge
a symbol of man so great, even the gods shall bow to it?"
–Zotikos

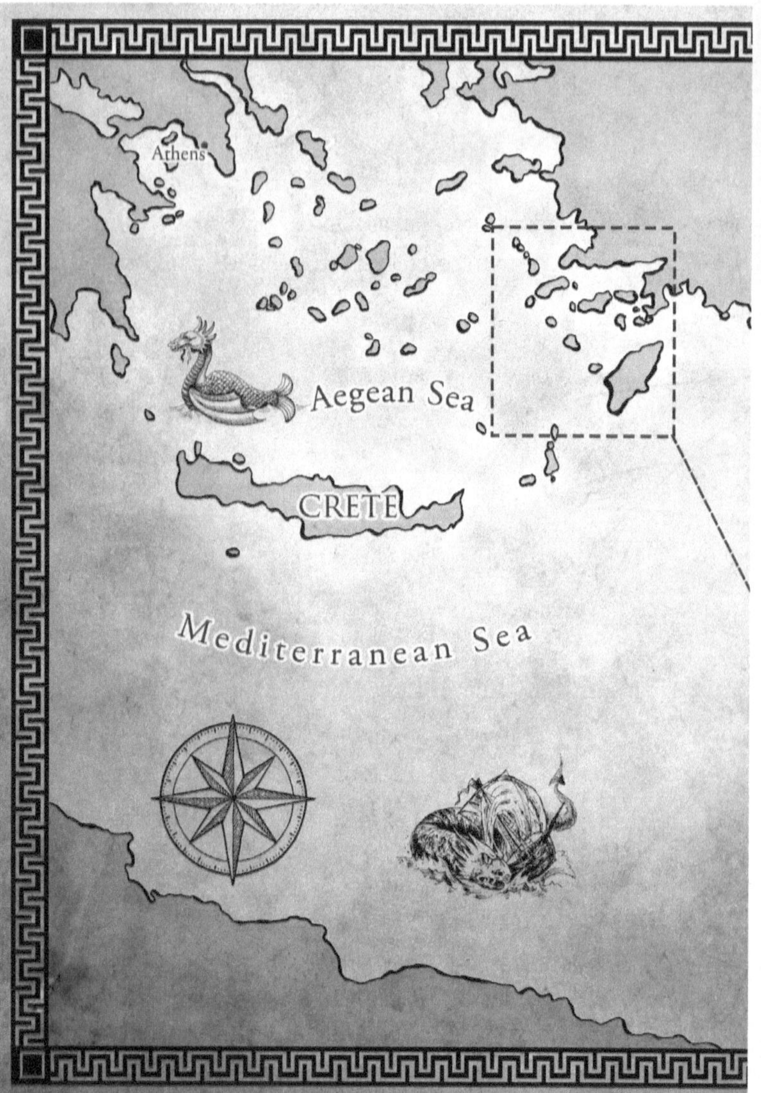

Athens
Aegean Sea
CRETE
Mediterranean Sea

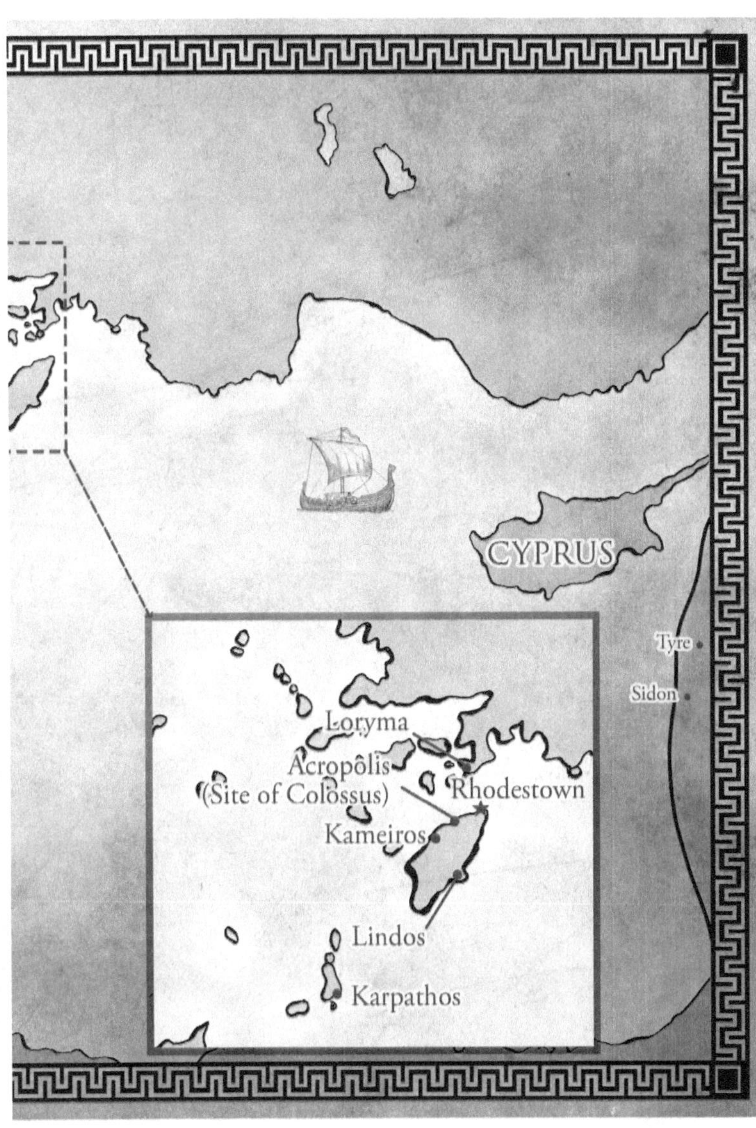

CYPRUS
Tyre
Sidon
Loryma
Acropôlis
(Site of Colossus)
Rhodestown
Kameiros
Lindos
Karpathos

CHAPTER 1

T HE WORLD OF MAN WAS smaller, the Earth vastly empty compared to the world we know today. It was a time when people were counted by thousands, not millions. Traveling from one city to the next was measured by weeks, not hours. While philosophers shared their doctrines and their theories of man's existence, others searched feverishly for a sign from the gods and worshipped things from the mighty sun to a wooden figurine found in the dirt. As centuries passed and no sign came, man created gods of their own until the sun, stars, Earth, and all upon it became man's. Empires soon formed and weaker civilizations were crushed.

The empire of Alexander the Great proved no different. Extending over three continents and millions of square miles, a significant portion of the world's population fell under his rule. After his untimely death while his only child was still in the womb, Alexander's empire cracked. His most trusted general and companion, Antigonus, fought to keep the Macedonian empire intact while declaring himself the new king and rightful heir of Alexander. The separatists, Ptolemy, Cassander, and Seleucus, began establishing kingdoms of their own.

In the middle of the struggle sat the small island of Rhodes. Its people remained neutral through the conflict, careful not to disrupt their many trade routes. However, the friendship between the magistrate of Rhodes and Ptolemy became of major concern for the new Macedonian king. Antigonus feared the island's many merchant and warships, the largest fleet in the Mediterranean, could be easily garrisoned by the separatists. After a failed assault against Egyptian ruler Ptolemy, Antigonus ordered his son Demetrius to attack the island and its many vessels. And so it was in the year 305 BC that Demetrius left the seaside village of Loryma and, with his three hundred and fifty vessels and sixty thousand soldiers, closed in on the merchant island of Rhodes.

The sound of creaking boards and oars smacking the water surrounded the men as they rowed in perfect unison. The wind pushed hard into the sails as the fleet moved hastily across the Aegean.

In the lead vessel, Demetrius stared into the distance, waiting for the island to appear on the horizon. "We'll make these Rhodians pay for not joining our cause, General," he said to the tall, dark-haired man standing beside him.

"Yes, we will, my lord," General Alkomis replied. "There is no doubt they will be informed of our approach by the merchants."

"I suppose, but no matter. They only have a garrison of a few thousand men," replied Demetrius. He pulled his sword and held it in front of him. "I will drive this sword into the heart of the Rhodian magistrate for turning his back on us." He swiveled his sword in his hand, then lunged forward, piercing the air. "Ptolemy, Cassander—they will all pay." He returned his sword to the baldric hanging over his left shoulder.

"They will indeed, my lord," replied Alkomis as the two men fixed their gaze across the Aegean.

Moments later, Demetrius spotted the island in the distance and ordered the banner up to signal the ships. He placed his hand on Alkomis's shoulder. "Prepare the men for a land battle, General. I will see to it the harbor and vessels crumble to the depths of the Aegean."

Alkomis kneeled before Demetrius. "Yes, my lord," he said before rising and spinning on his heel to board a skiff that would carry him to his quadrireme warship, a massive vessel featuring two rows of oarsmen with two men on each oar.

Demetrius tightened his armor, then adjusted his crown upon his thick brown hair. Made of bronze, the crown fancied a smooth one-inch band with several two-inch appendages rising from it. These attachments were also cast in bronze, in the shape of deer antlers. He stared across the water before noticing the long, dark hair of Alkomis and his shiny armor passing by on the small skiff.

The man stood, holding his helmet to his side, then raised his hand upon spotting his lord.

Demetrius raised his hand in return and grinned before stepping toward the stern to stand alongside the helmsman.

With the blow of a horn, the men scurried across the deck to their battle positions. The sails were lowered on the supply ships, letting the war vessels lead the way. Nearly half of the vessels followed Alkomis while the remaining ships followed Demetrius as he navigated to blockade the harbor.

The turquoise water of the Aegean surrounding the rocky heights, tranquil coves, golden beaches, and seemingly endless warm, sunny days made life on the island of Rhodes calm and fulfilling. The island remained far away from the constant threat of war like the landlocked empires and unfortunate city-states caught between them. They had a democratic system of government with a simple and relaxed approach to life. The Rhodians owed their comforts to the island's creator and protector, the sun god Helios. As an independent city-state with several small villages and ports around the island, they were free to trade among all nations surrounding the Mediterranean Sea. Their vast network of ships carried goods across the waters, establishing many trade routes. By 305 BC, almost all of the goods delivered in the eastern Mediterranean were delivered by Rhodian ships.

It was in the island's best interest to remain neutral during the recent fighting between Alexander's top generals. When approached by Antigonus to supply ships during his attack of Ptolemy in Egypt, Leonidas, the island's magistrate, had refused. After Antigonus's embarrassing defeat a few months later, the Rhodians were on edge, fearing the Macedonian king would seek revenge against the island. In preparation, the city-state reinforced its defenses by placing artillery along the city walls and on ships specially outfitted with raised platforms to support the weapons. They also fortified two small peninsulas reaching out into the harbor and added sentries and hundreds of hoplite soldiers to the garrison, bringing the total to just over five thousand.

Among these new soldiers was a man by the name of Chares who lived in the small fishing village of Lindos, located on the eastern shore of the island. He didn't consider himself a soldier and really wanted no part of it. However, in response to the growing threat facing the island, all able-bodied men were trained and outfitted.

Chares, a sculptor by trade, attended the school of Argos and Sicyon and was a pupil of the famous Greek sculptor Lysippus. He spent most days making busts for the wealthier civilians of the island, but for now, he had to put his craft aside for hoplite training and phalanx formation, known as *othismos aspidon*, the push of shields. After a grueling month, he realized his lack of skill as a soldier would put him in harm's way if they were indeed attacked by the well-seasoned Macedonian armies. On his final day of training, his use of the spear and sword seemed to be none better than when he'd started. In light of that, his plan remained simple. Hide.

After the day's training ended, his battalion leader, Lykus, had the new recruits line up for their positions. Lykus walked along the row of men, handing each a metal token signifying not only where they would be positioned but the weapon they would use.

As Lykus neared, Chares anxiously awaited his orders. Understanding a garrison of reserves would be placed in the heart of the city, he prayed to Helios that he would be positioned there.

Lykus stopped in front of Chares and handed him a bronze token marked *Spear-Infantry IV*. Area IV was on the eastern mole, extending into the harbor and well beyond the city walls. It was considered the most dangerous position and expected to suffer the highest number of casualties.

Chares's heart sank, and he stuttered, "C-Com-Commander, sir." He stepped nervously toward Lykus, holding out his token while pointing to the writing on it. "Sir, this says infantry four and—"

The battalion leader faced him and pointed toward the ground. "Back in line!" he shouted.

Chares immediately took a step back and stood up straight.

Lykus continued walking, stopping in front of the next soldier in line.

Still distraught, Chares's brow creased while he bit his lip.

After the final man received his orders, the commander addressed the men. "Fall out and form a line to acquire your weapons. I need all area one and two to report over there," said Lykus, pointing to his left. "And three and four over there," he added pointing to his right. "Now move!"

Lines of soldiers scurried to the armaments area and stood waiting their turn to receive their weapons. Helmets and armor were only for the soldiers who could afford it. Luckily, Chares had completed a few busts the month before and had the money to buy a full outfit.

"What position did you get?" asked Chares to the man standing next to him.

The soldier showed Chares the token he'd received. "Area two."

The man's position at the wall along the catapults and archers was not the perfect spot, but much better than his own. "Would you like to trade?" asked Chares, holding up his token.

The man glanced at the coin and chuckled. "No, I certainly would not," he replied, stepping away.

"I will make a fine bust for you, if you reconsider?" asked a desperate Chares.

The man kept walking, shaking his head.

Chares then noticed a man who lived just down the street

from him in Lindos. He had befriended the man and his wife several years ago, during a festival honoring Helios. As the man came slumping by, Chares called to him, "Kleitos!"

The man stopped and raised his head.

"What area did you get?"

Kleitos drew a deep breath. "Spearman, area four," he replied in a monotone voice and continued walking.

Chares sighed. "Ugh, you're with me. Sorry to hear that." He tapped his foot, observing the men gathering around the weapons table while looking for a young, strong, and fearless recruit who would possibly trade him. Moments later, he was pushed from behind.

"What's the matter, soldier? You need a special invitation?" grumbled Lykus.

"No, Commander, sir. I'd like to thank you for positioning me in four," replied Chares, regaining his stance.

Lykus smirked. "Is that right?"

Chares nodded. "Oh, yes, sir. It's just wonderful." He turned and stepped forward.

Lykus grabbed his shoulder, stopping him. "Glad to hear it, soldier. I personally saw to it you received position four, same area I'm stationed, so I will see you there," he said, releasing Chares's shoulder. "Now, go get your fancy uniform."

Chares stood frozen as Lykus stepped away, then he rubbed the back of his neck, realizing his idea of trading positions was no longer a possibility. He was the last to receive his spear, helmet, and armor. The shiny armor and helmet were decorated with an eagle accent fastened to it. He grinned at the bronze breast plate's squarish sculptured chest as he lowered the piece over his shoulders.

A few men standing nearby took notice of his uniform and laughed.

Chares glared at the men. "You will be wishing you had this armor and helmet once the battle begins," he said confidently, placing the helmet on his head. After securely fastening the uniform, he lifted his spear and made a few lunges. He glanced over at a soldier still staring at him.

"What a waste of armor," the man said, pointing and laughing once again.

Chares shook his head. "Imbecile," he mumbled under his breath. He looked to his left and noticed his battalion leader glaring at him.

Lykus then looked down the line of soldiers. "Having completed your hoplite training, you men are free to return home. When you hear the horn, you will return here. Do you understand?"

"Yes, sir," the soldiers replied.

"I assure you, any man who does not return will face something far greater than the Macedonians. Got it?"

"Yes, sir."

"All right then, move out."

Chares dropped his shoulders and stepped toward the gate. As he strolled through town in his uniform, many people stared. Confident no one could recognize him with his helmet on, he walked with purpose and gazed stoically ahead, pushing out his chest as he followed the dusty city street to the winding road leading directly to his home. As he walked, he felt something he'd never felt before. Tough. Soon, the houses he passed became more familiar, until he finally saw his own in the distance.

Chares's home sat a couple hundred cubits from shore

in the small village of Lindos. The two-bedroom home constructed of wood and stone consisted of a dining room, kitchen, sitting room, and central courtyard. He'd purchased the place upon first arriving in Rhodes a little over eight years ago. In his early twenties at that time, he'd met Pythia and been smitten by the young woman. He eventually gained favor of her father by routinely helping the man maintain his fishing vessels. After a series of gifts were exchanged between them, a dowry was given to Chares by Pythia's father, approving the match. She moved in with Chares a month after they were married. Pythia, by most accounts, carried herself rather well. She had dark hair, chestnut eyes, full breasts, and long legs. Among her many physical attributes, he enjoyed the woman's quick-witted sense of humor and boisterous laughter the most. From a charming giggle to her unrestrained full belly laugh, Chares simply could not get enough of her. To his concern though, the wandering eyes of men gravitated her way quite frequently. She was rather tall, standing nearly four cubits, and even though Chares claimed to be taller, deep inside, he knew they were about the same height.

The happy couple both wanted children, but as the years passed, they lost all faith that it would ever happen. They did quite well financially for a while, but work had slowed for Chares and money became tighter. Pythia had a voracious appetite for jewelry, figurines, and garments, making it difficult for him to keep up with her spending habits. She additionally provided money to a religious cult following the deities of Cabeiri and Telchines gods and was also friendly with a gymnosophist named Zotikos who similarly always had his hand out. Chares greatly distrusted Zotikos and his constant presence around his wife bothered him terribly. Between the cult, Zotikos, and the constant financial strain, the once loving and inseparable couple had slipped into a bickering and unhappy partnership.

CHAPTER 2

P YTHIA SAT ON A BLANKET in the central courtyard located directly behind her and Chares's home, pouring wine for herself and Zotikos, who lay beside her. The two spent most of the afternoon together like they had many times before. She kept a close watch on the door leading to her elderly neighbor's home because she also frequented the courtyard. As she lifted the cup to her lips with her right hand, her left hand fondled him. He asked her to do so to understand the struggles of man, which had been presented to her as another lesson. After setting her cup to the floor, he asked her to disrobe and lay beside him. She did as he instructed, and within moments, his hand caressed her breast.

Zotikos smiled at her while resting on his elbow, his head in his palm. "Close your eyes, Pythia," he said, moving his hand slowly along her stomach. "The feeling you have right now is a constant of man," he explained. "The feeling of not knowing right from wrong, impulse and equanimity." He put his lips to her nipple, gently biting.

She slowly rotated her hips, closing her eyes. "That feels good," she whispered.

Moments later, she heard the front door opening.

"Pythia, I'm home!"

Pythia released the man's phallus, scurrying to her feet and wrapping a robe around herself. Zotikos, on the other hand, calmly laid on his back with his hands behind his head. Realizing he had no intention of hiding his erection, Pythia hastily left the courtyard, still adjusting her robe, to greet Chares inside. Upon entering their home, she shut the door behind her and crossed the room toward the kitchen just as Chares came through.

"Oh my," said Pythia, covering her mouth at the sight of him in uniform.

Chares stopped and stood up straight, holding the spear to his side.

Unable to contain herself, Pythia laughed.

Chares's shoulders dropped.

"I'm sorry," said Pythia. "It just caught me off guard."

"This is the required uniform for my level of soldiery," said Chares, narrowing his eyes.

"Please, come out to the courtyard. I want Zotikos to see you," said an excited Pythia, opening the door.

"What's he doing here?" Chares asked, raising a hand to his side.

"Oh, don't be like that. He enlightened me on the struggles of man," she replied, placing a finger to her chin. "I never realized a man's life could be so *hard*?" she giggled.

Chares clenched his jaw, clearly irritated.

"Come now," insisted Pythia, reaching for his hand and pulling him toward the door.

Once outside, a naked Zotikos lifted himself to his elbows.

Eyes wide and grinning ear to ear, he said, "Chares, that is some outfit you have there."

Chares leaned his spear to the wall, then looked back at the man while pulling off his helmet. "What would you know about outfits, Zotikos?"

"Nothing," the other man replied with a smile.

"I'm surprised I didn't see you at the barracks today. Or does the passion of nakedness exclude one from soldiery?"

"My value is not in war, Chares. My words are much more valuable than any swing of the sword," explained Zotikos, leaning back on the blanket and resting his head on his hands.

"Well, maybe so, but how about you keep your swinging sword away from my wife?" Chares replied, stepping toward the man.

"Chares!" shouted Pythia, placing her hand to her hip. "You will not talk to my guest that way. Now, you go inside and take off that silly uniform," she insisted.

Chares glared at Zotikos as the man smirked and waved goodbye to him.

"Right now!" said Pythia, pointing toward the door.

Chares reached for his spear and walked inside.

"I am sorry, Zotikos," she said, clasping her hands in front of her chest.

"Oh, my lovely Pythia, the only thing we have to be sorry about is being interrupted by such a simple-minded man." Zotikos rose to his feet to stand before her. He pulled her robe away from her chest and looked down at her breasts before gazing back into her eyes and releasing the robe. "I do hope his sour mood failed to distress my lady's heart?"

Pythia smiled, reaching down to caress his manhood. "Of course," she whispered.

Zotikos raised a brow while brushing his fingers along her cheek. "Shall we continue our lesson tomorrow?"

Pythia sighed. "Today was Chares's final day of training. He will be home all day tomorrow," she said, fixing her gaze on the floor.

"Meet me in the morning, on the beach. It will be exhilarating," said Zotikos, lifting her chin and stealing a quick kiss. He stepped around her as Chares walked out of the house and back into the courtyard, no longer in uniform. "That's much better," said Zotikos, glancing at Chares.

Chares shifted his eyes to the man's erection and shook his head as Zotikos continued walking in the other direction. "I think I will put a good word in for you to Lykus, my battalion leader. He's looking for a few more men," he said. "And it looks like you already have your own spear."

Zotikos waved his hand over his head, dismissing Chares's threat.

"Why do you treat him that way, Chares? You know he is my friend. And he did plenty for your sister-in-law after your brother passed," explained Pythia.

"Yeah, I bet he did," replied Chares, rolling his eyes. "The man is twisted and delusional, and I don't want him here when I'm not home," he insisted, pointing to the floor as if to make his point more sternly.

"Some kind of man you are, Chares. You know he offered to look after me while you are away fighting the Macedonians?" said Pythia, reentering the home with Chares on her heels.

"Oh, that's very kind of him. I am sure he will keep all intruders away from you," replied Chares, gripping his privates.

"You are a sick man, Chares," Pythia said, turning on her heel to head for the door.

"Where are you going?"

"The agora," she replied.

"Don't buy anything. We can't afford it!" he hollered as she slammed the door behind her.

Chares sighed, then shook his head. *Why did I ever marry that woman?* he thought, stepping toward the kitchen. He stood by the table and poured a cup of wine, then grabbed a chunk of bread resting by the oil lantern before meandering toward the courtyard. Once there, he glanced to the floor at the blanket left by Zotikos, curled his lip, and then sat in a nearby chair. The courtyard was one of Chares's favorite places. With the constant sound of waves and birds singing, he found it quite relaxing. There were several tables and comfortable chairs throughout the courtyard, as well as his work bench where he did his sculpting.

At the end of another warm and sunny day, the bright rays slowly waned below the sea. Chares stared across the water, taking in its beauty before closing his eyes. After a few moments, he opened his eyes and raised his glass to his lips. He smiled, embracing the fact that the training had finally ended. Now, he could go back to his art of sculpting. At least until the horn blows, signaling the enemy's approach and his return to the capital.

He dipped the bread in his wine while looking over at his workbench on the other side of the courtyard, about a dozen cubits away. A block of limestone on the bench sat waiting, and he decided to make a bust of himself in his new helmet and armor. He placed the last bite of bread in his mouth and walked toward the bench, setting his glass of wine upon it.

Turning the block in several directions, he looked for the best side to begin. He picked up his chisel and hammer, about to make his first strike, when he heard a banging on the door. He sat his chisel and hammer on the bench, walked through the house to the door, and opened it. There stood his nosey elderly neighbor, Medeia.

"I heard a lot of strange noises coming from the courtyard this afternoon," she said, adjusting her cloak.

"Hello, Medeia. How are you today?" asked Chares.

"Well, not very good, if you must know," replied Medeia, squinting her eyes and peeking around Chares to gaze into his home. "Is Pythia here?"

Chares shook his head. "She went to the agora."

"Well, I heard all kinds of moaning and shouting," she said, taking a step back.

"Pythia was meditating with her friend."

"You mean that pervert Zotikos?" she asked.

Chares smiled while shutting the door slowly. "Good day, Medeia."

While the woman continued her complaining, Chares listened by the door until her voice faded off in the distance. He turned and walked back to the courtyard. Upon returning to the bench, he took a sip of wine and picked up his hammer and chisel. He struck the hammer several times, sending small chunks of limestone falling to the dust-covered bench.

After an hour of chiseling and drinking wine, he grew tired. He cleaned up the workbench and himself before lying on his kline. Just about to fall asleep, he heard the door open. Chares could hear his wife carrying in items she'd purchased, and he shook his head in disappointment. Moments later, she walked into the bedroom with several new garments in hand.

"I told you not to buy anything," said Chares, turning away from her as she held the garments out for him to see.

"Yeah, just lie there, you drunk," she said, leaving the room.

"I will," replied Chares with a smile. Moments later, he fell asleep.

In the early morning, Chares awoke, rubbed his eyes, and glanced around the room. Standing from the kline, he walked to the table and lifted the vase that rested upon it. Only a few drops rolled into the cup.

"Pythia, we need water," he said, setting the vase on the table. He listened for a moment, before calling for her again. "Pythia, wake up!"

The home remained silent. He sighed, walking to her room. Upon entering, he glanced around and discovered it empty. He walked out into the shared courtyard where Medeia sat knitting.

"She left just a bit ago, heading toward the beach," she said, not lifting her head.

"Thank you, Medeia," replied Chares, spinning on his heel and reentering the house.

He picked up the large water vase and walked out the front door, then along the busy street to get fresh water. Many women were gathered around the public fountain filling their vases. Several glanced at Chares as he bobbed his head and waited his turn. A woman by the name of Alyna also stood in line, only a few other people between them, and he'd always had a soft spot for her. He had met her several years ago, and they'd became acquaintances, so he promptly said hello to her.

"Hello, Chares," she replied with a smile. "How is Pythia?"

Chares blinked repeatedly. "You see me standing here, don't you?"

Alyna chuckled, covering her mouth.

An older woman in front of her turned around and made a mean face.

"Hello, Egina," said Chares as the woman turned away.

Chares shrugged and refocused on Alyna, their gazes locking for several moments. Alyna had long dark hair with dark, compelling, lash fringed eyes. She had a broad and infectious smile. Sometimes, the light-colored chitons she wore allowed the sun to shine through, exposing a silhouette of her curvaceous figure. By all accounts, Chares found her nothing less than beautiful. Her husband Kleitos, also recently trained and garrisoned, belonged to the same group of spearmen as Chares.

"Did Kleitos tell you—"

He stopped speaking when the woman turned, stepped forward, and filled her vase. Hoping a spot next to her would open before she finished, Chares anxiously looked around the woman in front of him.

"Excuse me," the woman said, crossing her arms.

"Sorry," said Chares, stepping back.

Alyna carried her full vase of water away from the fountain as Chares curled his lips in a smile. He found himself lost in thought as he gazed at her, watching her walk away before being pushed from behind.

"Move it!" a woman said.

Chares turned and smiled. "Sorry, Lois."

The woman shook her head. "I don't think Pythia would appreciate you gawking at Alyna like that."

Chares raised his brow. "What do you mean?"

Lois tapped her foot. "Just go, and pay attention," she said, fanning him forward.

Chares chuckled, placed his vase under the fountain, and searched for Alyna in the distance, but he could no longer see her.

"Chares!" Lois yelled.

He glanced over his shoulder at her. "What now?" he asked, getting irritated by the woman.

"It's full," she replied.

Chares looked to his vase to see the water overflowing. He waved and stepped away from the fountain as several women scowled at him. "Good day, ladies," he said, walking backward while giving them a nod.

He bumped into Egina, making her drop her vase, where it broke into several pieces on the ground.

"Oh no," said Chares.

The big woman glared at him with fiery eyes. She curled her fist as he backed away, sensing she would pounce at any moment.

Chares held his vase out in front of him. "Here, take mine!"

Egina curled her lip and stepped toward him.

He turned and ran, hearing giggles from the women gathered around the fountain. Chares continued running through town, spilling some of the water out of the vase. He looked behind him several times to make sure Egina wasn't closing in on him. He slowed and chuckled about what had transpired at the fountain, then looked back one more time, thankful of the empty street behind him. Chares wasn't too afraid, knowing he could easily outrun the hefty woman, but he certainly would not be returning to the fountain anytime soon.

More than delighted with his chance encounter with Alyna, he was even more pleased she had left before he'd run away from Egina. The thought of her kept a smile on his face the rest of the way home. Upon entering, he filled his cup and set the vase on the table. He emptied the cup and then refilled it, before stepping out into the courtyard.

Medeia, still sitting there knitting, glanced up at him. "She hasn't come back yet."

Chares nodded, taking a drink of water. He strolled over to his workbench and set his cup down.

"I hope you are not planning on working right now," said Medeia.

"Excuse me?" asked Chares.

"I don't want to hear all that clanking and hammering."

Chares drummed his fingers on the bench. "No, of course not." He glanced at the limestone block, lifting his cup, then rested his back against the bench.

Medeia peeked up at him, then refocused on her knitting.

Chares sighed. "Well, I guess I'll join Pythia for a stroll on the beach," he said, placing his cup upon the bench.

As he walked out of the courtyard, Medeia tilted her head but didn't look up. "Uh huh," she mumbled.

⚊⚊⚊⚊◆⚊⚊⚊

Zotikos lay in the high grass about sixty cubits from shore, enlightening Pythia about the end of man and the time of the precipitates, as he called them.

"The precipitates will fall from the sky like rain and destroy all men," he explained. He reached for her face, directing it toward him. "Climb on top of me. I want you to feel the end of man."

Pythia licked her lips and straddled him, guiding his phallus inside her. She rocked back and forth as he reached up and caressed her breasts. He pulled her close, putting his mouth to her nipple. She glanced to her left only to see Chares walking in their direction.

"Are you kidding me?" said Pythia, slowing her hips and leaning forward.

"What is it?" asked Zotikos, raising his head from the ground.

She rolled her eyes. "It's Chares," she said, leaning to the side as his member slowly slid from inside her.

Zotikos turned to his side and began to stand up.

"No, stay there," said Pythia, fixing her undergarment and then reaching for her cloak. "I will see you later." She kissed his cheek before standing.

Chares wasn't more than thirty cubits away as she exited the brush and walked toward him. She waved as he raised his brow and stared into the brush.

"Whatcha doing in there?" he asked in a soft tone.

"I had to pee," she replied, now just cubits from her husband.

Chares looked around her toward the brush, but she turned his head and kissed him. She placed her arms around his neck as she pulled her lips from his.

"Were you missing me?" she asked, as Chares smiled. She reached for his hand, leading him back the way he'd come.

"What have you been doing out here all morning?" he

asked. He raised his palm. "I had to fill the vase at the fountain. It was quite the ordeal."

Pythia shrugged. "Oh, just walking and thinking."

Chares glanced at her. "Thinking about what?"

"Oh, mainly about us and a little about precipitations." She looked up at the sky. "Or was it precipitates?"

Chares drew his chin toward his chest. "About what?"

Pythia re him. "It's nothing. Just something I overheard," she replied, dismissing it. "But what's most important is that I am sorry."

"Oh yeah? Sorry for what?"

She shrugged. "Running off to the shops yesterday and spending money." She stared out across the water before focusing on the sandy ground in front of her.

"Well, it's all right," said Chares. "We just have to be careful, but now the training is over. I can return to sculpting."

Pythia looked away, rolling her eyes, before glancing back at Chares. "That's great, my love. It will all work out," she said, beaming at him.

"Well, if things go the way I hope, I'll get the proposed statue job in the square. It's of Poseidon holding a trident."

Pythia glanced over at him. "How tall?" she asked.

"From the acme of the trident to the base of the pedestal, about eighteen cubits," he replied.

Pythia sighed. "Well, that will help, but it's not near enough to fix our financial woes," she said, shaking her head.

"I will still have my bust work. I am sure the—"

A horn blew in the distance, bringing the conversation to a halt.

Chares froze, staring intently in the direction of the sound.

"What does that mean?" asked an alarmed Pythia.

Chares lips trembled. "They're here," he said under his breath.

"Who?"

"The Macedonian army," replied Chares, looking at his wife.

Seeing the fear in his eyes, Pythia embraced him. "C'mon," she said, releasing him before pulling him along in the direction of their home. "Let's get that shiny outfit back on you."

Chares and Pythia ran toward home, then through the courtyard as Medeia stood listening to the horn. They rushed past her like she wasn't there. Once inside, Chares put on his new tunic and armor, and Pythia handed him his spear.

"I don't know when I will return," said Chares with tears in his eyes.

Pythia smiled, placing her hand on his face. "You can do this, Chares. Be brave, but most importantly, be safe," she said, kissing him on the cheek. She placed the helmet on his head. "Look at my Chares, the soldier."

He chuckled as a tear rolled down his cheek. "I will try to keep you informed about what is happening, but stay inside until you know it's safe."

"Don't worry. I will have Zotikos here to protect me."

Chares sighed. "I have to go. I love you." He reached for her hand and kissed it before walking toward the door. He turned back as he opened it, staring at his wife for a few moments and then drawing a deep breath. "Here goes nothing," he said, steeling himself as he walked out the door.

CHAPTER 3

C HARES RUSHED THROUGH THE CHAOTIC streets of Lindos, as did many other men heading in the direction of the capital. Women were scooping up their children and taking shelter in their homes. In the distance, Chares saw a wagon with several men climbing inside. He raced in their direction, but the wagon pulled away.

"Wait!" shouted Chares as the wagon continued toward the capital. He looked in both directions hoping to see another wagon, but there were none.

He dropped his shoulders and walked briskly toward the capital. Once entering the city walls, Chares noticed many men already in position. He looked around and spotted the glare of Lykus in the distance. The battalion leader pointed to the ground in front of him, and Chares raced toward the man. Once within four cubits, Chares stopped and stood at attention.

"About time, soldier. A few minutes longer and you might have missed your chance to fight," said Lykus.

Chares tilted his head, wondering if what the man said

was true. If so, he certainly would have taken much longer to arrive at the fort.

"Are you paying attention to me, soldier?" asked Lykus, clenching his fist and taking a step toward him.

"Yes, of course," replied Chares, taking a step back. "I was just trying to remember if I shut the front door, being in such a rush, you know." He bit at a fingernail.

Lykus curled his lip. "Get your ass over there!" he shouted, pointing to a group of soldiers in the distance.

Chares walked toward the men.

"Move!" shouted Lykus, and Chares picked up his pace considerably.

Once reaching the soldiers, Chares greeted them, taking in the sight of his fellow countrymen. Most everyone had similar looks of fear written across their faces. One man shivered, and it was none other than Alyna's husband, Kleitos.

Chares called him by name and placed a hand on his shoulder. "Hello there. Did Alyna tell you I ran into her at the fountain?" He secretly wondered if the man had heard anything about his episode with Egina.

Kleitos shook his head, shaking and paying little attention to Chares.

"What were you doing at the fountain? That's the woman's job to fetch water," another man said.

Chares nodded. "Well, that's true, but I believe we should split the duties. I understand a man has his responsibilities, and while that may never change, I person—"

"Will you shut your mouth and get in line!" shouted Lykus, pushing Chares into the men as two of them kept him from falling.

His spear fell to the ground, and Lykus quickly reached

down to pick it up. He punched Chares in the chest with spear in hand. "Take your weapon and don't lose it again, understand?"

"Yes, Battalion Leader," replied Chares with wide eyes. He barely felt the punch with his armor on, making him feel a bit more confident about the coming fight.

Lykus walked along the row of men, counting them. He centered himself in front of the unit. "Men, we will be the farthest from the safety of these walls and the first engaged. At no point will we retreat. At no point will we surrender!" he shouted as the men raised their spears and swords. "There are already nine hundred men on the moles, not including the fifty standing here. When this battle is over, there will be nine hundred and fifty men on those sea walls. We might all be dead, but that's where we will be," he shouted, glancing at Chares and the rest of the men. "Do you understand me?"

"Yes, Battalion Leader," the men responded.

"All right, let's move!"

The men filed out of the gate, into the harbor, and onto the eastern mole. Chares and the soldiers marched to their positions where fortifications had already been prepared weeks earlier. Among the defenses were three catapults and dozens of archers lined up behind the rampart. Chares and his fellow spearmen filed along an unearthed area, providing shelter from enemy fire. He found himself surprisingly calm, staring across the harbor at the city about three hundred cubits away while keeping an eye on the archers and ballista being readied. Glancing out across the water in all directions, he didn't notice a single enemy ship. He focused on several Rhodian ships that had been converted into floating artillery. At least a half dozen ships had been outfitted with catapults and bronze plating to deter the likelihood of being set on fire with arrows. To his relief, he felt convinced they could hold off the Macedonian attack.

Lykus walked up and down the line, addressing the men and checking their positions. He pointed and shouted at least a hundred times in a few minutes, as Chares wished the man would be quiet. Before long, the men were in their positions and ready.

As the minutes crept by, they sat in silence as Lykus watched the wall where the sentries signaled with flags to report the enemy's movements and the number of cargo and warships approaching.

Lykus kept his men informed as the details came in. "Looks like three hundred warships coming our way," he said.

"Three *hundred?*" said Chares, leaning forward.

The men all stared at each other, mouths hanging open.

"Don't worry, men. We have the advantage of defense," Lykus explained, taking notice of the soldiers' apprehension.

Chares sighed heavily. His courage and faith in victory rapidly dissipated just thinking of the size of the approaching army. He knew most trireme warships could carry two hundred men. A cargo ship could carry almost twice that number. Doing the math in his head, he drew in his chin. "That's more than sixty thousand," he muttered to himself.

Seated next to him, Kleitos looked over with tremendous fear in his eyes and jaw trembling. "Sixty thousand *what…* soldiers?!" he asked.

Chares raised a brow and nodded.

"Oh my," said Kleitos, shifting to look over the dirt formation, at the enemy.

Chares, seeing the man's fear, decided to calm him a bit.

"It's going to be all right, Kleitos. We have the advantage," he said confidently.

Lykus walked by moments later, and Chares called to him. "Battalion Leader, I think I can speak for everyone and say we are glad you are leading us today," he said with a nod.

Lykus glared at him, walking away.

"Geesh," said Chares, glancing back at Kleitos. "You would think for a group of men about to die, they would appreciate a little friendly conversation."

Kleitos bowed his head and wept.

"Oh, sorry, not you, Kleitos. We will make it out of here together. You just stay close to me," said Chares, glancing back toward Lykus now about ten cubits away.

Kleitos looked over at him and bowed his head once again.

Chares shrugged. "Well, not much to do but get comfy and wait." He shifted his weight, finding a more relaxing position.

Another fifteen minutes passed as Chares watched the other soldiers continuously glance over the mound to see the enemy ships, but there were none. He sighed, removing his helmet to set it on the ground next to him. He closed his eyes and thought of Pythia, likely worried sick about him.

Pythia sat in the courtyard eating grapes and drinking wine. It had been a few hours since Chares left for the capital, and she was already enjoying her time alone. Her cult leader, Tanis, had stopped by an hour ago to inform her the group planned on meeting in a few days at their usual location.

The group converged twice a month and spent hours discussing their mother goddess Axeirus, protector of sailors and promoter of fertility. Their meeting place remained hidden to the public as their group was not widely accepted. Pythia had always fulfilled her monetary obligations, but the responsibility of giving birth had eluded her. The groups initiations included a promise to have many children. Pythia believed Chares's lack of manhood and unworthy seed remained the primary reason for their failure to produce a child, an idea championed by Zotikos.

Pythia had first met Tanis at the fountain while gathering water. The two women had chatted after running into each other several times. They eventually became close enough for Tanis to share information about her group, and Pythia, who always looked for purpose and belonging, had quickly embraced them and their ideas.

Chares knew of her allegiance to the group but did not understand it or even try to. He considered them to be much like Zotikos, always looking for a free handout. He hadn't hid his dislike for Tanis the few times he'd met her either. During the last occasion, while she'd talked briefly about the group to him, he'd walked away from her in mid-sentence, saying. "Yeah, that's great. How much is it going to cost for the mother goddess to protect me?"

Tanis's face had turned red, and she'd never called him by his name again. Now she only referred to him as *That Man.*

As Pythia took a drink of wine, Medeia walked into their shared courtyard and glanced over at her.

"Hello, Medeia," said Pythia, crossing her arms.

Medeia gave a small wave and found a seat.

Pythia stared at the old woman for several moments, well-aware Medeia did not like her or her friend Zotikos. "What a terrifying day, with the enemy at our shores. Thank goodness my friend Zotikos will be here shortly to protect me from the raiders," said Pythia with a smirk. She raised her glass, taking another drink of wine while eyeing the woman seated across the courtyard.

Medeia tilted her head and raised a brow but didn't respond.

Pythia glared at her a moment longer and sighed. "Well, I am going inside to refill my cup. I think it's going to be a long night," she said, rising from her seat and stepping toward the door.

She glanced at the woman, but Medeia remained quiet, lounging in her chair.

Pythia entered the home as the front door opened. She glanced around the corner, looking toward the entrance. "Zotikos!" she said, racing toward the man now standing near the dining area.

The two embraced, and Pythia kissed him several times. Zotikos glanced around the room, and Pythia said, "He is at the capital. I don't think he will be coming back for several weeks, maybe never," she explained, reaching for his hand and moving it toward her privates. "Touch me," she whispered, leaning her head against his chest.

"I can't stay. I have a lecture at the village square," said Zotikos.

Pythia lifted her head from his chest. "Can you come by after?" she asked.

"Of course," he responded.

"I want you to stay with me tonight," said Pythia.

"We'll see. Just have the wine ready, and we will have a lesson you will never forget."

Pythia closed her eyes as Zotikos kissed her forehead. "See you in a couple hours," he said, pulling away.

Pythia dropped her head, showing her disappointment.

"I'll be back soon."

"Fine. But I have a favor to ask when you return."

Zotikos tilted his head. "Ask now," he insisted.

"My group meets in a few days, and I would like you to come with me. I think it would be of great interest to you," she explained.

"I can do that. I have a couple group exercises we could try," said Zotikos, his gaze wandering about the room in what appeared to be deep thought.

Pythia placed her hand to her hip. "I would like you to hear the words of our highness, Tanis. Her wisdom is inspiring."

Zotikos's brows drew close. "Is it now?" he asked with a smirk.

"Not as inspiring as yours, but her ideas and visions are highly respected," said Pythia, sensing his apprehension.

"I'll see you later, and we will discuss it more then," he said, taking a step backward toward the door.

Pythia gazed at the man's phallus and smiled. "Don't you want to cool down a second before you leave?" she asked.

Zotikos glanced down at his erection, then back at her. "No, the body does what the body does. Besides, with the men protecting the capital, it might help the attendance at my lecture." He shrugged, followed by a chuckle. "Probably could count on more women being present," he explained as Pythia's smile dissipated. "Don't fret, Pythia. What many may want, you already have." He turned and walked out the door, closing it behind him.

Pythia walked to the table, filled her wine glass, and raised it to her lips with a smile on her face.

CHAPTER 4

FTER TWO MORE HOURS OF waiting, Chares
wondered if the Macedonian ruler had changed his
mind about attacking the island. *How grand that would be,* he
thought.

Moments later, they heard the blow of the horn. The men
rose to their feet while looking away from the harbor, toward
the open water. Countless rows of ships could easily be seen in
the distance, and Chares moaned as fear coursed through his
body. Up to that point, he'd felt fairly calm, but the situation
had just become very real. His whole life he'd never wanted
any part of fighting, wars, or soldiery. Yet here he stood on the
front lines, facing sure death.

Early on during his training, Chares had convinced himself that he could find a safe place to hide when the fighting
began. However, on the mole in the harbor, there was nowhere
to run. Any attempt to flee would certainly be noticed by
Lykus or the sentries along the city walls. As the ships drew
closer, the commanders began steeling their men for the impending battle.

Chares stood alongside Kleitos with his eyes closed, drawing in deep breaths. He truly didn't understand why the Macedonians wanted to attack the island. The idea of war seemed quite strange to him. Men fighting and killing each other. *For what?* he thought.

"Is there really so much war in this world that it can't be avoided?" he mumbled, drawing the attention of Kleitos.

"What's that?" the nervous man asked.

Chares shook his head. "Oh, nothing. Just talking to myself." He looked out across the water and saw the first of the enemy's ships a few hundred yards away. "Oh, man," he said before sitting back down.

Kleitos looked over the mound as well. He fell to the ground, placing his hands against his forehead. Chares watched the man and remained a bit perplexed by why Kleitos seemed so afraid. He wasn't a small man and appeared tough. Before seeing him shiver in fear over the last few hours, Chares would have thought twice about tangling with Kleitos. But now, he seemed far less formidable. Chares became convinced that inside the man lived a sheep in wolves clothing.

Still, feeling bad for Kleitos, he reached over and placed his hand on the man's shoulder. "Remember, we have the advantage," said Chares, before standing and looking over the mound again.

The ships were now a couple hundred yards away and beginning to group. It appeared they were fitting cargo ships with artillery. Chares sat on the rocky ground and looked at the line of men, before spotting Lykus walking in his direction. A large group of soldiers followed close behind him.

Once the battalion leader got within a dozen cubits, he stopped and addressed the soldiers. "They are mounting ballista to the cargo ships. This would be a perfect time to send out a few biremes and strike their supply boats," he explained. He pointed at several men. "You men, there…and you four." He looked at Chares and Kleitos. "And you two. Leave your spears and come with me." He turned to walk along the mole toward the harbor.

Chares and Kleitos glanced at each other, then stood and found their place in the line of men following the battalion leader. Once they reached the harbor, men from both necks of land filled the warships.

"We need at least a hundred men on each ship," said Lykus.

Chares glanced over at him and raised his palms. "Sir, I am not a sailor. I have only been trained on a spear and very little with a sword."

Lykus clenched his jaw. "You know how to row, don't you?"

"Well, yes, but there has to be men better for the task, who are trained sailors."

"I will be frank with you, Chares. I selected men I could spare. The chances of you returning are slim," said Lykus.

Chares's eyes grew wide. "Slim? Then why would we do it?" he asked.

"How about you get your ass on that boat and do what you're told!" shouted Lykus.

Chares spun on his heel and climbed aboard.

"Listen up," said Lykus, addressing the men. "Under the cover of darkness, we'll paddle out and target their supply boats. Hopefully, we will be able to hit a few before their war-ships take notice."

Lykus turned and walked toward the front of the ship, standing alongside the bow officer. About a half hour later, he gave the command to row, following the other two warships out of the harbor.

Chares gripped his oar and rowed in unison with the other soldiers.

The helmsman navigated the vessel, steering clear of the enemy's warships. After fifteen minutes of steady rowing, they were no more than a hundred yards from their targets. The other two Rhodian biremes set out in different directions, putting distance between them. Still stationed at the front of the ship, Lykus continued signaling their path to the helmsman.

Chares watched as best he could from his position, until just moments later when they were ordered to stop rowing.

Lykus surveyed the area, finding the best target. He knew the challenge would not be striking the enemy vessels but getting past the Macedonian warships and returning safely to the harbor. If the enemy's ships were alerted, the chances of making a safe return were near zero.

The supply ships they targeted were unmanned and anchored, most towed there by other ships. The Macedonian army would only return to the vessels to get rations, weapons, or siege equipment. Although sinking the supply ships would not hurt the Macedonians strength in numbers, it certainly would disrupt their preparations and shorten the length of time they could besiege the city.

For the Rhodians, it could be a costly gamble. The island could afford to lose a few warships, but the soldiers were in low numbers already. However, Lykus strongly agreed with the plan to strike first. He felt it could have a psychological effect on the attackers, believing the Macedonians were overconfident that the island would lay down their arms and surrender. But this early offensive would let them know the Rhodians would do no such thing.

Over the calm water hovered a light layer of fog.

"Forward, slow and quiet," said Lykus.

The men paddled soundlessly.

Lykus looked for the other two Rhodian warships, taking note of their position. Seeing they were closing in on the cargo ships, he gave the order to row full speed, and the Rhodian bireme raced across the water, moments from impact.

The cargo ship Lykus selected appeared unmanned. He braced himself as he gave word to the men to stop rowing and raise their oars. The paddling fell silent as the bireme whisked across the water. Seconds later, its bronze plated ram smacked into the side of the cargo ship. A loud crash and breaking of wood carried across the water, and Lykus immediately gave the order to back paddle. As the ship pulled away, he saw the huge hole in the enemy's vessel swallowing large amounts of water. After he searched for their second target, he ordered the men to row full speed and pointed to his right, signaling the helmsmen. He glanced over at the cargo ship they had rammed, watching it capsize. The crew paddled as the boat raced across the water. Lykus again ordered the men to hold their oars and brace for another impact.

Bang!

Lykus gave the order to back paddle while keeping an eye out for enemy warships. He could faintly see one of the Rhodian bireme's heading for the harbor. Just as Lykus prepared to give the order to return to the seaport, he spotted another enemy cargo ship nearby. He pointed in its direction and commanded his crew to row full speed. In minutes, they raced across the water and slammed into the unmanned vessel. They hit it with such force, their own ship rose upon it.

Lykus shouted to the crew to backpaddle, but their ship remained attached to the sinking vessel. He leaned over the bow to assess the situation. His men kept rowing, but the ship remained wedged. Lykus needed the cargo ship to take water so it would lower itself from the ram.

The glow of fire caught his eye in the distance in the direction of the harbor. A stream of fire arrows raced across the sky, into one of the Rhodian biremes. The boat caught fire and seconds later, another round of fire arrows flew through the sky, striking the other Rhodian vessel.

Lykus ordered his men to stop paddling and remain quiet. The burning Rhodian ships were soon rammed by a Macedonian trireme, as sounds of shouting and cries for help carried across the water. Smoke from the burning ships blanketed the harbor. A few minutes later, the flames disappeared and neither bireme was visible any longer.

The bow officer looked at Lykus with fear in his eyes. "What do we do?" he asked.

Lykus stood staring stoically in the direction of the harbor. "We wait. Keep the men quiet."

He glanced over the bow, seeing the cargo ship still taking in water but hadn't lowered much since impact. He remained reluctant to order his men to row until he became certain they could break free from the ill-fated vessel.

The enemy warships circled, waiting for more Rhodian ships to make a run for the harbor. To do so would be certain ruin. Speed remained the only advantage Lykus knew he had. The enemy's warships were trireme or quadrireme vessels. They were slower than the smaller bireme ship he commanded. If he could get past the enemy's vessels, they would have little chance of catching the smaller Rhodian ship.

Lykus listened to the many shouts of men in the distance. He heard the command to row, as the enemy soldiers bellowed out in unison with each stroke. Sensing they were coming his way, he ordered his men to backpaddle. The creaking of wood and splashes of water filled the air. If the Macedonian warships didn't know they were there before, they certainly did now.

The bireme inched away from the sinking cargo ship. Once cleared, Lykus ordered the men to row full speed. He could see several warships emerging from the smoke layered water in the distance. Moments later, the fire from the many arrows lit up the night sky, aimed in their direction. He instructed a full turn to the helmsmen as the arrows raced across the sky.

"Take cover!" shouted Lykus.

The men rushed to the lower level as the arrows stormed the ship. Luckily, from the last-minute maneuver, many arrows missed their mark. After a few moments, the men filed back up to the top deck and promptly extinguished the small fires.

"Row, men!" shouted Lykus, rushing back toward the bow. He looked to the stern, seeing three enemy warships closing in on them, and pointed toward the many supply ships a little over a hundred yards away. "Head into their supply line. They will hold their archers, knowing they could hit their own vessels."

As the bireme reached the line of cargo ships, the helmsman steered through the idle fleet.

Upon reaching a clearing in the middle, Lykus ordered the men to turn around and head back the way they'd come. "Port side!" he signaled to the rowers on the left to paddle while the other side dragged their oars.

The ship turned and headed directly toward the enemy vessels navigating through the anchored cargo ships.

Lykus contemplated the chance of colliding with the approaching vessels. However, this being their best opportunity to escape, he had no choice but to risk it.

Seconds later, he caught the first glimpse of an enemy vessel, relieved it sailed safely outside their own course. A second ship also emerged from the darkness, they too not in harm's way. The third Macedonian ship appeared as the other two turned around. The third vessel had time to see the fast-approaching Rhodian vessel and aimed there ship directly at them.

Lykus ordered his men to row full speed as the ships barreled toward each other. While standing near the bow instructing his men, he would signal left, but to turn it starboard. Once the ships were withing a hundred cubits of each other and visible to the enemy, Lykus gave the command. The bireme ship swiftly turned to the right as the enemy ship steered in the other direction before correcting itself. The Rhodian bireme out maneuvered the larger vessel and within moments slipped into the darkness.

"Full speed, men!" shouted Lykus, pointing toward the harbor. He looked to the helmsmen. "Take us straight to the eastern mole. Once we get close, we will have support from our archers," he said, before turning and walking to the lower deck. He stopped and glanced back at the man. "Stay on that horn, so they know it's us."

"Where are you going?"

"To help row." Looking around the deck of the ship at the

small group of men, he added, "I need everyone except the bow officer and helmsmen on a paddle." He hurried below where the exhausted soldiers stared at him with fear written across their faces. "Keep rowing, boys. We're almost home," he said as he knelt, finding an oar. He glanced over to his left and spotted Chares rowing with great determination. "I knew you were a sailor," he said with a chuckle.

A few minutes later, the sound of a horn was heard from above.

"Okay, boys, just a bit more. Give me all you got," said Lykus.

The men continued rowing until they heard the much-anticipated sound of the hull dragging on the bottom. The men released their oars as cheers erupted from inside the boat and along the mole. The men clasped hands, celebrating their success against such unlikely odds. They paraded off the vessel as the men standing along the eastern mole raised their spears and swords in celebration of their victory and safe return.

Lykus wasted no time ordering the men back to their positions. He smiled, looking out across the water at the three enemy warships lurking in the distance. His smile widened, thinking about the six cargo ships the Rhodian biremes had sent to the bottom of the Aegean Sea, three from his vessel alone.

CHAPTER 5

T HE NEXT MORNING, AN EXHAUSTED Chares awoke to Kleitos pushing against his shoulder.

"Wake up," he said urgently.

Half dazed, Chares looked around. "What is it?"

"Macedonians. They launched an attack on the western mole."

Chares stood to his feet and looked out across the harbor. There were men fighting as arrows from ships and the city walls flew through the sky. He glanced around the eastern mole, making sure they were not being attacked as well. As he searched for enemy ships and soldiers, he noticed Lykus walking his way. Chares stood at attention when the man stopped in front of him, and the group of soldiers gathered nearby.

"C'mon, men, they need help over there. They are losing the mole."

Chares sighed, then picked up his spear and helmet. As he walked by Lykus, the man smirked at him.

"What's wrong, soldier?" Lykus asked.

"Nothing, sir."

"Then move," shouted Lykus, shoving him forward.

Chares stumbled, then picked up his speed. *What a fine way to be awoke,* he thought, breathing heavily and following the line of men.

Upon reaching the western mole, the soldiers moved into attack formation. A couple hundred cubits ahead of them raged the hand-to-hand battle.

"Spearmen, form a line right here," Lykus instructed, pointing toward the ground. "Hold it at all costs." He waved to the other men standing nearby. "Swordsmen, come with me."

Lykus led the charge toward the enemy, and at that moment, Chares felt grateful he had been made a spearman. The rain of arrows subsided as the battle became man to man. The Macedonian ships that had carried the soldiers to the mole backed away, leaving their men with no choice but victory or death. The Macedonian swordsmen not only outnumbered the Rhodians, but their combat skills were superior.

Both sides fought gallantly, but the Rhodians were pushed back toward the city. When the enemy line had moved to under sixty cubits from Chares, he and the other spearmen dropped to one knee and raised their spears. Chares's eyes widened, being quite impressed with his courageous leader, Lykus, and his skill with a sword. However, the man's successes were overshadowed by the many Rhodian swordsmen falling around him.

Now a mere dozen cubits away from the outer edge of the battle, Chares's hands shook. Six men from his line turned and ran, among them Kleitos, as a few others moved back.

"Hold the line!" shouted Chares.

Lykus, now half a dozen cubits away, motioned to his spearmen. "Charge!" he shouted.

The spearmen lunged forward into the mix.

Chares's spear caught a Macedonian soldier in the side. The man turned toward him before collapsing to the ground. The battle fell quiet for Chares, hardly noticing the enemy troops closing in on him as he stood frozen, staring at the dying man. Seconds later, he was delivered a serious blow to his head. He dropped his spear and tumbled to the ground. He pushed himself up from the rocky terrain, while shaking off the heavy hit. He squared his helmet and stood to his feet, quickly reaching for an enemy soldier's arm, as the enemy swung a sword at a fallen comrade. After successfully stopping the man from delivering the blow, the two locked arms and wrestled each other to the ground. Chares dropped to his knee as the man drew back his weapon, only to be hit in the neck by the sword of Lykus. The blade pierced through more than half of the man's neck, splattering blood on Chares's face. The enemy soldier reached for his throat to cover the wound, blood racing between his fingers, before he fell lifelessly to the dirt.

Lykus reached for Chares's hand, pulling him up from the ground. "Here," he said, picking up the dead man's sword and handing it to Chares before returning to the fight.

Frozen, Chares watched Lykus take several shots to the chest and back. The smack of the iron sword against bronze armor echoed in his ears, as did the shouts of men on both sides. Realizing Lykus was about to be overrun, Chares leaped into the fray, swinging his sword wildly. Within moments, he took several strikes to his chest and head. No longer clean and shiny, the armor and helmet were battered and covered in blood and dirt. An enemy soldier kicked Chares in the chest, and he dropped his sword and rolled down the rocky seawall to the edge of the water. He lay there drawing deep breaths as the sounds of the battle filled the air above him. In no rush to return to his feet, he closed his eyes, feeling the cool water run through his fingers. Minutes later, the sounds of the battle subsided as the Macedonians withdrew.

Chares opened his eyes and rose to his feet, climbing the embankment to the top of the mole. To his delight, the enemy forces continued backing away from the Rhodian line. Both sides were exhausted, and the battlefield fell quiet except the cries for help from the wounded and dying.

Outnumbered and exhausted, Lykus did not order another attack. Instead, he formed a line of spearmen no more than sixty cubits from the enemy. "Hold them here, boys," he said, adjusting his armor and wiping the blood of his enemy from his arm.

For now, the battle of the western mole had ended, but the Macedonians held ground less than a hundred cubits from the city walls. Several spearmen who had retreated returned to the line. Lykus swiftly moved toward them, striking a soldier with the butt of his sword and throwing the man to the ground.

Fearing the soldier might be Kleitos, Chares peeked over from the corner of his eye. His fears came to fruition as he watched the helpless Kleitos slowly climb to his feet. He reached to the ground, picking up his spear and standing at attention with blood trickling from his forehead. The battalion leader glared at the nervous man and the other soldiers who had fled. Chares wanted to step in but knew that would be a dangerous endeavor.

"Cowardly bastards, to the front of the line. Now!" shouted Lykus before refocusing on Kleitos and pushing him along.

As the men moved past the other soldiers, Kleitos and Chares locked eyes.

"It's all right, Kleitos. We have the advantage," said Chares.

Kleitos and the others found their new positions directly across from the enemy's line.

Since many soldiers had moved from the eastern mole to reinforce the western side, both seawalls were now in jeopardy of falling to the enemy. The battalion leader journeyed to the capital to receive his orders. After returning a short time later, and to Chares's dismay, he informed the men that they would hold both peninsulas if possible.

Before being positioned outside the city walls, Chares remembered Lykus telling them, *"All nine hundred and fifty men will be on the mole, even if they are all dead."* And so far, he was half right.

CHAPTER 6

A FEW DAYS AFTER THE BATTLE of the western mole, not much had changed. The Macedonians still held a good portion of it, while keeping just out of reach of the Rhodians archers along the city walls. The Macedonian soldiers were supported by the trireme warships and Cretan archers, making an attack from either side a dangerous proposition.

The Macedonians continued focusing on mounting ballista onto their cargo ships. They had started the process a week before and were nearing completion. Each of the massive catapult towers were mounted on a platform across several cargo ships, standing four stories high and capable of launching hundred-pound boulders.

Chares, still located on the western mole, hadn't gotten much sleep since the battle. Still bothered by taking a man's life, while constantly worried of another attack by the Macedonians, made sleeping near impossible. When Chares did manage to fall asleep, he would have a nightmare and wake up startled with the other soldiers staring at him.

Chares wasn't the only man having trouble sleeping. Kleitos also struggled. Convinced the man hadn't eaten or slept a wink in three days, Chares felt bad for the man. Knowing how frightened he had been when first positioned on the eastern mole, now placed so close to the enemy must be horrific for him.

The sun, less than a couple hours from setting, cast its rays across the sea. Chares closed his eyes leaning back against the dirt formation. He smiled as his thoughts drifted to his home in Lindos and his wife Pythia. Even though the two bickered often, he truly missed the woman. Those thoughts were soon interrupted by discussions and movement of men around him. He cracked an eye, noticing several soldiers looking out toward the harbor.

"What is it?" asked Chares, glancing up at a man standing nearby.

"They're bringing the catapults forward," he replied.

Chares rose to his feet and looked in the distance at three amphibious siege towers being moved into position by several enemy warships. The sound of a horn rang out from the city and soldiers scrambled. Lykus moved up and down the line, preparing his men while keeping a close eye on the enemy soldiers.

The triremes released the cargo ships and they coasted closer, until within striking distance. Four boulders fastened to rope were pushed off the platform by several soldiers anchoring the siege-carrying cargo ships. Chares took a long look at the amphibious siege engines and could see the bronze plating reflecting in the sun, protecting them from Rhodian fire arrows. He glanced back at the city walls as the soldiers prepared the catapults.

It fell eerily silent as Chares and the men around him glanced back and forth, anticipating the bombardment to begin at any moment. He spotted torches moving along the line of archers lighting their arrows. The orange glow reflected into the harbor as hundreds of archers prepared to fire. At the blow of a horn, the Rhodian archers drew back their bows and held. The Macedonians did as well, and for a few seconds, it remained completely quiet.

A thundering clatter surmounted the silence, as all three Macedonian catapults launched their projectiles.

Almost simultaneously the Rhodian archers let their arrows fly as did the Cretan bowmen, followed by the release of Rhodian catapults.

An awestruck Chares gazed across the harbor, taking in the sight and sound of massive rocks and hundreds of fire arrows piercing the sky. Never in his life had he seen such a splendid display of man's military might, in just one instant. Two of the Macedonian catapult's missiles struck a cargo ship fitted with artillery. The larger of the siege engines found its target, as a thundering sound echoed across the harbor. The boulders slammed into the wall, and many archers fell to the hard ground below. Chares fixed his gaze on the three Macedonian siege vessels, as the Rhodian arrows bounced harmlessly off them. The rocks hurled by the Rhodian catapults seemed to fare better, damaging the enemy's ballistae. Chares heard men shouting and swords clattering. He placed his helmet on his head and followed the line of soldiers heading toward its source.

The Macedonian army located on the mole advanced on their position, and a hand-to-hand battle ensued. The fighting became intense as men swung their swords wildly, delivering grotesque injuries to one another. Chares, spear in hand, came to a stop forty cubits from the center of the battle. The advancing Macedonians were cutting down the disorganized Rhodian hoplites. Lykus shouted at the men trying to bring calm while waving the pikemen forward. Many stayed put, not willing to advance any closer to the melee.

Chares, locked eyes with Lykus.

Lykus's piercing glare, enough to make any man find the courage, ordered Chares and the spearmen around him to move forward as he commanded, "Make a line right here!" Then he drew his sword and turned to face the enemy.

The situation became dire as at least fifty Macedonian soldiers advanced rapidly toward Chares and the line of eighteen spearmen.

"All right, men, on my word!" shouted Lykus.

Chares's hands shook as the last of the Rhodians in the center of the struggle fell. The Macedonian swordsmen raced toward his line. Chares closed his eyes and prayed to Helios. A moment later, he heard a stream of arrows sent by the city's archers fly over his head and directly into the approaching enemy's ranks. At least half of the Macedonian soldiers fell to the ground. Relieved, Chares smiled as he glanced back toward the city, raising his fist in the air.

"Charge!" shouted Lykus, pushing him forward.

Chares turned facing the enemy with renewed confidence. He ran straight at the withering Macedonian advance, he and the other spearmen plunging into their ranks followed by Lykus and the swordsmen.

The Macedonian advance halted.

Chares's spear pierced a soldier in the stomach, and the man staggered and collapsed. He withdrew the spear and continued forward until he caught another soldier in the leg, followed by the blade of Lykus's sword into the man's chest. The

Rhodian soldiers continued pushing the enemy back toward the end of the mole.

"Halt!" shouted Lykus.

Chares glanced around feverishly for the reason Lykus had stopped the attack.

"Fall back!" he shouted.

The men moved back as a volley of arrows from Cretan archers barreled toward them. Chares ran as fast as he could, eventually dropping his spear. The arrows hit several of the men, but many escaped thanks to Lykus's quick decision to disengage the enemy. The men ran another thirty yards before stopping and catching their breath near the line they'd held a couple hours ago.

Chares looked in the distance, watching closely for enemy soldiers, then glanced at the several men lying dead around him. To his dismay, he spotted Kleitos lying motionless nearby. He scurried across the ground toward him, knelt, and lifted his head. The man's eyes opened widely as he gasped for air. Chares pulled the blood-soaked tunic to the side, exposing the man's chest and finding a deep wound.

"It's gonna be all right," said Chares, while looking in all directions for Lykus.

Kleitos tried to talk, but instantly coughed, as blood shot from his mouth. He gripped Chares's hand.

"Hold on, Kleitos," said Chares. "Battalion Leader!"

Lykus walked toward him and stood by his side, looking at the injured soldier. He knelt and examined the injury. "It looks mortal. Leave him or put him out of his misery."

Chares shook his head. "No, sir, I couldn't do that."

"Then leave him. We're falling back." Lykus stood. "Move back, men!" he said, walking away.

Kleitos looked up at Chares with a tear running down his cheek.

Chares placed the man's hand over the injury. "Keep pressure on the wound. I will come back for you."

Shaking his head, Kleitos gripped his hand tighter.

Chares wriggled his hand from the man's grip. "I have to go. I'll be back, Kleitos. I promise."

He stood and rushed toward the group of spearmen walking away in the distance. As they neared the walls, he could see they were severely damaged in several areas. As the sun set and darkness fell across the land, visibility diminished.

After marching to just over a hundred cubits of the city walls, Lykus ordered the men to stop. "Let's take cover here. Keep an eye out for enemy soldiers."

Chares found a soft piece of ground and watched the city exchange blows with the Macedonian catapults. Moments later, a horn sounded from the enemy's flagship and the ropes were cut, releasing the siege-carrying cargo ships. They were towed away from the harbor and disappeared into the darkness, the day's battle finally over.

Lykus and his men stood watching the enemy ships retreat from the harbor. Exhausted, he was thankful of the darkness. Not only could he and his men rest, but they could now move freely along the peninsula. The Macedonian soldiers still holding a part of the mole had suffered tremendous losses, and much like Lykus's unit, they were short in numbers. They both would need reinforcements if another fight were to come in the morning.

Lykus examined his few injuries as a messenger arrived.

"Battalion Leader, the commanders would like to send three warships to pursue the fleeing enemy, targeting the siege vessels."

Lykus shook his head. "Soldier, they are not retreating. They only stopped their attack because it's too dark to see their targets."

The soldier shrugged. "Sorry, sir, but after your recent success sinking the supply ships, they are requesting you to lead the vessels."

Lykus adjusted his armor. His tone fiery, he said, "Me and my men have been fighting all day. Have them bring up the reserves from inside the city wall."

"Sir, they are readying the ships now," explained the soldier, raising his palms.

"Damn it," said Lykus, clenching his jaw. He glanced around at his men just starting to relax from a hard day of fighting. "Attention, battalion," he shouted.

The soldiers gazed at him while slowly climbing to their feet.

"We are going to pursue the enemy," Lykus continued, placing his helmet on his head.

"Battalion Leader, can I retrieve the injured soldier farther up the mole? I'll be quick, sir," asked Chares.

"What do you think?" replied Lykus, placing his hand to his hip. "Now get your ass moving. We are heading out." He stepped toward the harbor.

Lykus led his men to the waiting bireme ship. There were also two other ships loaded with soldiers, garrisoned from the moles and ready to depart. Lykus and his men climbed aboard and took their positions. His soldiers scurried below to their rowing stations as Lykus walked toward the bow. Near the front of the boat stood another commander, whose men were also manning the oars.

"Some mission we have here," said a disgruntled Lykus.

"What do you mean?" replied the man.

Lykus realized the commander might of have had part in the decision to pursue the enemy, so he simply shook his head and gave the order to row. The men paddled the vessel out of the harbor, followed by the other two warships.

"If we can hit the outside cargo ship, the tower shall lean and fall into the sea. If we even sink one siege vessel, our mission is a success," the man said.

Staring ahead into the darkness, Lykus rubbed the back of his neck. The ships left the safety of the harbor, and he ordered the men to stop rowing and lift their oars. He listened carefully while looking out in the distance, making out the silhouette of several ships. From the darkness emerged orange lights as the enemy's torches lit the archer's arrows.

"Drag your oars, back paddle!" shouted Lykus, rushing to the safety of the lower deck.

The archers aboard several Macedonian warships released their arrows with deadly precision, and all three Rhodian biremes were set ablaze. Within moments, the catapult towers they were pursuing released their weapons on the biremes as well. The ship rocked violently from a blow to the port side. Several soldiers were injured by the impact, and water rushed through a gaping hole.

"Abandon ship!" shouted Lykus.

The men hurried from their seats and reached for the ladders to the upper deck. As they scurried up the ladders, Lykus removed his helmet and armor, tossing them away. They skidded across the wooden planks before he leaped into the sea.

Many soldiers followed his lead, jumping from the ship into the dark water as the vessel listed.

The burning ships reflected across the water as the floating men were targeted by the Cretan archers. Lykus dove to avoid the barrage of arrows. When he reemerged to the surface, his ship was only moments from disappearing into the depths. He noticed a soldier half a dozen cubits away, struggling to stay afloat.

Lykus swam toward the man. "Release your armor!" He reached for the soldier's helmet, pulling it off and tossing it.

Chares struggled to loosen the buckle securing his armor, and Lykus pushed his hand aside, assisting him. Once free of the additional weight, the man treaded the water easily. Lykus glanced at an approaching warship paddling toward them, while men leaning over the rail speared the Rhodian soldiers who struggled to stay afloat.

"C'mon, soldier, we have to swim," said Lykus, pulling Chares in his direction.

The two men swam the open water as the fires of the sinking vessels faded behind them. The cries of soldiers drowning and being speared could be heard in the distance as they swam to the safety of the eastern mole. Once reaching its rocky edge, Lykus looked across the water but didn't see a single soldier swimming his way. He glanced at Chares lying on his side, drawing deep breaths, and looking up at him.

The sound of footsteps caught Lykus's attention as he glanced to his right. Several Rhodian soldiers rushed toward them, descending the rocky hill to the water's edge. They helped their exhausted leader and Chares to the safety of the camp. Once there, Lykus contemplated taking out a small skiff to look for survivors, but in his heart, he knew there were none. If any men survived, they would have reached the mole already.

Of the nine hundred and fifty men garrisoned on the seawalls, less than fifty remained. After putting on a dry tunic someone handed him, Lykus angrily walked toward the northern gate of the city.

CHAPTER 7

PYTHIA AWOKE TO THE SNORES of Zotikos beside her. Usually, the woman and man slept in separate rooms, but Zotikos insisted on sleeping in the same bed. Although not fond of sharing, Pythia smiled as she looked at the man still in deep sleep.

She stood and walked to the table, pouring a cup of water. A grin came across her face thinking of her night with Zotikos. Not only did the man please her physically, but emotionally and intellectually as well. She trusted him more than any person she knew, including her husband, Chares. It occurred to her in that moment that she loved Zotikos more than her husband and would give anything to share a life with the man.

A few moments later, Zotikos came stumbling into the room half asleep.

"Good morning," said Pythia, handing him her cup and kissing his cheek.

"Good morning," he replied, raising the cup to his lips.

"Let's go sit in the courtyard," she said, reaching for him.

The two strolled outside holding hands. Pythia sighed upon spotting Medeia sitting outside knitting.

The elderly woman glanced up at them, then shook her head after refocusing on her work. "I imagine, your husband would not appreciate you galivanting around with other men in his absence," she said.

Pythia stopped walking and turned toward the woman as Zotikos found his seat on a bench behind her. "I imagine that's none of your business," Pythia replied sternly.

Medeia kept knitting and tilted her head. "Your husband is risking his life to protect our island. At least show him some respect." The old woman lifted her eyes from her work to meet Pythia's.

The two women stared at each other for several moments.

Medeia turned toward Zotikos who had a blank stare across his face. "Why aren't you out there with him?" she asked, raising a brow.

"My words are more important than any swing—"

Pythia raised her hand to the man. "Don't answer to this hag," she asserted, curling her lip. She faced the woman with her hand to her hip. "He is here to keep me safe in my husband's absence. Chares is well-aware of that fact."

"Yeah, and how do you repay him for keeping you safe?" the old woman asked, smirking.

Pythia clenched her jaw and sneered at the woman. She raised a brow and stepped back toward Zotikos. She found her seat next to him while continuing to gape at the old woman. "I pay him like this," she said, moving her hand across his lap, to his member, and massaging it.

The old woman peeked up. Startled, she dropped her needle and thread.

Pythia smiled as she leaned closer to him, cupping his

scrotum with her other hand. "And like this." She moved her mouth toward his phallus.

Medeia shrieked, stood from her seat, and rushed inside.

Zotikos shook his head. "I don't know if you should have done that," he said, scratching his cheek.

"What difference does it make?" she replied, smiling. "Chares won't make it out of there alive, and even if he does, I am yours now."

Zotikos leaned his head back as she once again placed his member in her mouth. He closed his eyes and reached for the back of her head, and within moments, he erupted.

Lykus walked through the corridor of the palace to meet with the commanders and his magistrate, Leonidas. It had been a hard week of fighting for the seasoned battalion leader, and his body ached with each step. Still angry about the catastrophic decision to send the three bireme warships to pursue the Macedonians, Lykus decided to control his emotions.

As he approached, a soldier held the door open and he entered the war room. There were four commanders, council members Cadmus and Takis, and His Magistrate, Leonidas. The men turned toward Lykus as he approached the table.

"Good to see you well, Battalion Leader," said Leonidas.

"Thank you, Your Magistrate, gentlemen," said Lykus, nodding while finding his seat.

"How many men do you hold," asked Leonidas.

Lykus cleared his throat. "Just what's left on the eastern mole. Maybe thirty."

Leonidas sighed, bowing his head.

"If both peninsulas are lost, they will have free rein to

bombard the city," said Councilman Takis while glancing at Leonidas.

"The only way to secure the moles is to take soldiers from the city garrison and redeploy them outside the walls," said Commander Ares seated to the right of Lykus.

"We cannot afford to send more troops outside the city walls. We need every single one of them for the growing threat to our southwest," said Councilman Cadmus, leaning forward.

"If we do not reinforce the mole, we can expect a full assault on the harbor, the ships, and the city walls within the next few days," explained Ares.

"We have lost over one thousand men and the battle has just begun. We have less than four thousand men at our disposal against a force of nearly sixty thousand," said Takis, raising his palms.

"We don't need reminding that we are heavily outnumbered, sir. What we need is a solution," said Leonidas. "Now, there is one man here who has been in every battle we've had so far, and I'd like to hear his thoughts," he added, fixing his gaze on Lykus.

"Well, the western mole is still occupied by the Macedonians. Any troops we send to push them off will be under heavy fire by the Cretan archers. The eastern mole we control but with very few men. If the enemy attacks there, our troops will be easily overwhelmed," explained Lykus, raising his hands from the table. "If there are no available troops to reinforce the eastern mole, I believe we should concentrate our forces within the city walls. Hopefully, our ballista and archers can hold them back."

"Wishful thinking," said Takis.

Lykus glanced at him. "Their siege equipment was damaged during the bombardment. It's my guess they will repair them before they attack again. I say we use the time to find more men," he said.

Leonidas raised his brow. "Men from whom, from where?" he asked.

"Ptolemy," replied Lykus.

"We already sent word of our situation and requested soldiers and ships weeks ago," explained Leonidas.

"What about the slaves?"

"What about them?" asked Cadmus.

"If we spend a few days training them, it will free up our seasoned soldiers to fight outside the walls," said Lykus.

"Why would the slaves fight for us? They would be more likely to turn against us once we give them weapons," said Takis.

"Maybe by offering them something," replied Lykus.

"Their freedom?" asked Leonidas.

Takis chuckled. "That's ludicrous. Our whole economy rests on the shoulders of the slaves."

The commander to the right of Lykus scratched his chin. "Maybe we wouldn't have to offer freedom, but rather a small daily wage?" he said, shrugging his shoulders.

"Three days of training will not be enough. Many of those men have never held a sword," said Takis.

Leonidas glanced at the councilman, then nodded. "I agree. Is there another service they could be of?" he asked.

The men sat quietly for a moment. "We could use them to man a few warships. Surely they know how to row," said Lykus.

"What use is a few warships?" asked Ares. "Especially after

what happened to the last three we sent out to attack the siege engines."

"It's absolutely of no use," said Takis.

Leonidas looked over at Lykus, tilting his head. "I have to agree with him, Battalion Leader."

Lykus tapped his fingers on the table, thinking. "In a few days' time, its more than certain Demetrius will launch a full attack on the city from the harbor. He certainly will target the ships, merchant and war alike."

"What's your point?" asked Takis.

Leonidas raised his hand to the man, signaling him to remain quiet. "Go on, Battalion Leader."

"Let's use the slaves to drag two warships on shore and hide the ships along the brush, concealing our movements under the cover of darkness," explained Lykus.

"Then do what with them?" asked Ares.

"Use them to attack the cargo ships carrying the siege weapons. Without his artillery, Demetrius will be forced to call off the attack, or foolishly carry out his invasion without them."

"We still have his forces to our southwest preparing to advance," said Leonidas.

Lykus nodded, raising his brow. "Yes, but we must deal with that regardless when the time comes. I am talking about our more immediate threat."

Commander Ares shook his head. "Battalion Leader, you conducted an attack against those same siege vessels yesterday and you know the outcome. Why would you even consider such a thing?"

Lykus raised a brow. "Yes, I did, but I will tell you now as many may already know, I was not in agreement of the attack.

Demetrius knew we would be coming and prepared. Once we were in range, six warships carrying Cretan archers fired upon us, not to mention the catapults on the cargo ships we were targeting."

"And why would this second attack of the siege vessels be any different?" asked Leonidas.

Lykus raised his hand slightly from the table. "They won't be expecting it."

Ares nodded. "He's right," he said, looking over at Leonidas.

"When they launch their next attack, they will certainly target our warships. If they believe all the ships are neutralized, they will have their guards down," explained Ares, placing his hand on Lykus's shoulder. "Nice job."

Leonidas smiled. "Yes, nice work, Battalion Leader."

Takis ran his fingers through his hair. "Even if the battalion leader's idea is successful, we must fend off the Macedonian attack before we can even attempt it. There is still no guarantee we will," he said.

"What do you say to that, Battalion Leader?" Leonidas asked.

"I say, he's right. If we cannot fend off their attack, the plan will be useless."

"Do you have any ideas to help us hold the city?" asked Leonidas.

"Have the slaves begin repairing the walls and constructing a new wall about two dozen cubits inside the current one. Place every soldier and archer we have on it, and keep what ballista we have left firing," replied Lykus.

"A second wall?" asked Takis. "Where would the manpower come from to do that? Not to mention the money and materials."

"Put all the men we have on it. Slaves, civilians, and soldiers alike. Even you, Councilman," replied Lykus, glaring at him from beneath drawn brows.

Takis dropped his chin toward his chest as Lykus fixed his gaze on Leonidas.

"We can use the boulders we gathered for the artillery since many of the catapults were destroyed," Lykus said.

"What would be the importance of the second wall?" asked Leonidas.

"It's not a matter of *if* anymore but *when* they breach our walls, the city will surely fall," Lykus explained. "The second barrier would slow their advance. They would have to move up their ballista to knock down the second wall, buying us precious time."

"Time for what?" asked Cadmus.

"Refortify our positions and repair our artillery." Lykus raised his hands and tilted his head. "Maybe time to hash out terms for a cease fire."

"That's out of the question," said Takis, leaning back in his chair and crossing his arms.

Leonidas thought for a few moments while stroking his beard, then nodded. "Fine, we will begin construction of a second wall." He tapped his fingers on the table, fixing his gaze on the battalion leader. "If we hold, Battalion Leader, it will be on you to lead the warships, targeting the siege vessels."

Lykus turned his gaze to the man. "I expected as much, Your Magistrate. I will be happy to do so."

Leonidas summoned his servant and the man placed cups in front of everyone at the table. After the cups were filled with wine, Leonidas rose from his seat lifting his cup and the others followed suit.

"To our soldiers and commanders, may they each fight with the strength of a thousand men and with the courage of one, our battalion leader, Lykus." Leonidas smiled, before raising his cup to his mouth.

"To Lykus," said the commanders.

Lykus bowed his head slightly and raised his cup.

CHAPTER 8

Early the next morning, Chares and several other soldiers gathered supplies, weapons, and their fallen comrades from the eastern mole. Much to Chares's relief, he would be positioned inside the city walls for the remainder of the battle. With the eastern mole now almost cleared, they would soon head over to do the same on the western. Chares remained anxious about his return to the western mole battlefield, still holding hope of finding his friend Kleitos. The chances of the man being alive were slim, but he'd vowed to return and certainly planned on keeping his promise.

The city council had announced that family members of the soldiers could visit for a few hours along the eastern wall of the city. Although the families would not be allowed inside, the soldiers were free to line up along the barrier. Chares remained hopeful but knew it unlikely that Pythia would make the twelve mile trip from their home in Lindos. After helping several soldiers pull the last wagon of lifeless men to a burial site being dug by the slaves, Chares wiped his brow and walked to the harbor, splashing water up on his face and neck.

"Head inside, soldier. I will take you to your new position."

Chares wiped the water from his eyes and looked up at Lykus standing a few cubits away. "Yes, Battalion Leader," he said, stepping toward the man. He stopped and pointed. "Sir, aren't we going to retrieve the men and supplies from the western mole?"

Lykus shook his head. "Still occupied by the enemy," he replied, looking out across the western mole as he walked toward the gate. "If we advance on that seawall, Cretan archers will unleash on us."

"Sir, I think we could safely make it to the first checkpoint, where we held them the last time," said Chares, placing his hand on his chin.

Lykus stopped and faced him. "You want to go get your friend."

"Yes, I do. I promised I would return for him," replied Chares. "There is a chance he is still alive, sir."

"Sorry, soldier, can't risk it," said Lykus, stepping away.

Chares rubbed the back of his neck. "Sir, I could take a hand cart and one other—"

"Enough!" shouted Lykus, glaring at Chares. "You want me to risk more men, for what? To rescue a man who deserted us in the middle of battle! Where was he when we needed him?" Lykus face turned red as his eyes bulged.

Chares immediately stood at attention.

Several soldiers stopped what they were doing and looked over at Lykus and Chares.

"Yes, Battalion Leader. I understand, sir," replied a nervous Chares.

"Then move your ass inside those walls, soldier," said Lykus, pointing.

Chares turned and hurried toward the gate as several men gawked at him.

Upon catching up to a waiting Chares, Lykus led the way to a ladder placed along the northeast corner of the wall facing the harbor. He grabbed a rung and swiftly ascended to the top of the wall, Chares following behind him.

Once on top, Lykus pointed out into the harbor. "You see that stake out there along the western mole?"

Chares squinted and nodded. "Yes, Battalion Leader."

"That is the range of the weapon you will be in support of. It can fire up to sixty-pound projectiles." He pointed to a pile of boulders toward the middle of the yard. "The slaves will continue to place the boulders there, and it will be your job to get them up here to the weapon," he said, placing his hand on the catapult. "Now, there are three ways you can do this. One is the ladder." He then tilted his head. "But I doubt you could carry them up." He pointed to a pully with a large rope and basket attached to the end. "You can crank them up using that, but be careful not to let your hand slip. If it spins out of control and drops, it could be damaged." He pointed to a ramp with small boards nailed across it for footing. "That's your third option. Rolling them up that ramp." He turned, looking out into the harbor before returning his attention to Chares. "When the horn blows, this is where you will be. Understand?"

"Yes, Battalion Leader," replied Chares.

"I personally don't care which way you bring those stones up here, but make sure of one thing, soldier—they don't run out," said Lykus, walking toward the ladder. "My advice is start bringing them up now, so they are well stocked."

"Yes, Battalion Leader," replied Chares, before once again

looking out across the harbor. He fixed his gaze about halfway down the western mole, trying to spot Kleitos. After a few moments of searching, he shook his head and stepped toward the ladder.

Later in the afternoon, Chares cleaned up after an exhausting day. He'd managed to move twelve of the boulders. He was tired, and his hands and back were aching. However, the families had arrived and he wondered if Pythia came to see him. After drying his face and hands, he strolled to the eastern wall.

Many soldiers had already lined the barrier, and several were waiting their turn to climb the ladder. Chares found his place in line and in a few minutes began to climb up. He searched the groups of families congregated along the wall for Pythia, glancing up and down each line without seeing her anywhere. After a good half hour of searching in anticipation, he found a seat and settled for listening to nearby soldiers talking to their wives and children. For some families, the occasion wasn't joyous. Too many had to be informed their sons or husbands had fallen in battle.

A couple of hours before sunset, the families began to disperse. Feeling he'd waited long enough, Chares stood and stretched his arms over his head, followed by a yawn. He turned and took several steps but then froze when he heard his name being called.

"Chares!" said an old woman, walking his way with her hand in the air.

He squinted as she got close. "Medeia?"

"Chares, you have to come home immediately," she said, shaking her head and watching her step as she approached.

"Medeia, what on earth are you doing here?" he asked.

"It's your wife, Pythia."

"Is she okay?" asked a concerned Chares.

"No, she is not!" replied Medeia, lowering her brow.

"Is she hurt?" asked Chares, eyes wide.

"You have to come home," she said.

"What's going on?" he asked.

"It's bad, Chares. Really bad."

"Medeia, please, tell me what's going on?"

"It's that foul man Zotikos. He has been at your house day and night with her. Walking around naked."

Chares rubbed his hand over his head. "Medeia, that's her friend. He's a gymnosophist, so of course he's naked," he explained.

"No, you don't understand. They came into the courtyard early in the morning. I am sure he stayed with her all night."

"He's watching after her, is all," said Chares.

"I asked her how she pays him for looking after her, and she began rubbing his penis."

"Medeia, she asked him to keep—" Chares drew in his chin, blinking repeatedly. "What was that?" he asked, tilting his head.

"I said, she is rubbing his penis!" said Medeia much louder.

Nearby soldiers and families grew quiet and turned toward her. One woman covered her son's ears and made an angry face before walking away.

"What in the world are you talking about?" asked Chares, shuffling to the very edge of the wall to get as close as possible to the woman. "And keep your voice down, please."

Several soldiers stepped closer to eavesdrop on the conversation.

"Will you guys get back? This is a private discussion here!" he shouted.

The soldiers turned their heads and stepped away.

Chares fixed his gaze on Medeia. "Please, go on."

"I was saying, I asked Pythia how she pays him, and she said, 'Like this,' and began rubbing his penis," explained Medeia, moving her fist up and down.

"Stop that!" said Chares, looking over his shoulder to make sure no one was nearby.

"It gets worse, Chares," said Medeia, lifting her brow.

"It does?"

"Yes, she placed her head between his legs and—"

"Okay, stop," said Chares, raising his hand.

"You have to come home right now," she said urgently.

"Medeia, I know you never cared for Pythia. But I need you to tell me you really saw this with your own eyes?"

"As sure as I'm standing here, I did," she replied. "Now, get your things. We're leaving. I have a horse drawn cart waiting for us."

Chares shook his head, still reeling from what the woman had told him. He glanced at Medeia. "I can't just leave. It doesn't work that way," he explained.

With all his might, Chares didn't want to believe the woman, but intuition told him she was not lying. He'd never trusted Zotikos and always suspected he was up to no good. Pythia seemed mesmerized by the constant philosophical garbage spewing from the man's mouth. His eyes filled with tears as his thoughts drifted to Pythia and how much in love they once were. He'd waited two hours on this hard wall to see her face for just a few minutes. But instead, he'd gotten Medeia and the awful news she'd brought with her.

Chares dropped his shoulders and looked back at the woman. "I thank you, Medeia, for journeying here to tell me, but I have to go," he said rising to his feet.

"Chares, tell them you have an emergency and have to go home. You will see it for yourself when you arrive unannounced."

Chares sucked his teeth. "Do me a favor and don't mention that you came here today."

"I won't say a word to that filthy woman," she replied.

Chares closed his eyes and sighed. "Thanks, Medeia."

He turned and walked to the ladder, climbing down as several soldiers gawked at him, obviously aware of his conversation. He walked through the yard to the soldier's quarters and searched for a comfortable spot along the ground. He stared off aimlessly, thinking about Pythia's betrayal and how bad he wanted to confront that bastard Zotikos. Moments later, a soldier called his name.

"What?" replied Chares.

"There's a woman asking for you at the wall," the man explained.

"Let me guess…an ugly old woman?" asked Chares.

"No, a younger woman, quite pretty actually."

Chares sat up, hurrying to his feet. "Thanks," he said as he passed the soldier.

Once reaching the ladder, he climbed up and stood on the wall to look for the woman he suspected was Pythia. Soon, a woman called his name. He glanced to his left to find a woman in a light purple chiton waving at him. Chares squinted as she continued walking in his direction.

"Alyna?" he muttered.

As she stepped a little closer, he recognized the head turning walk, hair, and smile that certainly belonged to Alyna.

"Chares," she said. "Have you seen Kleitos?"

He raised his brow while shifting his eyes side to side. "Not today," he replied, shaking his head and feeling a bit caught off guard by the question.

"I asked a few other soldiers, and they hadn't seen him either," she explained, stepping closer to the wall. She bit her nails as worry washed across her face.

"He's probably still out on the mole. I will go check the first chance I get," said Chares, followed by a nod.

"Can you go now?" she asked.

Chares shook his head. "No one's allowed in or out till tomorrow."

"But I walked most of the way here. I don't know when my next chance to see him will be," she explained.

Chares felt bad for the woman. Not knowing what to say or do, he bit his lip and then scratched his cheek, thinking.

"Chares?" she said, tilting her head.

He glanced behind him, pointing to his right. "Meet me at the gate," he said, turning and walking toward the ladder. He climbed down and approached the gate leading outside where Alyna stood.

Two guards lowered their spears.

"No one in or out," the man said.

"Please, let me have a minute with the woman," said Chares.

The guard pushed him back. "What don't you understand?"

Chares tried to scurry around the man before being

grabbed by the other guard. "Let go of me!" he shouted as the two men tackled him to the ground.

Chares became enraged and threw punches. The guards were quick to throw their own, and the three tussled. Finally, the two guards got the upper hand. One man held Chares while the other landed several punches to his face.

"What's the meaning of this?" said Lykus, grabbing the guard who had hurled the punches and shoving him to the dirt. He sneered while pointing at the other guard. "Release him, now!" he shouted.

The man let go, and Chares quickly fell to his knees, blood streaming from his nose and mouth.

"He tried to exit the gate, sir," said the guard who had released him.

The other guard stood to his feet, examining the scrape to his forearm.

Lykus glanced at Chares. "You know better than that. Where were you going?"

Chares wiped his mouth, pointing to Alyna standing at the gate. The woman appeared stunned at what she'd witnessed, her hand over her mouth and eyes wide.

"Is that your wife?" asked Lykus.

Chares shook his head.

Lykus glanced back at the woman. "Is that the wife of the soldier out on the mole?" he asked.

Chares nodded, climbing to his feet.

Lykus pointed to the barracks. "Go get cleaned up. I will inform the woman about her husband," he explained.

"Battalion Leader, could I please be the one to tell her?" asked Chares.

Lykus stopped and drew a deep breath, placing his hands

to his hips. He turned toward Chares and took a step toward him. Chares anticipated being thrown to the ground, a skill the battalion leader refined and used often. To his surprise, Lykus simply said, "You've got five minutes, soldier."

Chares stepped in the direction of the gate, as did the guards. One man glared at him as they walked, curling his lip. Once he reached the iron gate, Alyna stood back as the guard unlocked and opened it. Chares stepped out while wiping his face with his tunic.

"What in the world was that about?" she asked, wiping the blood still trickling from his nose with a handkerchief.

Chares took the handkerchief and pressed it to his face, tilting his head back slightly. "I only have a few minutes, Alyna," he explained. He shook his head slightly, removing the rag from his nose. "It's about Kleitos…"

Alyna's mouth fell open as her eyes widened. "What is it?" she asked, placing her hand over her mouth.

"He got hurt out on the mole, and we had to retreat," he said, raising his hands. "I tried to go back for him, but they wouldn't let me."

"Was he captured by the Macedonians?" she asked.

"I don't know, but that's highly possible. That area is occupied by the enemy."

A tear raced down Alyna's cheek.

Chares reached for her, and the two embraced for several moments. "I will try to reach him, Alyna. I promise you, I will."

She nodded and pulled away, then reached for his hand and closed her eyes. "Please find him Chares," she said, opening her eyes. "The thought of him out there, injured, hungry, and scared, is more than I can bare."

"First chance I get, I promise."

Alyna pursed her lips as more tears streamed down her face.

"Inside, now!" shouted the guard.

Alyna released his hands and embraced him again.

"I will get word to you the minute I find him," said Chares.

"Now, soldier!" shouted the guard.

"I have to go," he said, backing up toward the gate.

"Thank you, Chares," said Alyna.

"You're welco—"

He was grabbed by the guard and yanked inside the city walls. The guard shut the gate and pushed him farther inside. Chares stumbled backward but kept his footing.

"Go on, get out of here," said the guard.

Chares scowled at the man, raised the handkerchief to his nose, and walked away. He strolled back to the entrance of the barracks and lifted a pot of water, then leaned his head back and poured it over his face.

Strolling back to his spot in the camp to lie down, his jaw ached and he pushed on his teeth to make sure they weren't loose. He rubbed his cheek as the pain became a little worse. He closed his eyes and found his thoughts were not of Pythia, but Alyna. Although he'd received several punches for his efforts, seeing Alyna brought a smile to his battered face.

His thoughts then shifted to Kleitos, and he wondered how he could reach the man without getting caught by the Macedonians, or even worse…Lykus.

CHAPTER 9

O N A WARM AND SUNNY afternoon, Pythia and Zotikos walked along the alley to a metal gate. A woman standing on the other side promptly opened it for them.

"Hello, Pythia," said the woman before fixing her gaze on Zotikos.

"This is my friend. He will be joining us this afternoon," explained Pythia, tilting her head toward him. "Zotikos, this is Nysa," she said, motioning to the woman.

The man smiled and kissed her hand. "It is said a beautiful woman has more power over man than the greatest of kings but with twice the malice."

Pythia glanced at Zotikos, then to Nysa as the woman's eyes narrowed. Pythia chuckled, reaching for his hand. "Follow me," she insisted, leading him away from the woman and into the courtyard. "I'd like you to meet Her Highness, Tanis," she said, looking around.

With the men fighting the Macedonians, a much smaller group showed up for the ceremony. There were about fourteen, all of them women besides Zotikos and an old man who sat in a nearby chair. Pythia waved upon spotting Tanis, and the woman walked toward them.

"Refer to her as Your Highness," she whispered.

"You seem to have lost your tunic?" said Tanis, looking Zotikos up and down.

"Your Highness, I am a man of simple things and sometimes, no things," he replied with a grin.

"This is Zotikos, my friend and gymnosophist."

Her Highness glanced at Pythia and then back at Zotikos. "Welcome. A friend of Pythia is a friend of ours," she said. "Now, come have a seat. The ceremony is about to begin."

As Tanis turned and walked away, Pythia looked over at Zotikos. "Isn't she great?" she asked, beaming.

Zotikos narrowed his eyes as Pythia led him to a blanket laid out on the floor. The other members found their places as well. Her Highness lit several candles, raised her hood, and raised her hands out from her side while closing her eyes.

———

Tanis opened her eyes, smiling as she looked around the room at the group. "Peace be with you," she said.

"Peace be with you," replied the group in unison.

"In these desperate times with our men fighting the enemy along our shores, we call on Gaia, and our great mother, Axeirus, for guidance," she said. "We ask Pontos and Ceto to summon great sea beasts and destroy the Macedonian warships. We call on Aphrodite to bring love and passion to our lives, even with the absence of our men," she continued, raising her hands higher. "Peace be with you." She closed her eyes.

"Peace be with you," replied the group.

Her Highness motioned toward the far side of the room,

and a woman stepped forward carrying a lamb. The animal writhed as she held it firmly down on the alter. Her Highness drew back a knife and extended it over her head.

"We ask of you these things," she said, forcing the blade into the side of the animal.

"We ask of you these things," said the group.

Tanis raised the knife again. "We ask of you these things." She brought the knife down a second time, and the animal squealed and shifted as the other woman continued holding it on the alter. "We ask you to awake the beasts of the sea and destroy our enemies," she said, bringing the knife down yet again.

The animal now lay motionless as she stabbed it repeatedly. Blood covered her hand and forearm and dripped from the pedestal to the floor. She reached for a cup and placed it along the altar, collecting some of the animal's blood before facing the group.

"Peace be with you," she said, raising the cup to her lips. After taking a drink, she handed it to the woman next to her.

"Thank you, Your Highness," said the woman, then she took a sip before passing it to the congregation.

Each member took a drink of the animal's blood. When the cup reached Zotikos, he stared at it momentarily before Pythia nodded her encouragement for him to drink. He raised it to his mouth before passing it along.

"As many of you know, a few women here are without a child. We beseech Great Mother Axeirus to give them the gift of maternity." She glanced around the room until her eyes fell on Pythia. "Our sister Pythia and *that man* she is bound too have yet to create. We beg of you, Great Mother, to hear us and place life inside her," she pleaded.

"Hear us, Great Mother," said the group.

Her Highness reached for a towel and fixed her gaze on Zotikos while wiping her hand. She noticed the man's constant glare as if he had something to say. "We have a new member here today. I wonder if he would like to share a few words?" she asked, tilting her head and placing the rag upon the lifeless animal.

Zotikos kissed Pythia on the cheek and rose to his feet. "Thank you, Your Highness," he said, stepping toward the alter and standing beside the woman. He glanced at the lifeless lamb before fixing his gaze on the members. "There is no doubt Gaia, Axeirus, Pontos, Ceto, and Aphrodite will hear your pleas," he said, nodding. "The question is will they act? And if so…when?" he asked, raising his hands. "I look around this courtyard and see many lonely women. I see many hearts filled with worry, not only for their husband's wellbeing but of their own. Our safety and the very island we call home may perish if the battle is lost." He motioned to the alter. "The words of man are like the blood of the sheep. They are continuous to the gods, but I fear they tire from both."

Her Highness crossed her arms. "We have always sacrificed to the gods, and they have rewarded us time and time again," she asserted.

"Have they?" replied Zotikos, widening his eyes. "Well, our very own Pythia is still without a child, and the entire Macedonian army is at our gates. And let's be honest, when's the last time you've seen a sea beast?" he asked with a smirk. He faced the members. "What will become of you women?" He raised his hands to his sides. "Will you not be raped with a sword to your neck?" He raced around the room, stopping directly in front of several members and putting his face just a handsbreadth from their own, using his hand to simulate a sword being held to their throats.

"All your belongings stolen?! Your homes destroyed?!" Zotikos shouted, waving his hands wildly and contorting his body. He fell to his knees and pounded his fist to the floor several times before drawing several large breaths. "My dear friends, the few who survive will become enslaved and sent to distant lands." He wept. "I cannot stomach the mere thought of it." He wiped his cheek with the back of his hand.

The courtyard fell silent as the members had a look of shock on their faces.

Tanis glanced wide-eyed at Pythia, her mouth hanging open.

Pythia grinned, then held up a finger gesturing for her not to interrupt the man.

Zotikos rose to his feet and stepped in front of the alter, shaking his head. "The blood dries and so does the mouths of those who spill it." He faced the congregation. "Make no mistake, all things created by man are the furthest things from the gods. Why would it be man's creations that inspires them, and not what is given?" he asked, raising his palms. "The fate of man rests solely on those who worship him, and I assure you it's not the gods." He raised his chin and widened his eyes. "The people of Rhodes did not ask for war." He pointed to the sky above. "But as sure as the sun shines on us today, we certainly have it." He peered at the frightened members, staring each of them in the eyes. "Just as the gods placed the Macedonian child inside the mothers of our attackers, the gods led them to our very shores."

Many in the room gasped.

Sliding a table to the center of the courtyard, Zotikos

stepped toward Her Highness and touched her long black hair, running his fingers through it. "I believe we can do more to gain favor of the gods than slaughtering lambs," he said, motioning toward the table. "Please, disrobe and lie down."

Tanis stood stoically and glared at the man, her fists clenched.

"Please, Your Highness, the gods are waiting," said Zotikos, raising his brow.

The woman glanced about the room, slowly sliding off her chiton, then found her seat.

Zotikos placed his hand under her legs, assisting her as she lay flat on her back. "Perfect," he said, facing the group. "Please, disrobe and join me."

The members did as he instructed and stepped toward the table.

Pythia stood next to him, biting her lip and fidgeting with her necklace.

He took his hand and ran it along Tanis's thigh, spreading her legs apart. "Don't be shy, everyone. Please join in," he insisted, lifting Pythia's hand to the woman's breast.

Pythia smiled, reaching with her other hand and massaging the woman.

"Your husbands are away, but that doesn't mean we shouldn't still have pleasures. Our pleasures will please the gods," he said.

CHAPTER 10

I T HAD BEEN A FEW days since Alyna came to the fort looking for Kleitos. Chares had had no opportunity to leave the city and search for his friend. Now that several more days had passed, he accepted the fact that Kleitos was most likely captured or had succumbed to his injuries. It was just an hour after sunrise in what was sure to be another hot day when Chares relaxed along the wall near his post, gazing across the harbor.

The Macedonian siege engines seemed to be repaired as the enemy's vessels closed in on the city once again. The sound of a horn coming from the ramparts signaled their approach. Chares took one final glance around the harbor and noticed a soldier lying motionless near the western mole. Placing his hand above his eyes, he squinted against the sun to get a better look. It certainly looked like Kleitos from where he stood.

Convinced, Chares spun on his heel and rushed toward the ladder. After descending, he sprinted for the gate where the two guards stood. He moved past them, but they stopped him before he could reach the gate.

"Not you again."

"There's a man out there. He's one of ours," explained Chares.

The guards grabbed his arms and pulled him away from the gate.

"Please, let me get him. He's by the harbor, near the western mole."

"Get back!" shouted the man. "Return to your post."

"It will take just a few seconds for us to get him," explained Chares.

A guard shook his head. "Why is it always you trying to leave the city?" he asked. "We have orders not to open these gates for anybody. What don't you understand?"

The man glanced at the other guard. "Go get Lykus."

Chares raised his hands in front of him. "No, there's no need for that. I'm leaving," he said, backing away.

The two guards watched Chares as he distanced himself from them. He turned and rushed to the ladder, returning to his position on the wall and looking again for the man he felt was Kleitos.

"Will you get down?" shouted a soldier. "The enemy is approaching, and their archers will aim right for us."

Chares descended the wall and stood by the pile of rocks he'd gathered the days before. He heard a roar of men in the distance followed by the sound of a siege weapon releasing a projectile. Men scurried for cover as several boulders smashed into the wall. Large chunks of rock flew in every direction, and Chares fell to his knees and covered his head. His ears rang from the loud crash as a large plume of dust filled the air. The city's ballista returned fire at a steady pace. The pile he had gathered was disappearing rapidly.

Chares descended the ladder and reached the rocks in the

yard, rolling a boulder toward the ramp. Upon reaching it, he looked around and spotted Lykus talking to the guards. The men pointed at Chares.

"Oh, great," he muttered, before refocusing on the task at hand.

As he rolled the rock up the ramp, a shower of arrows came over the wall and Chares took cover behind the boulder. Several men were hit, as another thundering crash of rock pummeled the city wall and Rhodian artillery. The weapon Chares supplied took a direct hit, and the main beam split in half.

As an exhausted Chares reached the upper deck where he'd put the boulders, Lykus followed right behind him barking out commands. He climbed the wall and pointed, ordering the archers to fire. He examined the catapult and shook his head before glancing at the men standing nearby.

"Repair this catapult, soldiers. We need to keep fire on those siege weapons," he ordered. He glanced at Chares. "What's a matter, soldier? The guards informed me you were trying to leave the capital again. Don't tell me you were trying to reach that coward out on the mole?"

"Sir, there was a soldier…"

Lykus pointed to the catapult. "Give them a hand, soldier," he insisted, stepping away. He walked along the line, ordering the men to fire as rocks and arrows bounced off the wall in the area around them.

Chares gazed at the man, impressed by his courage.

"Are you going to just stand there or give us a hand lifting this?" asked a soldier.

Chares faced him. "Oh, sorry," he said, kneeling beside the man and lifting one side of the catapult.

Another man wedged a boulder under it. The soldiers untied the ropes that secured the damaged frame of the catapult. The enemy's bombardment continued relentlessly, triggering the men to stop and take cover several times. Once they got the damaged frame removed, two soldiers hurried to find a replacement.

Chares stood, then scurried to the outer wall and slowly peeked up over it, fixing his gaze on the harbor. Many of the Rhodian ships were ablaze, and enemy vessels unloaded soldiers less than a hundred cubits from the wall. Chares ducked behind the barrier and hurried back to the catapult being repaired.

The other soldier kneeling nearby glanced over at him. "What's it looking like out there?"

Chares shook his head. "Not good. The Macedonian soldiers are landing not far from the wall."

After the other two soldiers returned with the new frame, they fastened it in place. The men lifted one side of the catapult as two other men dragged the boulder out from under it.

Lykus returned from the other end of the wall, stopping only a few cubits away and then crossing his arms. "Fire your weapon, soldiers."

They lifted a boulder into the basket and released it a moment later. The men hurried to load another boulder as Lykus watched the projectile barrel toward the enemy ships.

"Raise the fulcrum a click. We're overshooting our target. Keep them supplied, soldier," said Lykus, placing a hand on Chares's shoulder. Then he stepped toward the next group of soldiers manning another catapult about a dozen cubits away.

Chares moved toward the ladder, climbing down to the pile of rocks. When he returned with another boulder, a huge projectile slammed into the wall a short distance from him. Fifteen cubits of wall collapsed and several men fell, quickly crushed by large chunks of stone tumbling down after them. Chares covered his head as debris landed all around him. One helmet sized piece of rock bounced off his shin, and he shouted before reaching for his leg. He saw a deep cut and dark spots, but it did not appear to be broken. He grimaced, holding his leg.

Lykus appeared and knelt beside him. "Move your hands," he ordered.

Chares released his leg, and Lykus examined the injury. "You'll be okay," he said, covering the wound with a piece of fabric and tying it tight. "Didn't you get a set of greaves with that fancy uniform?"

Still in pain, Chares squinted and then slowly shook his head.

Lykus chuckled. "Rest a few minutes, then get back to moving those boulders," he said before standing and walking along the wall, barking at discouraged soldiers still taking shelter. He ordered the men to return to their positions immediately, and without any obvious hesitations, the men scurried to their battle stations.

Chares looked at his leg, flexing his foot to see if it hurt to move. He glanced around at the dead and injured men scattered along the wall. The number of able soldiers and artillery was reduced to half of when the day's battles had started, and Chares feared the capital's defenses would collapse at any moment. Lykus did his best to keep the fatigued men firing the weapons, but the situation worsened by the minute. Huge gaps in the wall allowed enemy archers and ballista to fire into the heart of the city. Buildings collapsed as others were set ablaze by the fire arrows. Slaves and soldiers alike scurried to douse burning buildings with water, but their efforts were futile.

Lykus ordered the remaining archers to focus their arrows on the enemy soldiers just twenty cubits from the wall, but the enemy soldiers moved into a tight formation against the barrier, and the Rhodian archers were unable to find their targets.

Lykus peered over the wall at the enemy soldiers, then looked out across the eastern mole and the vessels unloading more men. He realized not only did the enemy's presence in front of the harbor pose a serious threat to the capital, but also his plan to attack the siege engines by using the warships hidden in the brush days before. If the Macedonians held this ground at day's end, it would be impossible to launch the warships in the harbor without being detected. His only option would be dragging the ships to the west beach over a quarter mile away. Such a maneuver would require a massive amount of manpower, not only to move the ships but to clear a path through the high brush and trees. With the presence of the Macedonian army to the southwest, they certainly would hear the vegetation being cleared. The only chance of success in sinking the siege ships was the element of surprise.

"Archers, hold your fire. I am leading a group of soldiers to clear the enemy from the wall. You men focus your ballista on the enemy ships." Lykus turned and raced down the ladder and across the yard to the much-depleted reserves of soldiers. "Men, prepare for battle. We are moving out," he said, fixing his gaze on the southern wall.

"Sir, we have orders to stay here and protect the square," replied a soldier.

Lykus faced the man. "Well, those orders have changed, haven't they?" he replied, raising his brow. "Now gather your weapons and report to the eastern gate."

He walked toward the southern wall where the fresh troops waited for the impending land battle. The commanding officer of the southern wall noticed Lykus and strolled toward him. Once the men were in close proximity of each other, Lykus pointed to a few rows of swordsmen seated along the wall.

"I am commandeering those men, Ares," Lykus informed him.

"Those men are protecting the southern wall," Ares replied.

"Protecting it from what? The fight is on the north side of the city."

"Look over that wall, Lykus. There are ten thousand enemy soldiers preparing for battle."

Lykus clenched his jaw. "I know what's out there, Commander. But we have to move the troops to the most pressing areas."

"Has the northern wall been breached?" he asked.

Lykus placed his hands to his hips. "Order your men to the eastern gate. We are going to push back the enemy from our walls."

"You are planning an attack outside the city walls? It was made clear not to leave the capital by His Magistrate, and from what I remember, your own recommendation."

"Circumstances have changed, Commander," said Lykus, stepping toward the rows of soldiers.

Ares reached for Lykus's shoulder. "You can stop there, Battalion Leader. I will not order my men outside the safety of our walls until instructed by His Magistrate and the war council."

Lykus stopped, pushing the man's hand from his shoulder. "There is no time!" he shouted before turning away from Ares and standing in front of the soldiers. "You men grab your weapons and follow me!"

The men rose to their feet.

"Stay where you are!" shouted the commander, now standing alongside Lykus.

Confusion raced across the soldiers faces as they nervously returned to their previous position.

Lykus shoved the commander. "Stand down. These men are now under my command," he shouted.

The shocked man stumbled backward before losing his footing and falling to the ground.

Lykus faced the soldiers. "On your feet," he ordered, grabbing a soldier by the breast plate and pulling him up.

The other soldiers swiftly rose from the ground and stood at attention.

"I am reporting you to His Magistrate, Battalion Leader," shouted Ares, hastily walking toward the palace.

Lykus glanced at the man before fixing his gaze on the soldiers. "Follow me," he said, stepping away.

Upon reaching the gate, the reserves were in wait of the battalion leader's orders.

"Open it," said Lykus to the guards.

They opened the gate, and Lykus, followed by a little over two hundred men, filed outside the safety of the city walls.

Chares sat in anticipation, glancing back and forth between

Lykus and the soldiers leaving the city and the forces on the eastern mole still advancing. He was more than relieved the man had not asked him to join in the risky campaign. Although there would have been an opportunity to reach Kleitos, he remained comfortable on waiting for another occasion to search for the man.

The few remaining Rhodian catapults continued firing on the enemy vessels. Fifteen minutes later when Lykus and the soldiers met the enemies along the wall, Chares leaned over the edge as far as he could to witness the battle. The sight of men delivering blows to each other became horrifying as the situation grew more chaotic. This made him even more relieved of his current position.

The ground looked as if it were alive and churning, and the understanding of which soldiers were Rhodian and which were Macedonian became more difficult. Chares searched for Lykus but could not make him out among the clusters of soldiers. He noticed the enemy on the eastern mole running toward the fray with their swords drawn.

"Take aim at the approaching soldiers," said Chares to the archers while pointing.

"We were instructed to hold our fire, soldier," replied a man nearby.

"Ordered to hold fire where *our* troops are. I am talking about over there, you fool," shouted Chares.

A moment later, a blow came to the back of Chares's already injured leg. He shouted in pain while securing himself from falling off the wall. Still grimacing in pain, he lowered himself from the wall to the ground.

"You shut your mouth, soldier. This is not your command!

You're just a meek, useless, hoplite," shouted the man, wielding his sword.

Chares glanced up at him with his jaw clenched, then lowered his head, still holding onto his leg and trying to shake off the blow from the man's sword. He sat listening to the shouts of soldiers fighting outside the city walls in between the deafening rumble of projectiles still pounding the city.

As another hour passed, a horn sounded in the harbor and the attack halted. The city fell silent. After waiting a few minutes, Chares climbed the rubble, taking great care with his injured leg, and looked out into the harbor. He saw the amphibious siege weapons being towed away while the Rhodian vessels in the harbor were either sunk or burning. He could also see the enemy still held the western mole, but the eastern seawall and forces directly in front of the city were cleared. Looking along the wall, he saw there were only two working catapults and the archer corps were heavily depleted.

Not entirely sure why the attack had stopped, Chares felt relieved it had. If the bombardment continued much longer, the city would surely be lost. He fixed his eyes on the eastern gate as the guards opened it, then he watched in anticipation to see if Lykus had survived the vicious battle. As the soldiers entered, helping the injured along, the last to enter the safety of the city was the battalion leader, Lykus.

Chares smiled at the sight of the man walking in under his own power. He only counted twenty-six men when the guards closed the gate. Doing the math in his head, he figured only one of every ten men had survived. Even though Chares took a blow to the leg from one of his own men, he remained certain he would have died if he had taken part in the battle.

He looked at his leg, assessing his injury as he heard footsteps approaching him.

"Help the wounded soldiers," said Lykus, tossing Chares a bundle of rags.

He glanced up at his commander. "Yes, Battalion Leader. It's good to see you well," said Chares, struggling to get to his feet.

"Is that small injury to your leg still bothering you? C'mon, soldier, toughen up," said Lykus.

Chares looked at the soldier who struck him and squinted. "That man hit me with his sword on the back of the leg, sir," he explained, pointing to the soldier.

The man raised his hands. "Battalion Leader, that hoplite told us to fire our weapons after you gave us clear instruction not too."

Lykus refocused on Chares. "Is that so?"

"Yes, Battalion Leader, but I asked them to target the soldiers on the eastern mole as they approached your position. We had a clear shot on them, sir," explained Chares.

"That certainly would have helped our situation out there," said Lykus, turning toward the soldier. "Could you not see that?" he asked.

"We were following orders, sir."

Lykus nodded. "Well, it's a sad day when a spearman has frame of mind to see opportunity that our seasoned soldiers cannot, yet is powerless to communicate them," he said, turning away from the man. He stopped and looked over his shoulder at the soldier. "You touch one more of my men, and I will throw you from this wall. Understand?"

"Yes, Battalion Leader," replied the soldier, standing at attention.

Lykus descended the ladder.

The man faced Chares, scowling at him.

Chares smiled and limped toward the ladder.

"We'll see each other again, hoplite."

"Yeah, I suppose. Unless you are thrown from the wall before then," replied Chares, shrugging his shoulders.

Slaves carried away the dead soldiers from the siege. Just by taking a brief inventory, Chares saw at least a few hundred men being piled up. As the sun set in the west and most of the dead were rounded up and wounded tended to, Chares noticed Lykus talking to a large group of slaves by the pile of bodies. He turned and locked eyes with Chares. The battalion leader called for him, and the two walked toward each other.

"Find twenty able men and come to the western gate," said Lykus.

Chares nodded. "Yes, Battalion Leader. What's going on?"

"Just do as your told and meet me at the gate."

Chares sighed.

Lykus glared at the man and pointed toward the barracks. "Go!" he shouted.

Fifteen minutes later, Chares arrived at the gate with the soldiers. There were a couple hundred slaves there already and Lykus as well.

The battalion leader opened the gate and led the way along the city wall, toward the harbor, and arriving about sixty cubits from the bay where two warships covered with brush waited. Lykus instructed the slaves to uncover the vessels and all the men gathered around lifting and sliding the bireme ship, while others pulled on a large rope fastened to the bow. Chares found his spot alongside the men helping move the vessel. Every ten cubits, the men had to stop and rest.

One soldier pulling on the rope glanced at Chares and to the men around him. "I wish Chares's wife was here. I heard she can pull some rope," he said, followed by a laugh from the other soldiers.

Chares reached for the man's chest while drawing back his fist.

Lykus grabbed him before he could swing and pushed him away. "Knock it off," the man said through his teeth. He pointed at the soldier holding the rope. "One more word from your mouth, funny man, and I'll break that jaw." He glared at the men around him. "Now, let's move," he insisted, waving his hand.

They moved slowly and quietly until finally reaching the shore. Once there, they returned for the second ship and carried it to the harbor as well. With both ships in a few cubits of water, they laid a ramp from the shore to the vessels and the soldiers and slaves filed onboard.

Lykus walked to the middle of the bireme ship and addressed the men on both vessels. "Demetrius and his Macedonian army will again besiege our city in the morning. He has all but demolished our walls, half of our men are dead, and all our warships destroyed." He placed his hand on the rail of the vessel. "All but these two. This ship is called *Victory*." He glanced around at the men and pointed to the bireme next to his. "That vessel is called *Freedom*."

"I have requested to His Magistrate to free every man aboard these two ships," he explained. "You are free men, fighting for your island. If we die, we die not only protecting our land, but we die for freedom," said Lykus, placing his hand on a slave's shoulder. "We have only three siege vessels to sink, then we can return home to a hero's welcome. We will move silently in tight formation along the eastern mole. If we are successful, by the time they know what hit them, we will be returning to the safety of the harbor."

Lykus moved to stand beside the helmsmen and gave the command to row.

Demetrius and his generals sat around a table aboard the flagship, discussing the next morning's plan of attack. Among them, his top commander Alkomis who had been preparing for the land battle southwest of the city.

"The siege has not been without disappointments, but we have severely weakened the city walls along the harbor, destroyed their fleet, their ballistae damaged, and their archers are few in numbers," said Demetrius, lifting his cup. "Tomorrow, we will continue our attack from the harbor. Alkomis, you will lead the attack from land." He took a drink.

"My lord, the southwest wall is still intact and heavily garrisoned. If I lead an attack, we will suffer tremendous losses with no guarantee of success," replied Alkomis, raising his hands. "We should focus our attack from the harbor and once we destroy what's left of the wall, move up the troops and take the city from the north. We have control of both moles. Landing will be effortless."

Demetrius stroked his chin. "Commander, if we attack simultaneously, they will surely surrender and the battle will be over."

Alkomis rubbed his neck and nodded. "As you wish, my lord."

Demetrius placed his hand on the man's shoulder, standing from his seat. "Lead your men into battle at first light. We will commence our bombardment at the same time and begin our invasion of the harbor." He smiled. "Father will be pleased to know we took the island in a few short weeks." He refilled his cup, lifting it to his mouth.

There came a knock on the door.

"What is it?" asked Demetrius.

The door opened and in walked the bow officer. "My lord, our siege vessels are under attack."

Demetrius slammed his cup to the table. "Sound the alarm," he said, rushing toward the door. Once on the upper deck, he raced to the bow and stared in the direction of the siege vessels a hundred yards away. "To your stations!" he shouted. He heard a crashing sound and could see one of his siege vessels listing. "Row, men!" He turned toward his commander. "Ready the archers."

"Yes, my lord," the commander replied.

Demetrius looked at Alkomis. "Ptolemy ships?" he asked.

Alkomis shook his head. "Not sure, my lord," he replied. "It appears the vessels came from the harbor."

Demetrius glared in the distance. "The Rhodian ships were destroyed, unless they concealed a few on shore?"

Alkomis nodded. "That's exactly what they did, my lord."

The flagship raced toward the battered siege vessels and, once fifty yards away, one ship capsized, sending the siege engine to the bottom of the sea. The sound of cracking wood came and then another ship listed.

"Row faster!" shouted Demetrius. He walked to the helmsman. "We have to support the right side of the platform before we lose another engine."

The darkened sky made visibility difficult, but seeing a ship moving around the siege vessel, Demetrius gave the archers the order to fire. The whistling sound of arrows pierced the night sky toward the ship, striking it with precision just as a second siege vessel capsized.

"Ready your arrows," said Demetrius.

"My lord, that is one of *our* ships," said Alkomis.

Demetrius investigated the night sky, seeing men on the vessel waving their hands in the air. "Hold your fire."

Now just sixty cubits away, Demetrius gave the command to stop rowing. The largest and last siege vessel was also listing. He pointed toward it, instructing the vessel he fired upon to secure it. The men raced to their rowing stations and parked the corner of their vessel below the platform. Moments later, the siege tower slid a few cubits in the direction of the men's boat.

With the extra weight applied to the bow of their ship, the stern raised from the water. The men shouted as the tower slid a few more cubits, sending the platform just a handsbreadth above the water. Seconds later, the tower collapsed onto the ship and crushed many men. Within a few minutes, both the vessel and siege engine disappeared into the dark depths.

Demetrius searched the area for the enemy ships but saw nothing. Minutes later, there was a bright flash across the sky and a large rumble. The wind increased as a massive storm raged toward them.

"Tell all commanders to set their courses for the camp southwest of the city and keep close to shore!" shouted a fiery Demetrius.

"Maybe we should head for the harbor?" asked Alkomis.

"The amphibious attack is over. Now the real battle begins." Demetrius looked across the sky. "Full speed, men," he shouted, shoving a soldier out of his way. He raced toward the steps leading to the lower deck. "Come, Alkomis. I have an idea."

⊰━━━━━━━━━◆

After safely returning to port following the successful mission, the men clamored and celebrated. Lykus grinned as he looked out across the Aegean, seeing lightning in the distance. He became hopeful that Demetrius would lose even more vessels by the approaching storm. Smile widening, he thought of how shocked the Macedonian commanders must have been while watching their siege towers collapse into the sea.

Still surprised at how poorly Demetrius had conducted the invasion, Lykus remained confident that if the Macedonian army had placed all its ships in the harbor initially and hadn't called off the attack early on two separate occasions, victory would surely be theirs. Now that their siege weapons were destroyed, the enemy commander would have to rethink his strategy.

Although Lykus remained unsure of Demetrius's next move, he assumed it would be a land battle, though they still had plenty of warships left to launch another attack from the harbor.

"It was sure nice not having to swim back this time," said a soldier, suspending the commander's thoughts.

Lykus removed his hand from his chin and looked at the man smiling at him. He chuckled. "Yes, Chares, it certainly was," he said, placing his hand on the man's shoulder before stepping away.

A soldier emerged from the cities gate and rushed toward Lykus. "Sir, the magistrate is requesting to see you."

Lykus nodded. He'd more than expected to be summoned

after the episode with Ares, the commander of the southern wall. "All right, men!" he shouted.

The celebrations halted and the soldiers turned to Lykus, giving him their full attention.

"Move the ships back to the tree line and cover them," he instructed.

The men's smiles left their faces.

An exhausted Lykus walked up the short path to the city gate alongside the soldier.

Lykus heard shouting as he approached the door to the war room, but when he entered, silence reigned and all eyes fell upon him.

"Battalion Leader, come have a seat," instructed Leonidas.

The commanders at the table stood as he found his seat, glaring at him for a few moments before finding their own.

"Battalion Leader, it has been brought to my attention that you led an attack outside the city walls and assaulted our commander, Ares, who has worked tirelessly to prepare us for the Macedonian land forces," said Leonidas, his brows drawing close.

Lykus nodded. "Yeah, that sounds about right," he replied, crossing his legs and clasping his fingers behind his neck.

His Magistrate drew his chin to his chest. "Would you care to elaborate on the reason why?" he asked.

"We lost over two hundred men by that decision," said the commander sitting to his left.

"You severely compromised our defenses!" shouted Councilman Takis, his eyes bulged and face bright red.

Leaning back in his chair, Lykus fixed his gaze on the man.

"Wait," said Leonidas, raising his hands from the table. "Give him a chance to speak."

Lykus removed his hands from behind his neck and placed them on the table. Though irritated to have to defend his decision, he calmed himself and looked at Leonidas. "The enemy held the ground on each mole and directly in front of the northern wall. If we were to have any chance at sinking their siege ships, we needed to catch the enemy by surprise. If we were spotted by their soldiers loading the biremes into the harbor, they would have certainly alerted the Macedonian warships and our vessels would have been destroyed before we left port." He shrugged. "So, I ordered an attack to clear their men from the eastern mole and the city walls." He then looked to the commander he'd shoved to the ground. "As for assaulting you in front of the men, I am sorry. But I needed those soldiers and time was of the essence," he explained, turning up his palms.

Ares tapped his fingers and gazed at him without expression.

Leonidas cleared his throat. "We have to work together, gentlemen. From now on, any changes in strategy will be approved by me and the council before they are executed." He glanced at Ares and then let his gaze linger on Lykus. "Understood?"

Lykus nodded. "Yes, Your Magistrate."

"Okay, now that is settled. How did it go out there? Were you able to sink a siege vessel?" Leonidas asked.

Lykus grinned. "All three of them."

Leonidas closed his eyes and smiled in relief. "Any casualties?" he asked, opening his eyes.

"None on our side."

"Great work, Battalion Leader," he said, smacking his hand on the table in excitement.

"What difference does that make now?" asked Takis, shaking his head. "We have less than two thousand soldiers. We cannot defend our city against the Macedonians once they attack from the south."

A loud rumble echoed through the palace as the vibrations of thunder shuddered the table.

"This storm," said Lykus, raising a finger, "could take a toll on the enemy's ships, especially the smaller supply vessels and biremes."

Leonidas placed his hand to his chin. "With what you know, what is our best-case scenario come tomorrow?"

Lykus tilted his head. "That Demetrius will foolishly attack the harbor again without the siege weapons. By morning, our men will have repaired most of the wall and artillery. We would have a clear advantage and deliver him a devastating defeat."

"And worst case?" asked Leonidas.

"Demetrius calls off his attack of the harbor and consolidates his forces to the south," Lykus replied.

Leonidas bit down on his lip, thinking. After a moment, he raised his hand from the table and said, "If they did in fact consolidate their army and attack the southern wall while in the meantime, we move our armaments from the northern wall to reinforce the south, what would be our chances of holding them?"

Lykus rubbed his chin, shaking his head. He looked from the table to the magistrate. "Little or none, Your Magistrate," he replied.

Takis exhaled forcefully, placing his hands to his head. "We have done what you asked from the attack of the siege vessels to building a second wall, yet you say we have no chance?" he exclaimed.

"If the wall holds, we certainly have a chance, Battalion Leader," said Leonidas.

Lykus rubbed the back of his neck. "The problem is that Demetrius still has at least thirty thousand men at his disposal. Even if they climbed the walls with ladders, they would eventually overwhelm our defenses."

Thunder once again rolled through the palace. Lykus pointed up, hearing it echo in the distance. "This storm is our best hope," he said. "If the storm reaches the enemy before they make it to the safety—"

A soldier rushed into the room, interrupting them.

"What is it?" asked Leonidas.

"Your Magistrate, there are warships approaching the harbor."

All men stood and rushed for the door, down the corridor, to a balcony overlooking the port. Sure enough, five trireme ships approached in the distance.

"I'll sound the alarm," said the commander as he turned to walk away.

Lykus placed his hand to the man's arm. "Hold on, Ares," he said. "I know Demetrius has made poor decisions, but why would he risk an attack at night, during a storm?"

The man stepped back toward the group staring out across the harbor.

Lykus kept his gaze fixed on the ships, but the rain and wind made it difficult to see until several flashes of lightning brightened the night sky, finally giving him a good visual.

"Ptolemy," he whispered.

Leonidas faced him. "Ptolemy?" he asked with raised brows and a smile crossing his face.

Lykus nodded, and all the men cheered, patting each other on the shoulder.

Ptolemy had not only sent five trireme war vessels, but nearly eighteen hundred soldiers, four hundred highly-trained mercenaries, and six pieces of artillery to strengthen the besieged city. With that, the Egyptian ruler had also brought much-needed hope to the severely battered capital of Rhodes.

CHAPTER 11

THE NEXT MORNING, CHARES AWOKE more than pleased to see new men filing into the city. The morale of the disheartened Rhodian soldiers all over camp had increased considerably by the mere sight of them. He rushed up the ladder and looked out across the water to see five Egyptian war vessels and not one Macedonian ship. He raised his hand and shouted, rejoicing at the sight of it alongside the many other soldiers cheering from the wall.

Celebration was short lived though, when Lykus climbed the ladder and ordered the men to disassemble the ballista and move to the southern wall. All but a handful of archers and soldiers were redeployed. Demetrius had failed to capture the city from the harbor, but he still commanded an army that greatly outnumbered the Rhodians.

After dismantling the weapons and being positioned in a similar role as before, Chares climbed the ladder and looked out across the field to the Macedonian camps. There were thousands of soldiers, and their ships lined the shore. He could see hundreds of men assembling enormous siege equipment.

Even with the reinforcements, he wondered how they could possibly defeat such a massive army.

Demetrius and Alkomis stood next to each other studying the southern wall of the city and trading ideas on how to carry out the attack. The storm had sent thirty-six vessels and eight thousand men to the depths of the sea, but with his forces still far superior in size and artillery, Demetrius was unmoved.

The men's discussion centered on the placement of the helepolis, a massive siege tower Demetrius had ordered be constructed. The gigantic tower would stand one hundred cubits high. Its bronze plating would push the final weight to one hundred and sixty tons. The tower would be armed with two 180-pound catapults, four 60-, and ten 30-pounders. The top floors would be garrisoned with archers and slingers.

To move the massive siege tower, it was mounted on huge casters with eight 10-cubit tall wheels under each. Even with the massive wheels and capstan, it would require three-thousand men to move it. Since the tower's mobility consisted of forward and backward, placement was crucial.

"Right here," said Demetrius, lowering his hand in front of him in a slicing motion.

Alkomis nodded. "Very well, my lord," he replied.

"The ground is smooth and sturdy and with the slight slope in the terrain, the tower should move easily," explained Demetrius.

Alkomis placed a hand to his chin, then faced the man. "My lord, with your permission, while the tower is being constructed, we could have men dig a tunnel to undermine the wall. Also, we could use the dirt to level the path for the helepolis."

Demetrius grinned, placing his hand on the man's shoulder. "A fine idea, General. You may proceed," he replied.

Stepping away, Demetrius sauntered toward the men standing nearby in charge of the construction of the tower. "Right there, men," he said pointing.

Now placed in full command of defense of the city, Lykus positioned the soldiers for the impending attack. He decided to place all the islands artillery along the southern wall, even the unusable ones that had been damaged defending the harbor. He figured if the enemy focused their attack on the decoy ballistae, it would draw fire away from the functioning engines. He also placed most of the archers there as well, only leaving a hundred back to defend the harbor. He placed the Egyptian mercenaries behind the second wall, planning to personally lead them into battle if both walls were breached. Even though still greatly outnumbered, Lykus became more and more confident the city would hold.

After every possible fortification was complete and each man understood their position and what was required of them, he allowed the soldiers to get some much-needed rest.

Being convinced the enemy's siege towers would take several weeks to construct, the families of the soldiers were allowed to visit yet again, this time inside the city walls. The morale of the men remained high. Even most of the freed slaves from the vessels *Freedom* and *Victory* stayed to defend their home and newly found freedom.

While the soldiers relaxed and enjoyed time with their

families, Lykus spent most of his days training and getting used to his new armor. The new defensive uniform featured a red cloak, reinforced breastplate, and a shoulder element for added protection. A red and black horsehair crest that rose high above the helmet made the already tall man seem giant. He also had greaves covering his legs from just above the knee to the ankle. In all, the entire outfit weighed over fifty pounds.

CHAPTER 12

I N THE SEVERAL MONTHS SINCE the battle of Rhodes began, life on the island became more relaxed. The enemy's troops still prepared for their invasion, but as each day passed, the civilians of Rhodes became more convinced their island would prevail.

While Chares and his fellow soldiers woke up every day wondering if it were their last, Pythia and Zotikos forged an unbreakable love. By her request, Zotikos had moved into Pythia's home two months before. Their constant companionship and common interests propelled their blooming romance to extraordinary heights. She could not have been happier as the two made plans to move away together once the war ended.

Their meetings with Her Highness also continued. Through Zotikos and his approach to pleasing the gods, their membership swelled considerably. The storm that had sent many enemy ships to the bottom of the Aegean was accredited to the man and his ideas. The group sex he initiated also became part of the ritual, as men and women pleasured themselves to keep the favor of the gods.

Pythia stood at the fountain filling a vase with water when

a woman called her name. She turned and spotted Alyna standing nearby, giving a friendly wave.

"Hello, Alyna," replied Pythia still filling her vase. Once full, she noticed the woman still hadn't moved and glared over in her direction.

"How is Chares?" she asked.

Pythia shrugged. "I don't know. I haven't seen him since the Macedonian army arrived."

Alyna dropped her gaze to the ground. "Oh, well, I saw him once when I went there to visit Kleitos," she stated, then glanced up at Pythia.

"That's nice," said Pythia. "How's Kleitos doing?"

Alyna bowed her head. "He was injured and left behind. No one has seen him since," she replied. "Chares searched but wasn't able to find him."

"Well, don't lose hope," said Pythia, stepping away.

Alyna quickly caught up to her. "I heard you are part of a group that does ceremonies to protect the men?"

Pythia bounced her head side to side. "Yeah, something like that," she replied.

"Would you consider asking the gods for Kleitos to return safely?"

Pythia stopped walking and stared at Alyna. The lovely woman would be a fine addition to the group, and she knew Zotikos would most certainly like to sample her. Pythia's gaze ran up and down the woman's body and she reached for her hair, running her fingers through it. Pythia became excited as the thought of seeing Alyna naked filled her mind.

The woman leaned away from her touch, and Pythia smirked, turned on her heel, and walked away. Moments later, the sound of footsteps closed in on her.

"Oh, please, Pythia," said Alyna.

Pythia stopped again and sucked her teeth. "I can help you, but you have to swear secrecy," she said, raising her brow.

"Of course."

"Okay, meet me at my house tomorrow before the sun sets. You will have a chance to meet Zotikos, and we will go to the meeting together," said Pythia.

Alyna tilted her head. "Zotikos, the gymnosophist?"

Pythia squinted. "You know him?"

Alyna shook her head. "No, but I have seen him in the square many times sharing his wisdom."

Pythia smiled as she turned and walked away. "He likes sharing more than wisdom," she muttered.

"Thank you," said Alyna.

Pythia kept walking and raised her hand over her head, acknowledging the woman.

Most soldiers along the wall kept their eyes on the massive tower in the distance, now nearing completion. Lykus, on the other hand, fixed his gaze on the pile of dirt amassing along the enemy's camp. He watched as several men emerged from behind the mound with carts of dirt. What the men did wasn't openly apparent, but Lykus became convinced that he knew what they were up to.

He glanced around before locking his eyes on a group of spearmen, then descended the ladder and walked toward them. "You men gather all the shovels and pickaxes you can find and meet me by the wall."

The men scurried to their feet.

He glanced over at a group of slaves eating their lunch.

"When you men finish eating, I need you to gather up as much wood as you can. Make sure they are at least four cubits long and this big around," he said, making his hands into a circle. He walked to the barracks where several officers were grouped.

"Battalion Leader," said one of the men, acknowledging him.

Lykus nodded, then placed his hands to his hips. "The enemy is digging a tunnel. I believe they are trying to undermine our wall."

"How do you know this?"

"By the mound of dirt growing alongside their camp."

"You sure they are not just excavating the ground for that siege tower?"

Lykus shook his head. "No, it's too far away from its path and they seem to be concealing their movements."

"What are you thinking?" the man asked.

"Well, drawing a straight line from where they are digging, I can pretty much predict their path," said Lykus. "I say we start digging and surprise them."

"Have a fight underground?" another man asked.

"Yea, possibly," replied Lykus. "We certainly will need to reinforce the ground below the walls regardless."

"That sounds good, Battalion Leader," said the man as the other officers nodded.

"We will have the slaves dig one and the soldiers another only cubits apart. Once we reach the enemy, we will have two lines to send in troops," Lykus explained.

"How far do you think we will need to dig?"

"Not far, just a good six cubits or so past the wall, maybe thirty cubits in all," replied Lykus.

"I will get the soldiers and slaves rounded up for the task," said an officer, stepping away.

Lykus then walked toward the palace to make His Magistrate aware of his findings and get his approval.

CHAPTER 13

T HE FOLLOWING EVENING, ALYNA KNOCKED on the door of Pythia's home and an elderly woman answered.

"Hello there. Is Pythia home?" she asked.

The woman curled her lip. "Next door," she said, slamming the door in Alyna's face.

Alyna drew in her chin before stepping away from the door, then she strolled the short distance to the home next to the unfriendly old woman. She knocked, and moments later Pythia opened it.

"Hello, Pythia," said Alyna.

"Hello." Pythia motioned her inside. "Come, we are having wine before we leave," she said, leading the way.

Alyna followed and moments later they walked through a second door, into the courtyard. Seated on a chair sat Zotikos. The man raised his cup to his mouth, keeping his eyes fixed on her.

"Hello, Zotikos. My name is Alyna," she said, smiling.

Zotikos lowered his cup, still studying her. He extended his arm and held out the cup.

"Thank you," said Alyna, raising it to her lips. She found a seat on a bench a few cubits away.

Pythia glanced over at the man, raising her brow. "I told you," she said.

"Indeed, you did," he replied.

Alyna felt immediately awkward as the two continued staring at her. She raised the cup to her lips again, taking another drink, but found her gaze gravitating toward the naked man's member, mostly out of simple curiosity but also partly because it was erect and quite large.

Pythia kneeled next to the man and stroked it.

Alyna turned away, hands shaking.

"Pythia mentioned your husband is missing," said Zotikos.

Alyna nodded, still looking in the other direction.

"Kleitos, is that correct?"

She gave another nod.

"Often in life, good things are hard to find when looking for them. Bad things, however, find us regardless, whether we are looking or not," he explained. "I would bet your husband is looking for something good amongst a sea of bad, while you are looking for something bad amongst a sea of good," he said.

Alyna faced the man. "You believe he is alive?" she asked, clasping her hands in front of her.

Zotikos smiled. "Of course I do. We will do good things, so he will only find good things," he replied, followed by a smile.

"We should get going," said Pythia, releasing his phallus and standing.

Zotikos kept his gaze on Alyna. "You are quite beautiful," he said, tilting his head. He looked up at Pythia. "Not as lovely as you, but still, incredibly pretty."

Alyna smiled and turned away, feeling the heat of her cheeks flushing.

"C'mon, Zotikos, we should go," said Pythia urgently.

"Wait just a minute, my love," he replied. "We have to make sure she is prepared for the ceremony." He fixed his gaze on Alyna. "Do you know what we are going to do tonight?"

Alyna's eyes darted back and forth as she thought. "Pay homage to the gods and ask them to protect the soldiers and my husband?"

Zotikos nodded. "Yes, that's exactly what we are going to do. Do you know *how* we will pay homage to them?"

Alyna thought about it and shook her head. "A sacrifice?" she answered, then shrugged.

Zotikos raised his palms. "Yes, probably, but to get their attention, we must do more than that."

He stood and stepped closer to her, then knelt and touched her leg as she jumped at his hand caressing her thigh.

"We please the gods with pleasure," he said, looking at her legs and rubbing his hand along them.

Alyna closed her eyes and shook her head slightly.

Pythia sat beside her. "It's the only way to be in the good graces of the gods and have them return Kleitos to you," she said, reaching for the woman's hand.

Alyna's eyes watered as she looked over at the woman.

Pythia smiled. "You can do this. I have seen the gods answer our calls many times," she explained, brushing her hand across the woman's cheek.

Zotikos placed his hand on Alyna's arm and smiled up at her. "I'll tell you what," he said, rising to his feet and massaging his manhood. "Turn around and I will penetrate you here, so when we arrive at the ceremony, you will feel more comfortable."

"Zotikos, my love, we really should be going."

He reached out his hand for Alyna, and she accepted. "This will only take a minute, Pythia," he said, spinning the woman around and bending her over the bench.

Pythia reached for Alyna's garment. "Wait, let's at least get this off her first," she said, helping to remove the chiton. Pythia also disrobed and sat on the bench. "Lean toward me," she said, pulling Alyna close.

A nearby door opened and out popped the head of the elderly woman next door. She yelped and hastily slammed the door as Pythia laughed.

Zotikos increased his speed and shuttered as he came inside her, then he pushed away from Alyna and found his chair. Alyna turned and found her seat next to Pythia. Zotikos and her both drew deep breaths as a smile washed across the man's face.

CHAPTER 14

LYKUS STOOD NEAR THE OPENING of the tunnels being dug by the slaves and soldiers. The men had already mined about twenty cubits from the wall and were now right under it, placing several posts to support their fortification. After digging another six cubits, they connected the two tunnels, opening an area underground of twelve cubits square, then left the tunnel and were replaced by Lykus and nine mercenaries.

Lykus and his men sat quietly, listening for the sound of the enemy digging. After waiting an hour, he heard the first scrape of a shovel and figured they were no more than a few cubits from them. He and his soldiers readied their weapons and waited, careful not to make any noise.

The sound of shovels and pickaxes grew louder as Lykus became convinced they would appear any moment. He pulled his sword from the baldric, gripping it with both hands. The battalion leader stared fiercely at the far side of the underground lair, clenching his jaw. Moments later a pickaxe came through and a large amount of dirt fell around it.

The surprised Macedonians peeked their heads inside and were instantly met by Lykus and the mercenaries. The unprepared enemy had no chance against the Rhodians and were quickly cut down. Macedonian soldiers scurried through the tunnel toward their camp but were pursued and captured before being dragged back to the Rhodian side.

Lykus walked two prisoners out of the cave while the other soldiers stacked the bodies of the enemy in the lair. "Place these men in chains and keep them under guard," said Lykus. He looked over at a group of spearmen standing nearby. "Follow me, men." He reentered the tunnel as did the spearmen, leading them to the lair. "You men guard this position and defend it at all costs. Understand?"

"Yes, Battalion Leader," they replied.

Lykus motioned for the mercenaries to follow the tunnel toward the enemy's line. He lifted his torch near the entrance, about to leave the lair, but instead paused. He glanced behind him at the spearmen standing nearby, then focused on one of them. "Chares, you come with me," he said.

The soldier ran his fingers through his hair, then rubbed the back of his neck, stepping toward him. "Yes, Battalion Leader," he replied.

The mercenaries were now well over thirty cubits ahead of Lykus and Chares, and the two moved steadily to catch up. They continued through the narrow tunnel, hunched over while they walked. At more than a hundred cubits inside the tunnel, they neared the enemy's line.

Lykus heard swords rattling and grunts of men in front of him. Moments later there were several shouts from the enemy alerting their commanders. He continued toward the sound until the mercenaries came running back his way.

"They are collapsing the tunnel!" shouted one of them.

Then Lykus heard the thuds of many soldiers as swords

and spears poked through the ground above him. He ordered his men to stay low. "To the lair, men," he said, waving for the mercenaries to follow him.

The group turned, scurrying the way they'd come as dirt tumbled down from above.

"Hurry," said Lykus, pushing Chares along.

Two spears came down in front of Chares, stopping him.

Lykus reached forward, placing his hand on his back. "Stay still," he whispered.

It was dark and quiet as the mercenaries laid to the floor of the tunnel. Another spear came racing down, stabbing the dirt just a handsbreadth from the battalion leader's shoulder. With widened eyes, Lykus and his men restrained any reactions as the spear was slowly pulled from above. Although Lykus could not hear the enemy, he knew there were several just above them, waiting for any movement of the lances still stuck in the ground in front of Chares.

"Try to move between the spears. Be careful not to touch them," whispered Lykus, figuring the enemy above had his hand to the weapon, waiting to feel any vibration.

Chares stayed frozen, jaw trembling.

"It's okay, Chares," whispered Lykus, fanning the man forward.

Chares looked toward the spears, then back to his commander. He was about to say something, but before he could, Lykus clenched his jaw and pointed.

"Move," he said through his teeth.

Chares rubbed his hand across his face, then turned toward the spears blocking his path.

Before the soldier could move, another spear raced down and hit a mercenary a few cubits behind them. The man shouted, and Lykus pushed Chares. "Go!" he said, glancing behind him only to see many more spears and swords come racing down from above. The mercenary was struck several more times, his yelps carrying through the tunnel.

Chares wiggled through as did Lykus while more spears pierced the ground around them. After another thirty cubits, the sounds dissipated and Lykus and Chares stopped to rest. Their breathing labored, they watched behind them in the dark tunnel. Only two of the mercenaries appeared next to them, the other seven unable to escape. Hearing cries for help, Lykus started back toward the trapped men, but the sounds of thuds from above drew closer. He stopped and listened, and within seconds, the tunnel fell silent. Realizing the men were dead, Lykus wiped his brow and stared into the dark tunnel before turning back toward the safety of the Rhodian side.

After reaching the lair, he instructed the spearmen to stand guard. Exiting the cave, he ordered several slaves to carry boulders and seal the tunnel from the enemy. While the slaves carried the heavy rocks into the cave, Lykus, the mercenaries, and Chares used rags to wipe the dirt from their faces. Chares stared aimlessly at the ground, appearing to be in deep thought.

Lykus took note of the man's demeanor. "Whatcha thinking, soldier?" he asked.

Chares scratched his chin. "Instead of sealing the tunnel, what if we used their own idea against them?"

Lykus tilted his head. "What do you mean?"

"Well, what if we follow the tunnel as far as possible, then start digging horizontally, across the path of that massive siege tower of theirs?" explained Chares. "If we compromise the ground, surely the weight of the tower will collapse it."

Lykus smiled, placing his hand to the man's shoulder. "You are full of surprises, soldier."

He stood and walked toward the entrance, stopping the slaves from carrying more stones inside.

"Grab your shovels and pickaxes. We have more digging to do," Lykus insisted.

Several men rose to their feet, entering the tunnel with tools in hand.

Lykus glanced back at Chares. "Nice work, soldier," he said before entering the tunnel.

CHAPTER 15

A FEW DAYS AFTER ALKOMIS IDEA of undermining the city's wall failed, Demetrius made final preparations for their attack. With the helepolis now complete, he anxiously awaited the chance of seeing the siege tower in action. Alongside the helepolis were two smaller towers, thirty cubits in height, equipped with two 60-pound catapults each. Demetrius remained confident the Rhodians would surrender once the bombardment commenced, but no longer would he be willing to discuss terms of peace. The substantial loss of men and ships had hardened the man, and he was more determined than ever to see the Rhodians pay a heavy price.

Close to four thousand men surrounded the enormous tower, lifting ropes while others lined up to push it from behind.

"Forward!" shouted Demetrius.

The sounds of ropes tightening, wood creaking, and massive wheels squeaking filled the air as the tower inched forward.

Demetrius studied the ground, pleased to see the wheels riding smoothly on top of it. "Pull!" he shouted to the men holding the ropes.

The tower lunged forward for another hour, and then the helepolis reached striking distance. He heard the horn sound within the capital, signaling the garrison inside. Demetrius focused on his soldiers' movements along the wall as the Rhodians prepared their catapults and archers.

"Prepare to fire," shouted Demetrius at the men scurrying to ready the weapons.

"Ready, my lord," said Alkomis.

Demetrius raised his chin, strolling a safe distance behind the weapon. He raised his hand slowly while fixing his gaze on the city, then glanced over at Alkomis and brought it down quickly. "Fire!" the general shouted.

The siege towers launched projectiles into the air, hurling them toward the city. The helepolis released its largest boulders first, shortly followed by the 60-pounders and finally the 30-pounders. The Rhodians also released their weapons, filling the sky with flying rock and arrows.

Demetrius and his soldiers watched as the projectiles closed in on their target. A thundering crash echoed as the two 180-pound boulders each made a direct hit. A large section of wall collapsed, taking men and artillery with it. Many of the smaller projectiles also found their targets. The Rhodian catapults did return fire but fell short of the tower, while their arrows bounced harmlessly off it.

"Reload! Fire at will," shouted Alkomis.

Moments later, another round of ballista smacked into the wall, shattering another section of it. Demetrius smiled. After two rounds, the city already showed signs of collapsing. While the other towers stopped firing to reload, the helepolis fired continuously, always keeping a boulder in the air. In less than an hour, after introducing the massive siege tower into the battle, the Rhodian defenses were crumbling.

Demetrius walked from his bunker and stood alongside his powerful weapon. Knowing the Rhodians were so shocked by his assault, he watched the city closely, waiting for a flag signaling their surrender.

The towers fired round after round as the Rhodians returned little fire at all.

Alkomis walked up beside him. "Great work, my lord," he said. "We have crippled their defenses." He looked in the distance at the rubble, once a towering wall.

"Thank you, General," replied Demetrius. Now watching the remaining Rhodian catapults, he pointed in the direction of the city. "Why do you think those two catapults are not returning fire?" he asked. "They don't appear damaged."

Alkomis looked at where Demetrius pointed, studying the ballistae. "I don't know, my lord. Perhaps the soldiers manning it retreated farther into the city?" He placed his hand against his chin.

The sound of footsteps drew close, and Alkomis turned toward the approaching soldier.

Demetrius kept his gaze fixed on the enemy's catapults.

"Sir, there is a second wall," said the man.

Demetrius removed his hand from his chin and glanced over at the soldier and Alkomis. "That explains it. They are behind the second wall, waiting for our soldiers to advance on them," he said. He sucked his teeth. "Aim your artillery at the second wall."

Alkomis turned toward the soldier. "You heard him."

"We have, sir, but it's out of range," the soldier replied.

"Move up the towers, General," said Demetrius, still eyeing the catapults.

"Were moving up the towers," shouted Alkomis, waving to the soldiers farther back and out of harm's way.

The soldiers rushed to the siege weapons and within a few minutes, they rolled forward.

"You know, General," said Demetrius pointing in the direction of the capital, "I am convinced those catapults are fakes. Placed there to make us think we have destroyed their defenses. While the working ones are in the rear."

Alkomis squinted off in the distance. "I believe you are correct, my lord," he replied.

"No matter. Once the towers are in position, not an inch of the city will be safe from our artillery," stated Demetrius, stepping in the direction of his bunker.

The soldiers continued moving the towers forward when many shouts came from the men upon it.

"Whoa!" shouted one soldier, catching Demetrius's ear.

He fixed his gaze on the helepolis and saw the front wheels sinking into the ground. "Pull them back, now!" he shouted, racing toward them.

The men dropped the ropes, ran to the front of the tower, and pushed. The tower didn't budge. The two smaller siege weapons were also sinking into the ground.

"Push!" commanded an anxious Demetrius. "Grab the ropes and pull it back!"

As the helepolis leaned farther forward, sinking, the soldiers inside the towers streamed out. Many archers and slingers at the top fell to their death. In a matter of minutes, the daunting siege engines had been rendered useless.

Demetrius called on his entire force to unearth the engines, but not one could be saved. He looked over at Alkomis and narrowed his eyes. "The ground was undermined!" he shouted.

Alkomis nodded. "It was, my lord."

"Yeah, I wonder where they got that idea from?" he said, seething. He walked in circles, squeezed his fists, and glared at the man.

"My lord, we can disassemble a portion of the towers and pull them from those holes," said Alkomis, raising his hands. "It would only take a few days to do so."

"No!" shouted Demetrius, his brows drawn close. "Prepare the men," he said, walking away from Alkomis and shaking his head. "Commence your attack, General."

Seeing the towers leaning in the distance brought smiles to the faces of Chares and the Rhodian soldiers. Most cheered and raised their spears and swords in the air. Several men patted Chares on his shoulder and head, knowing his idea to undermine the ground in front of the towers had saved the city. Chares's own smile widened when Lykus placed his hand on top of his head and gave it a shake.

"Good job, soldier," the man said, walking to a ladder leaning against the second and much smaller wall.

After the celebrating slowed, an eerie silence fell over the Rhodian capital. A few moments later, a low rumbling sound of metal and marching feet carried across the field and through the battered walls of the city. As did many soldiers, Chares looked over the wall to see thousands of Macedonian men marching toward them.

"To your positions, men!" shouted Lykus. Then he motioned to his archers to fire. "Fire at will!"

Arrows and boulders stormed the rows of enemy soldiers, creating huge gaps in their lines, but they kept coming. Chares stared out across the field as the enemy soldiers picked up their pace, shouting as they rushed toward the capital. He climbed from the wall and got in line with the several rows of spearmen placed directly in front of the new wall. They would be the first to face the charging Macedonian army.

Chares glanced along his line, the third and final row. In all, there were close to fifteen hundred spearmen. Behind them, an equal force of swordsmen. The final rows of men were made up of mercenaries and archers. Chares's heart raced as the enemy neared. His hands shook, and he had to remind himself to breathe. Then came a loud roar from the approaching soldiers as they closed in.

Seconds later, hundreds piled through the gaps in the outer wall and crashed into the first line of spearmen. The clash sent several men flying backward into the second line. When their forces had broken through the first two lines, Chares readied his spear.

"Forward!" shouted Lykus, and his entire line advanced, placing their spears into the enemy.

Chares and his fellow spearmen delivered major losses to the advancing army, causing its attack to come to a stop. Hand-to-hand combat ensued as Chares raised his spear, striking several men before being hit himself. Without his armor, the blow to the chest sent Chares backward and to the ground.

Fighting men stepped on him several times as he tried to regain his footing. He struggled to breathe as the blows knocked the air out of him.

"Forward!" shouted the commander at the Rhodian swordsmen now in the fray.

Men fell all around him as Chares examined his chest for injury. There was a four-inch cut, but nothing life threatening. He reached for a spear on the ground next to him just, as a Macedonian soldier came down with his sword on Chares's leg. Chares shouted, jabbing his spear upward and catching the enemy under his breastplate, into his rib cage. The man fell backward, and Chares released the spear and reached for his leg, holding pressure to the wound while grimacing in pain. The shouts of men, shuffling of feet, and clanks of swords were constant, sounding like a thousand boulders tumbling down a hillside.

More soldiers fell alongside Chares as he tried to stand, but the injury to his leg kept him from doing so. A sword slipping from the hand of a nearby soldier caught Chares on the side of his head. The thundering sound dissipated, and his vision blurred. His head spun, and the side of his face smacked against the dirt.

***

Lykus and the mercenaries prepared for their turn in battle as the Macedonian soldiers came over the new wall at a steady pace. The archers did their best to take out as many as they could, but soon they were too numerous.

"Charge!" shouted Lykus, rushing into the enemy swordsmen.

The mercenaries were right behind him as they cut down their enemies. Lykus took several blows from the opponents' swords, but his armor kept him from injury. As the enemy continued filing over the wall, Lykus spotted a man urging them forward. Convinced it was their leading commander, he raced toward the man while drawing back his sword and then swung at him.

The commander raised his sword just in time to parry, but the force of it sent him backward. Lykus charged the man, and a flurry of swords swinging from both men followed. They each attacked and counter attacked until Lykus's sword caught the side of the commander's leg. The man dropped to one knee and glanced down at the injury. Lykus brought his sword down with tremendous force, severing the man's head and sending his body tumbling down the embankment behind him.

Lykus stepped toward his group of mercenaries still fighting a hoard of enemy swordsmen. The archers continued firing their arrows, thinning the attackers with each round. As the Macedonian soldiers continued falling, fewer came over the wall while others fled the city. The mercenary's skill with the sword had proven far superior against the attackers. Even though they initially outnumbered the Rhodians, it became clear the Macedonians were outmatched.

The Rhodian defenders pushed the enemy back out of the city. One by one they fell, were captured, or retreated. Lykus led all his able men into the field where a large group of Macedonian soldiers laid their arms to the ground and lowered to their knees. The sounds of the battle dissipated as the cheers of Rhodian men rose higher and higher.

Breathing heavily, Lykus sat near the captured Macedonians, keeping an eye on them. The Rhodian soldiers kept their swords on the men, as an exhausted Lykus leaned back against the ground and closed his eyes.

Demetrius squeezed his fists at the sight of his men racing across the field to the safety of their archers. Enraged at the sight of his army retreating, he raised his hand as the archers drew back their bows, ready to fire upon his retreating men.

"Hold your fire," he grumbled.

The man paced back and forth, his jaw clenched as he anxiously waited for General Alkomis to return and explain himself, but the general never came. After a good hour, most of the surviving men had returned to the camp. Demetrius kept his archers on high alert just in case of a counterattack but knew that would be highly unlikely. Both armies were short on men and exhausted.

The attack had resulted in a crushing defeat and cost the Macedonian empire tens of thousands of men and nearly a hundred vessels. Demetrius strolled through the camps as healthier men treated the injuries of the many wounded.

Hours later the sun set and as its light dissipated, so had any hope of Demetrius returning to Antigonia a hero.

Chares awoke to the sound of someone calling his name and kicking his foot. "Get up, soldier," the man said.

Now approaching nighttime, a blurry eyed Chares had trouble making out the man's face. He rubbed his eyes, placing his hand to the side of his head and grimaced.

"You okay, soldier?" asked the man.

Chares closed his eyes and nodded, now recognizing the voice.

"Since you slept through most of it, I figured I would let

you know we won," said Lykus, stepping away. "Now, get that leg looked at. We have a lot to do tomorrow."

Chares smiled. "We won," he mumbled. "We won?" He stood, raising his hands over his head, and shouted, "We won!" He squinted, his hand rushing back to his head.

Limping toward the barracks, Chares held his hand to his leg. Hundreds of men were being treated for their injuries. Upon arriving, a soldier looked over Chares's wound and cleaned it. He stitched his leg, poured water on his head and back, and tossed him a handful of rags.

As Chares wiped the dirt and blood from his face and hands, he began feeling better. His thoughts turned to the realization that he would soon be going home.

The next morning, Lykus sat on top of the wall watching the movements of the enemy. They showed no signs of attacking but instead appeared to be doing the same as the Rhodians. Waiting.

Lykus noticed three men walking toward the city. They stopped a hundred cubits from the wall and raised a white rag above their head. He scurried down the ladder and walked over the broken bricks and piles of stones toward the men. He called for two soldiers standing nearby to walk with him. Stopping a few cubits from the enemy, he placed his hands on his hips.

"My lord Demetrius requests an audience with His Magistrate," the man said. "If he accepts, have him and two men come to our camp. There will be no harm to them. My lord gives his word."

Lykus shrugged. "I will let him know," he said, before turning and walking back toward the city.

"Is he wanting us to surrender, Battalion Leader?" asked a soldier.

"Anything's possible, I suppose," said Lykus, heading for the palace.

Two days later, Leonidas walked through the east gate, to a horse drawn cart. He and two councilmen, Cadmus and Takis, climbed up and the horse stepped forward, taking the men to meet with Demetrius. The magistrate already had his mind made up that he would not surrender or align Rhodes with the Macedonian empire. The tiny island had taken on the largest empire in the world and held. Leonidas was confident the Rhodians would ultimately prevail if the fighting did in fact continue.

The attack on his city had crippled their trade network and destroyed most of their fleet while leaving the capital in ruins. He felt the Macedonians not only needed to withdraw immediately, but also pay for the damages and supply the island with new ships. However, he certainly wanted the battle to end. The attack that had started nearly a year ago would continue to affect the city for many more. The time had come to end the fighting and begin the healing.

The cart came to a stop, and the three men stepped from it. Leonidas looked at the driver and Lykus sitting beside him, before focusing on a man walking in their direction. They were soon after joined by the man, who led them to a skiff. The men climbed on board and after finding their seats, the soldiers rowed.

Anchored about fifty yards from shore rested the Macedonian quadrireme flagship. Once reaching the vessel, the men were helped onto it and then followed the man to the steps to Demetrius's quarters. Once entering, the men were directed to a table with several cups and a vase of wine upon it. They found their seats as the man walked to a door on the other side of the room and knocked.

Stepping toward the door they'd entered, the man said, "He will be right with you," then he walked out, closing the door behind him.

Councilman Takis reached for the vase.

"We will wait for our host," Leonidas instructed.

Takis placed the vase back on the table.

Moments later the door opened and in walked Demetrius, strolling toward the table while opening his arms. "Hello, gentlemen," he said, glancing at the magistrate before turning and bowing his head. "Leonidas."

"Demetrius," the magistrate replied.

Demetrius lifted the vase, filled four glasses, and returned it to the table. He slid a cup in front of each man and found his seat. "We could spend hours talking about how we got here, but I'd rather talk about where we are going," he explained.

"Fair enough," replied Leonidas.

"I must say, your men have fought bravely. They have surprised my men and more importantly, myself," said Demetrius, lifting his cup.

"There has been no shortage of bravery during the battle, on either side," replied Leonidas.

"What I hope to achieve here today is to find a way to put an end to this struggle, so more brave men don't have to die," said Demetrius.

"Well, from our side it's pretty simple. Your forces immediately leave our island and pay a fair restitution so we can rebuild," explained Leonidas, raising his cup.

Demetrius exhaled through his nose as he tapped his finger on the table. "A fair request. We will leave your shores tomorrow if you swear your allegiance to the empire. I am sure we can help rebuild your city."

"Rhodes, now for a long time, has been an independent republic. You know as well as anybody that our economic stability depends on neutrality," replied Leonidas.

Demetrius raised his cup again and glanced around the table. "You need to understand, the empire must stay intact. To do that, we must put an end to the separatists. Ptolemy in particular."

"Ptolemy has been no burden to us, and he surely hasn't attacked our island," said a fiery Takis.

Leonidas raised his hand from the table and glanced over at the man. "Please, gentlemen, let us not bicker. Instead, let us focus on the issues before us." He fixed his gaze on Demetrius. "We have defeated your navy, we have crippled your artillery, and we have turned back your army. If there is another attack tonight, tomorrow, or next week, our city will hold," he said, raising a brow.

Demetrius smiled, then chuckled. He sat in silence for several moments, focusing on the man. "I will bury our dead and leave your shores tomorrow. I am willing to leave behind a good number of ships. But you must promise to keep your island neutral and not align with Ptolemy," he said, leaning back in his chair. "That's the best deal I can give you."

Leonidas grinned as he rose to his feet and extended his hand across the table. "It's agreed."

Demetrius accepted his hand, then shook hands with each of the councilmen. "How many of my men did you capture?" he asked.

Leonidas turned toward the councilmen. "Maybe a few hundred?" he replied.

Demetrius scratched his cheek. "We have several hundred of yours, taken from the sea wall. I will return them to the harbor in the morning in exchange for our men and any remaining forces on the mole."

Leonidas raised his cup. "It's agreed," he replied as the men lifted their cups to their mouths. After setting his back on the table, Leonidas scratched his beard for a moment and then looked over at Demetrius. "What of the siege weapons?" he asked.

"I don't have the time to dismantle them," replied Demetrius. "Keep them as a reminder of our agreement."

Leonidas smirked. "Our crumbled walls are more than enough reminder," he replied.

⎯⎯⎯⎯⎯◆⎯⎯⎯

The following morning, the two armies exchanged prisoners as agreed upon the day before. Demetrius remained hopeful that Alkomis would be among them, but he was not. After gathering the last of his forces from the western mole, Demetrius sailed for Antigonia, returning to his father a failure.

For the Rhodians released, many men had injuries and needed medical attention. One man had a deep wound to the abdomen and struggled walking under his own power. The injured man was none other than Kleitos.

As the last of the Macedonian warships sailed away from port, the city raised their flag and sounded the horn, making the civilians aware that the battle had ended. And by the grace of the sun god Helios, the island of Rhodes had achieved the impossible. Victory.

PART 2

RISE OF *THE COLOSSUS*

CHAPTER 16

T HE WEEKS AFTER THE ISLAND'S success against the Macedonians were utilized burying their dead and repairing the city walls and other damaged structures inside the capital. The southern wall, which faced the devastating attack of the helepolis, was so badly damaged that the council decided to take it down completely before extending it farther into the plain.

Demetrius had left the island half of his remaining ships, just under a hundred in all. His Magistrate acted quickly to re-establish their trade routes, the economic lifeline of the island. However, the twelve-month siege had nearly bankrupted the capital and the road to recovery would be long and arduous.

Even facing the economic hardship, the mood of the island stayed jubilant over the unlikely victory. His Magistrate and councilmen planned for a great festival shortly after the Macedonian army retreated. After the debris had been cleaned up and structures repaired, the soldiers were free to return home, including Chares.

The returning soldiers were greeted warmly by the people of the island. Many were given wine, food, and colorful leis as they passed through town. A young woman had given Chares a vase of wine and a kiss to his cheek just after exiting the capital. Shortly followed by an older woman handing him a basket of figs and bread. By the time he reached his front door, his arms ached from carrying all of the gifts he'd been given.

Chares stood nervously on the porch, unsure of what he would find upon entering. It had been a year since he had seen his wife, and although angry about her infidelity with the immoral man Zotikos, he truly missed the woman. He opened the door and stepped inside. Glancing about the empty room, he found no Pythia and all the furniture was gone as well. As he strolled through the home, he noticed his wife's dowry also missing. The only items left were his clothes and kline.

Chares set the wine and bread to the floor and walked out to the courtyard. He browsed around, finding it mostly empty except for his workbench and sculpting tools. He ran his hand through his hair and walked back inside. He searched for a cup, but they were gone as well. He kicked off his sandals and sat next to the bread and wine with his back against the wall. He lifted the vase, taking a large drink as some dribbled from the side of his mouth and into his lap.

Chares reached for a piece of bread while thinking of his wife and all he had been through the last year. Over the next hour, almost half the wine in the vase was consumed and a drunken Chares passed out with a piece of bread hanging from his red-stained lips.

Chares awoke to banging on the door. He rubbed his head and slowly rose to his feet. As he approached the door, he wiped the breadcrumbs from his tunic. He opened the door, and there stood Medeia with a bowl of olives.

"Welcome home, Chares," she said, extending the bowl toward him.

Chares smiled, accepting the gift.

The woman peered around him.

"She's not here," said Chares, assuming Medeia looked for Pythia.

"I figured as much. I saw her and that disgusting Zotikos carrying items out last week. I was more than relieved to see them go," she explained. The woman gazed at him. "You look awful. Let me make you breakfast," she said, stepping toward him.

"No, that's okay," said Chares, scratching his head. "I appreciate it though."

"Stop by later. I have fresh figs and eggs," she said, stepping back.

"Thanks, Medeia," replied Chares, closing the door.

***

As the weeks passed, Chares kept to himself while keeping the wine closer. All the heavy drinking and lack of food gave him a sickly appearance, and each day became more of a struggle for the heartbroken, lonely man. Many days he would awake and just stay in his kline all day, unable to find the energy to even bathe. Trash and spoiled food filled the home. He also regularly missed the slaves collecting the pots of waste matter, giving the home an awful stench.

Since returning from the capital, he had not spent a single minute sculpting and his finances had diminished. One afternoon, as he lay on the floor near the sitting area after a long night of drinking, there came a knock at the door. Chares cracked an eye open but let his gaze wander aimlessly about the room.

"Chares, are you there?" asked the man as he knocked again.

Chares slowly pushed himself from the floor, wiping the drool from his mouth and staggering toward the entrance. He leaned against the wall. "Yeah, what is it?" he asked through the door.

"I was sent here by His Magistrate. He has a request of you."

Chares rubbed the back of his neck. "What does he want?"

"His Magistrate is asking the sculptors of the island to submit a detailed proposal for a new statue that will be built in honor of our triumph over the Macedonians," the man replied.

A naked Chares opened the door and leaned against it. "The Poseidon statue?" he asked.

The messenger at the door squinted and covered his mouth, obviously overtaken by the stench. Then he shook his head. "No, that plan has been scrapped. This will be a far grander statue, symbolizing our victory and honoring Helios," he explained.

"Far grander, huh," replied Chares, scratching his chin. "How long before I have to present?"

"One week," the man replied. "His Magistrate would like to announce it at the festival next month."

Chares yawned and stood back from the door. "Would you like to come in for a drink?" he asked.

The man peered into the home before taking a step back. "No, thanks. Have a good day," he replied, stepping away from the door.

Chares gazed at the messenger now walking away and glancing back at him several times.

About that time, another man walked by and shouted, "Put on some clothes or shut the door!"

Chares turned and scratched his butt cheek, closing the door behind him.

Alyna sat by the bedside of Kleitos, weeping. Her many prayers to the gods to return him to her were fruitful, but the man's injuries were too great. After weeks of struggling, he had finally succumbed to them. She spent an hour with her lifeless husband, then left the room and fell into the arms of her awaiting daughters of eight and ten years old. The three embraced, shared tears of grief rolling down their cheeks.

Kleitos's brother, sister, and mother were also present. The women bathed the man with wet rags and then dressed him in a fine tunic. They placed a coin to his lips to pay for passage across the Styx and into the underworld, then laid him unto a wagon lined with blankets and led his funeral procession through the streets of Lindos. Many emerged from their homes to give their final farewells to the man.

Chares had spent most of the day cleaning his home. Hearing a bell ringing outside, he stepped onto the porch to see Alyna and her family leading a cart carrying his friend, Kleitos. Chares stepped close to the wagon and placed his hand on his comrade's shoulder. His mind raced to the early days of battle when a nervous Kleitos had somehow helped him contain his own fear. Chares's eyes watered as he began to smile, thinking of the time Kleitos and a few others had fled in the face of the enemy only to return later and be berated by the battalion leader. Paying his respects to the man, Charles then approached Alyna at the front of the cart. She informed him of a banquet in honor of the deceased, and he embraced the woman and accepted the invitation. Releasing Alyna, he watched the caravan continue down the street as others emerged from their homes to pay homage to the man. After a few minutes, Chares turned and walked to his porch, then opened the door.

After spending some time getting the home back in order, he walked to the public bath and washed himself and his clothes. Upon returning home, he trimmed his hair and shaved his face. He not only looked like a new man but felt like one too.

Being informed of the proposed statue had motivated him greatly. He wanted to design something to not only please the Rhodians but awe the masses worldwide. As a soldier during the battle, when all hope seemed lost, Chares remembered calling on Helios, and every time, the sun god had answered his prayers. Chares became convinced, as were many others of the island, that their victory came entirely from the grace of the sun god. He knew if he could design something to not only symbolize the island's resilience but also pay homage to the god, he would surely be awarded the job. He searched his mind feverishly while considering the labor and material needed to build the statue. He knew not only the design would be important, but the costs of building were equally crucial.

After sketching several ideas on a piece of papyrus, he tossed them aside, frustrated. He instead focused on the banquet. After walking to the agora to get a gift for the family of the bereaved, he strolled toward the home of his fallen comrade. Still shocked and saddened by the death of Kleitos, those feelings were soon overtaken by his excitement to see Alyna.

Upon arriving, he greeted the woman and her family. After giving her the highly decorated lekanis he'd purchased at the agora, he strolled to the table where much food had been placed for the guests. He gathered bread, olives, and figs in a small bowl and meandered into the courtyard.

Of the many people there, Chares saw two he hadn't expected and had no want of seeing, none other than Pythia and Zotikos so fixed on each other they didn't even see him. He squinted as he felt the blood race to his face. The woman sat on the lap of Zotikos, feeding him grapes between several kisses. He forced himself not to beat the man senseless, knowing it was hardly the time or place.

He felt a warm hand touch his own and turned to find Alyna standing beside him.

"I am sorry, Chares. I should have warned you they might be here," she said, dropping her head.

"It's okay, Alyna. This isn't about me or them, it's about Kleitos," he explained.

The woman smiled and released his hand before stepping away.

He fixed his gaze back in the direction of Pythia and Zotikos to find them both staring directly at him with a surprised look on their faces.

Chares gathered himself and strolled toward them.

Pythia rose from the man's lap and found a seat next to him.

"Chares, you're alive. Quite the victory, huh?" said Zotikos, grinning.

"No help from you," replied Chares, fixing his gaze on Pythia.

The defiant woman smirked at him. "What do you want?" she asked.

"Just wanted to tell you we are hereby divorced." Then he motioned toward Zotikos. "This nasty pervert can be our witness to that." He refocused on Pythia. "And thank you for taking everything we had. That was really nice of you."

"We left your kline," said Zotikos. "It's quite comfy."

Chares glared at the man. "You know, Zotikos, someday you will have to answer for your wicked ways. And all the garbage that pours out of your mouth about the world of men ending, will not be for the masses, but just you." He curled his lip. "And I hope I am there to see it." He looked at Pythia and shook his head. "I feel sorry for you," Chares said before stepping away.

"You should feel sorry for yourself, you pathetic excuse of a man!" said a fiery Pythia, gaining the attention of several guests.

Chares walked back into the home and spotted Alyna by the table. He stepped close to her, placing his bowl upon it. "I am leaving, Alyna," he softly said.

Alyna reached for his hand. "I'm sorry. I know it must be awkward seeing them here together," she said, releasing him.

Chares smiled slightly and nodded.

"Before you go, I have something for you," she said, leading Chares into the sitting area. She raised a decorative vase from the table and slipped a piece of parchment out from under it. "Kleitos was in a great deal of pain after returning home. He drew to keep his mind from it," she explained, as her eyes filled with tears. "The day the horn blew, and he was leaving for the capital in his uniform. I called for him before he left and handed him a bowl of olives to snack on while walking to the fort," she said, wiping away a tear. She handed it to Chares. "Here, I want you to have it."

Chares looked at the simple drawing of a soldier holding a spear in one hand and a bowl in the other.

"He told me how kind you were to him during the battle," she said, with a smile.

"Thank you, but don't you think you should hang on to it?"

"I have plenty of other drawings. Yes, I am sure," she replied.

Chares smiled and gave her a quick hug. "If you need anything, let me know," he said, stepping toward the door.

After returning home, Chares kicked off his sandals and filled a cup full of wine. He thought of how much effort he'd spent getting ready for the banquet only to be there a few minutes. Seeing Pythia and Zotikos there together had made his blood boil. The woman seemed cold and almost angry at him.

What's she got to be mad about? He rubbed his forehead.

He lifted his cup, then walked into the courtyard and found a seat at his workbench. He reached for a small cup of water sitting on the desk and wetted a block of clay. After taking a drink of wine, he lifted his stylus and stared at the block for several moments. He started to draw, then shook his head and wetted his fingers, once again smoothing the surface.

Over the next hour, Chares repeated this sequence while becoming more and more frustrated each time. He threw the stylus to the desk and walked inside to get more wine. As he set the vase down after filling his cup, a drop of wine fell on the parchment he'd received from Alyna. He hurriedly lifted the drawing and shook the wine from it. He squinted at it for a few moments, rotating the parchment several times. The drop had landed upon the head of the soldier and gave the appearance of him wearing a crown. A great excitement came over Chares.

"That's it!" he said, his eyes widening.

He carried the cup of wine and the drawing to his workbench, picked up his stylus, and placed the tip upon the block. He chuckled and shook his head many times as the excitement continued to build. Several hours passed by the time he finally rested the stylus and lifted the block of clay, holding it up in front of him. His smile widened as he stared at it for several moments. He set it on the bench and dragged a block of limestone close to him. He raised his chisel and glanced at the drawing. He chipped away at the block as more hours flew by like minutes. Almost twelve hours later, exhausted but happy, Chares placed his chisel and hammer back on the bench. Although still needing to finish the pedestal and smooth out the rough edges, the fourteen-inch statue neared completion.

He rose from his seat and staggered toward the door. The morning sun peeked above the horizon as he hurried inside before its rays could reach him. He walked directly to his kline and lay upon it. Moments later, he fell asleep.

Later in the evening, Chares awoke and shuffled right back to his bench to work. After finishing the pedestal, he etched the limestone with the name of his statue. *The Colossus.*

A few days later, Chares waited in a hallway by the door of the board room where his statue, scroll, and concept drawing sat on display. He had placed a rag over the small statue before joining the other sculptors patiently waiting their turn to present. There were several other sculptors also there, including the well-known Priamus, who had shaped the *Praying Boy* statue located in the square near the palace. The sculptors greeted each other warmly, as most knew each other. Chares, on the other hand, remained quiet while nervously tapping his foot.

The door opened and a sculptor exited, glancing around at the waiting group. "Chares, you're next."

Chares rose to his feet, watching the man walk away with his head bowed. "Thanks," he replied, before stepping into the room.

There were six people seated on the far side of a long table, with a small stand in front of it. Chares set his items up on the small stand, then glanced up at the group. Seated among them were Leonidas, Takis, Cadmus, Ares, the city manager named Hermes, and Lykus.

Upon noticing him, Chares nodded to his former battalion leader.

"Hello, Chares. Good to see you," said Lykus.

"Good to see you too, Battalion Leader," he replied.

Upon finishing a discussion with the man next to him, Leonidas looked from the table toward Chares standing before him. "Okay, Chares, let's see what you have for us," he said.

Chares lifted the small statue, keeping the rag in place, and stepped toward the man. He placed the statue in front of Leonidas. "I give you, *The Colossus*," he said, lifting the rag.

The men studied the figurine of a man holding a spear and bowl by his side. The tiny soldier had the face of Helios and a crown with many points simulating the rays of the sun god.

Chares waited in anticipation as they each passed it around, studying it.

"Tell us about *The Colossus*, Chares," said Leonidas, his eyes still fixed on the small statue.

Chares placed his scroll on the table in front of the men and opened it up. "The statue will be made of bronze and have a crown honoring our sun—"

"What's this here?" asked Leonidas.

"That's the height," replied Chares.

The man leaned closer to the scroll. "Eighty-six cubits?" he asked, drawing his chin to his chest.

Chares widened his eyes. "Yes, with the pedestal, it would be close to two hundred feet."

The men in the room laughed, all except Lykus, whose eyes shifted back and forth between Chares and the men seated beside him.

"Where would we get enough bronze to build something like that?" asked Councilman Takis, raising his palms.

"Well, we could use the bronze plating on the helepolis, and the other siege weapons Demetrius left behind."

Lykus cleared his throat. "If we took all the bronze from those siege towers, how far would that get us?" he asked.

Chares scratched his chin. "Just past the knees," he replied.

Leonidas laughed again until he started coughing.

"What's the projected cost to build this Colossus of yours?" asked Cadmus, his brows drawing close.

Chares turned toward the man. "Five hundred talents."

The men laughed hysterically as Chares glanced over at Lykus, then lowered is head. The man stared stoically back at Chares before glancing to the men seated next to him. Chares rolled up his scroll and placed the rag back over the statue.

"Why don't we build a marble bridge to the mainland

while we are at it?" said Takis. He laughed so hard, he rocked back and forth in his chair, slapping his knee.

Leonidas wiped his eyes, still unable to catch his breath.

A red-faced Lykus stood from his chair. "Your Magistrate, gentlemen. I humbly remind you Chares was instrumental in stopping the helepolis and saving our island," he stated.

The laughing subsided.

He continued, "I know this man and maybe he is a dreamer, but his engineering and vision were exactly what we needed when he suggested digging the tunnel." Then he sat back down.

Chares glanced at Lykus, then at the floor and back to his defender, his appreciation and embarrassment warring for priority within him. "Thank you, Lykus," he said, picking up his belongings and walking toward the door. He got about half-way to the door and stopped, removed the rag from the statue, and examined it for a few moments. He rubbed his thumb over the name engraved into the pedestal, spun on his heel, and walked back toward the men. They were still fighting their laughter as Chares handed the statue to his battalion leader. "For you, sir," he said.

The man accepted the gift and smiled. "Thank you, soldier," said Lykus, placing the statue on the table in front of him.

As Chares turned and walked briskly for the door, Leonidas called out, "Chares, can you send in Priamus, please?"

Chares sighed as he left the room. Once in the hallway, the sculptors stared at him.

"What in the world was so funny in there?" one man asked.

Chares dropped his shoulders and walked away. "They will see you now, Priamus," he said. *I need a drink,* he thought.

Once outside the building, he walked to the agora, which had a taverna there. He had a cup of wine as his thoughts raced. He had spent the last week designing his statue to commemorate the victory over Demetrius, only to be laughed out of the room. One drink led to another until a drunken Chares slouched in his seat. He stood, staggering along the city street until stopping by a pine tree and resting his back against it. He closed his eyes, his mouth falling open.

Chares awoke to the sound of giggling as two young boys kicked his feet.

"You okay?" one asked.

Chares cracked an eye open. "Go on, get out of here!" he shouted as he stumbled and nearly fell, trying to get to his feet.

The boys laughed and ran off.

Chares squinted from the bright sun while staggering along the street, heading for his home. Over halfway there, he realized he didn't have his scroll or drawing of *The Colossus*. He briefly thought about heading back but quickly shunned the idea, thinking of nothing he wanted more than a cup of wine and his comfy kline.

CHAPTER 17

ALMOST THREE WEEKS AFTER CHARES met with Leonidas and the others about his statue, the mood on the island remained high. By the time of the festival to celebrate their victory, Chares had returned to his listless heavy drinking and his home returned to the filthy hole deluged by trash and stench once again.

He lay on his kline scratching several days since his last bath when a knock came at the door. He stumbled up and staggered toward it.

"Who's there?" he asked.

"Medeia," the woman replied. "Are you going to the festival tonight? Maybe we could ride together?"

"No, I am staying in," replied Chares.

"It's going to be quite special, and all the people of the island will be there," she explained.

"All but one," he replied, stepping away from the door. "Have fun, Medeia."

He walked to a nearby table, filled his cup with wine, and grabbed a handful of grapes before returning to his kline.

Alyna and her daughters climbed up on a horse drawn cart heading to the festival. Countless people filled the road to the capital for the much-anticipated event. There would be all kinds of games, food, and even a small-scale reenactment of the battle. Also planned, the announcement of the new statue to commemorate the victory. Alyna had not been back to the capital since going there to look for Kleitos. Her mind couldn't help thinking of the man as she rode along with her daughters by her side.

At the festival, Alyna and her girls snacked on baklava near center stage, watching a woman play a harp. After the performance ended and she left the stage, His Magistrate stepped up. Following behind him were several other men waving their hands, bringing the crowd close. People closed in and filled the entire square.

His Magistrate raised his hand to quiet the crowd. "Great people of Rhodes, we have a special announcement for you. To commemorate our victory over the Macedonians, we have decided to build a statue to honor our sun god Helios," he explained.

Two men beside him each held a corner of a large piece of fabric hiding what lay behind it. The crowd waited with great anticipation.

"I give you…*Phoebus!*" he said.

The men dropped the curtain, revealing a small model of the proposed statue. A column of marble supported a man's upper torso, arms holding a spherical bronze plate representing the sun.

He gestured to the small model and raised his hands. "It will stand twenty-four cubits high and be placed right here in the heart of our capital," he said, widening his eyes. "Designed and built by Priamus."

Some of the crowd cheered, but a great many more grumbled as Leonidas glanced around, seeming surprised.

"*Phoebus!*" he said again, getting even fewer cheers than the first time.

Puzzled, Leonidas raised a brow and talked to the other men beside him.

They shrugged.

A man made his way through the crowd. The onlookers stepped aside to let him pass. Leonidas glanced at him, as did many others gathered around the stage. The man walked right past Alyna as she pulled her daughters close. As he passed, she noticed a scroll in his right hand. Upon reaching the stage, the man held the scroll out for Leonidas.

His Magistrate reached for the scroll as the crowd fell silent. "What's this?" he asked, unrolling it before glancing from the man to the scroll. He gazed at the writings and drawings for several moments before turning to the group of men beside him.

"*The Colossus,*" he said.

A spontaneous roar of the crowd startled the man, and he nearly dropped the scroll.

"*The Colossus!* We want *The Colossus!*" the crowd shouted.

Leonidas turned to the men next to him, having a discussion as the crowd's chants grew louder. He raised his hand, and the crowd fell quiet.

"As His Magistrate, I have the responsibility to put the best interests of the island first," he said, gazing out at the crowd. "I have sworn an oath to do just that. This enormous statue is so far from anything man has ever created, it's not only unrealistic but borders on the impossible."

The crowd moaned.

"But we have done the impossible when we defeated Demetrius, and we shall do the impossible again!"

A thundering roar came from the crowd as they raised their hands in the air.

Leonidas opened the scroll and showed it to the crowd. "I give you, *The Colossus!*"

The crowd cheered and chanted for *The Colossus* once more.

Alyna squinted as she peered at the scroll the man held up. Her mouth dropped when she realized it was the exact drawing she had given Chares a few weeks before.

Puzzled, she shouted. "Who is the sculptor?" She pulled her daughters along, walking toward the stage. "Who's the sculptor?" she asked again, drawing the attention of Leonidas.

The man raised his hand, and the crowd became quiet again. "Excuse me?" he asked, leaning toward her.

"Who designed *The Colossus*? Who's the sculptor?"

Leonidas smiled, raising his hand and quieting the crowd further. "The sculptor is not only a master of his trade, but he also played an instrumental role stopping the helepolis," he explained. He leaned toward the man standing next to him as the man whispered in his ear. Leonidas nodded, then raised his hands. "Chares of Lindos," he said.

The crowd chanted. "Chares and *The Colossus!* Chares and *The Colossus!*"

Gasping, Alyna took a few steps back. She brought her fingers to her mouth, then walked opposite of the stage with her daughters in tow. As she reached the outer edge of the massive crowd, she caught a glimpse of Pythia and Zotikos in discussion.

"Can you believe this?" she asked.

Pythia and Zotikos faced her. Pythia clenched her jaw as Zotikos raised his hands.

"It can't be the Chares we know. It has to be someone else," he insisted.

"They said *Chares of Lindos*, and that drawing was the one I gave him from Kleitos," said Alyna.

Pythia rolled her eyes and pulled Zotikos by the hand, leading him away.

Alyna looked at her girls. "C'mon, we have to go home."

The girls pouted as she led them toward the horse drawn cart. A few moments later, the bewildered Alyna rode for Lindos, anxiously biting her nails all the way there.

Chares lay on the floor just moments from falling asleep when a knock came to the door. He pushed himself up and accidently hit his foot against the vase sitting nearby. The wine spilled out across the floor, as he pressed his fingers to his eyes. He glanced at the door as another knock came much louder and for a longer time. Annoyed, he kicked the vase and then glared at the door.

"What?" he shouted, and the knock came to a sudden stop.

"Chares?" a woman asked.

"Yeees," he answered in a slow, monotone voice as he stepped closer.

"Chares, it's Alyna."

His eyes opened wide as he glanced around his room, then

to his wine-stained tunic. His house was a complete mess, and he hadn't bathed in days. Alyna was the last person he wanted to see looking like this.

"Hello, Alyna," replied Chares with a cracking voice.

"Let me in. I have something to tell you," she said urgently.

Chares cleared his throat and looked about the room again. "Can I come by later tonight or tomorrow?" he asked.

"No, let me in. You won't believe what happened at the festival."

He bit on his lip, thinking. "I would rather you come by tomorrow."

"Chares, it's about *The Colossus*."

His eyes grew wide, and he quickly opened the door. "What about it?" he asked, tilting his head.

Alyna dropped her chin and stepped back. "My goodness, Chares," she said, covering her mouth. "What happened to you?"

Chares looked at the front of his tunic and rubbed his hand over his head, making his hair even more messy. "It's been a long day," he replied.

Alyna blinked repeatedly, still covering her mouth.

"How do you know about *The Colossus*?" he asked.

"Chares, I was at the festival and they announced the winner. A guy named Priamus had been awarded the job and the crowd yelled, 'We want *The Colossus*!' "

"Huh? Are you sure they were yelling *Colossus* and not *Proboscis*?"

Alyna's brows drew together. "Why would they yell that?"

Chares raised a shoulder. "Leonidas has quite a big one."

Alyna snickered. "Yes, I am sure. After I saw the scroll

that had a drawing of the man and the spear, I asked who the sculptor was and His Magistrate replied, 'Chares of Lindos.' "

Chares scratched his chin as he stared aimlessly at the ground.

"Chares, I was completely shocked. Who would have thought the spearman my Kleitos drew in his final days would be the design for the biggest statue in the world?" she said, her eyes watering. She leaned forward and embraced him, before hurriedly leaning away and covering her mouth again.

Chares smiled at the woman, still trying to wrap his head around what she'd told him. Then, raising his hands, he said rapidly and in an animated manner, "I don't understand it… I really don't. You gave me the drawing, and I sat it on a table. I spilled wine on it, got an idea, and showed it to Leonidas. He laughed me out of the room, so I got drunk and passed out. When I awoke, my scroll was gone."

Alyna shifted her eyes side to side.

"That's it," he said, placing his hand to his chin. "Someone must have picked up my scroll and showed it to the people around the capital," he explained, reaching for the woman and pulling her close. "Alyna, do you know what this means?"

"Chares," she replied, pushing against him. "It smells, and you're squeezing the air out of me."

"No, it means…" He pursed his lips in thought of how in the world he could build the gigantic statue. "It means… I have to think."

He released her as she drew a much-needed breath and took a step back. He peered at the sky in deep thought before looking at the woman again.

"It means you need to go take a bath and change your clothes," she said, placing her hand over her mouth.

Chares smiled as he stared into her eyes. "Alyna, you are the most beautiful and most amazing woman in Lindos." He bit his lip, surprised by what he'd just said to her.

Alyna chuckled. "You are just excited," she replied. "Now, get cleaned up and come over later," she insisted, stepping away from the door. "I want to know all about it."

Chares waved as she looked back beaming at him. He shut the door, then leaned his back against it. He had a smile fixed across his face. He glanced at the mess around him, and the smile quickly dissipated. He rushed about the home picking up dirty clothes and trash and emptied the waste matter from the pot into the ravine along the street. After making the home much more presentable, he grabbed a clean tunic, oil, and strigil and walked to the public bath. He was relieved to see no one there as he stripped and stepped in.

A man walking by shouted at him. "Put on some clothes or get in the water!"

Chares creased his brow and glared at the man before lowering himself into the cool water. Soon he heard many folks coming his way. As groups of people passed by the bath in what seemed quite a rush, Chares dove under the water to clean his hair. When he reemerged, folks were still filing by.

I wonder where they are going? he thought.

After stepping out of the water, he sat on the bench drying for a few minutes before slipping on his tunic. As he strolled home thinking about *The Colossus* and, of course, Alyna, he noticed a large group of people by his door. He stepped behind a tree to conceal himself and observe them.

What in the world are they doing?

He wanted to go home and shave before going to Alyna's but decided to go now. Once arriving at her home, the two strolled to the courtyard and talked. Hours passed like minutes as he told her all about *The Colossus* and his meeting with the magistrate.

The two joked and laughed as their conversation shifted from one topic to the next. There were also tears, as Chares shared the details of him and Kleitos during the battle. By the time an exhausted Chares left for home, the streets were completely dark. He was pleased to see one thing as he approached his door. No one.

CHAPTER 18

The next morning, Chares began the planning phase of building *The Colossus*. He had the specifics for the statue and pedestal but still needed to consider many other matters at great length. The internal framework, scaffolding, maintenance, manpower, and how to make it a functioning lighthouse.

Certainly there would be many questions, and he wanted to make sure he could address all of them confidently. After a few hours of working, he walked to the kitchen as a knock sounded at the door. He finished filling his cup and took a drink, then placed it back upon the table. He then walked to the door, pulling it open.

There stood the same messenger who had visited him weeks earlier and informed him about the proposed statue. The man quickly stood back and covered his mouth. He gazed at Chares, then peered around him and inside the home. He lowered his hand.

"His Magistrate wishes to see you immediately," the man said.

Chares looked past him at the horse drawn cart, then nodded. "Let me get my things."

He stepped away from the door and to the table where his drawings and schematics rested. After gathering his items, he slammed the rest of his water, then walked outside to the cart where the man waited.

As they rode through the streets of Lindos, many people pointed and waved to Chares. He beamed as many folks called out his name. He felt like a famous philosopher or even a king, as more and more called out to him. He rose from his seat and waved. After leaving Lindos, he sat with a smile fixed on his face, focusing his gaze at the man next to him.

"Were you at the festival?" asked Chares.

"Yes, it was quite a spectacle," the man replied.

"I wasn't there, but a friend told me about it," said Chares, looking out in the distance across the water. "It must have been quite embarrassing for Priamus."

"I suppose it would," the man replied, holding back his laugh. "I think His Magistrate will be interested to know how so many people found out about *The Colossus*."

"That makes two of us," replied Chares with a chuckle.

Once entering the busy streets of the capital, many folks turned toward them. They pointed and one man yelled, "Are you Chares of Lindos?"

"Yes, good sir," replied Chares, waving to the man.

Many flocked around the cart, following alongside it. They reached in, touching his head and shoulder while others shook his hand. The mob grew as people cheered.

"Chares and *The Colossus*!" they repeated several times.

His smile widened as the wagon approached the palace.

The guards there held the crowd back as the cart rode past the iron gates.

"Get back!" shouted the guards, pushing the group of people following the cart back outside the gates.

One man at the gate resembled the guard who had punched Chares in the face during family day. The two locked eyes, and Chares smirked, thinking how difficult it once was to get the gate open. Now they would open it any time he stepped near.

The cart came to a stop in front of the palace. The two men climbed down and walked to the entrance. Once inside, Chares knew right where they headed and began to lead.

"No, sir, we are going this way," the man said.

Chares stopped, turned, and followed him. They climbed up several steps into a much more decorated area, then to a courtyard with a vineyard, many vases, and flowers. It was much nicer than the last place they'd convened. Near the middle of the courtyard sat several men in fancy chairs with cushions covered in fine fabric. There were also several women serving them drinks and snacks.

As Chares approached, Leonidas stood and waved him over, then shook his hand. "Welcome back, Chares," said His Magistrate, before turning and gesturing to each man now standing. "You remember Commander Ares, City Manager Hermes, and Councilman Takis."

The men stepped forward one by one and shook Chares's hand. The last man to welcome him placed one hand to his shoulder and gave it a squeeze. "Good to see you again, soldier."

"Same to you, Battalion Leader."

Lykus motioned toward an empty chair next to his.

"Please, have a seat," he said, then waved to a servant. "Bring wine for our guest."

Returning to his chair, Leonidas gazed at Chares and chuckled. "My goodness, Chares. Were you at the festival?"

Chares shook his head as the servant handed him his drink, smiling at him. His eyes followed the beautiful woman as she stepped away.

"Have you been informed of what took place?" he asked.

Chares nodded, his gaze still fixed on the woman.

Lykus chuckled, reaching over and tapping Chares on the shoulder. "Easy, soldier," he said, pointing toward Leonidas.

"Huh?" replied Chares, glancing over at the man.

"Chares, please, have you been informed as to what transpired at the festival?"

"Yes, Your Magistrate."

"Do you have any idea how so many found out about *The Colossus* in the few short weeks after you left here?" he asked.

"None," replied Chares.

"Well, the man who approached the stage had your scroll. Did you give it to him?"

Chares shook his head and shrugged.

The magistrate leaned back in his chair and stroked his beard. "Well, how would he have gotten it then?"

"After I left here, I got drunk and passed out. When I awoke, it was gone," said Chares, lifting his cup to his mouth.

The magistrate leaned back in his chair. "That's not here nor there. I was just curious. What's important now is this colossus of yours," he said pointing at him. "The people of Rhodes are demanding we build it, so now we have to figure out how." He motioned to the servant to refill his cup.

The woman approached, and Chares quickly locked his

eyes on her again, getting him another nudge from Lykus. The woman glanced at Chares as she stepped away smiling.

"Chares, you said it would take five hundred talents to build. Is that still your number?" asked Leonidas.

"Yes, maybe a bit more," he replied.

"We are prepared to spend three hundred for the statue," stated Hermes.

Chares turned his gaze to the ground, then to the man. "It cannot be built for three hundred."

"What if we make it smaller?" asked Leonidas.

"How much smaller?" asked Chares, squinting.

"Fifty cubits," he replied.

Chares closed his eyes and shook his head. "You can't build a statue at fifty cubits and call it *The Colossus?*"

"Chares, you have to understand. After the battle, not only were hundreds of slaves set free, but we now pay a daily wage. We still need ships, and all the while, our economy is several years from recovering. Simply put, we don't have the money," explained Leonidas, raising his palms.

The councilman sitting next to Leonidas sucked his teeth, leaning forward. "Chares, this may seem like a strange question, but what would be the shortest statue you could build and still consider it a colossus?" he asked.

Chares rubbed his chin for a moment, thinking. "Seventy-five, maybe," he replied.

"Okay, and what's the height of the pedestal?" he asked.

"Fifty cubits," replied Chares.

"That still puts us over one hundred and twenty cubits," said Leonidas. "Chares, please, I am sure any statue over one hundred cubits in total height would be considered colossal." Leonidas closed his eyes and rubbed his temples.

"Chares, if you built a thirty-cubit pedestal and seventy-cubit statue, for a total of one hundred cubits," asked Ares, "would that put us closer to the total cost of three hundred talents?"

Chares tapped his fingers on the arm of the chair, then shook his head. "No, probably in the four hundred range," he replied.

"How long would it take to build?" asked Lykus.

"Fifteen years," replied Chares.

Leonidas placed his hand to his forehead. "You mean I might not be alive to see it?" he asked, being the oldest man there.

"Chares, you have put us in a serious position," said Takis, crossing his arms in front of his chest.

"Nobody but yourself put you in this position, Councilman," said a fiery Lykus. "He told us exactly the height and cost of the statue before you all laughed him out of the room." He raised a finger. "It was the council who told the crowd they would build the statue before discussing it with Chares first." He peered at the man as his breaths quickened.

Leonidas raised his hand. "Lykus is right," he said, pinching the bridge of his nose and closing his eyes.

Chares gazed at His Magistrate, understanding why he was upset. He wanted to compromise with him but remained certain that if they made the statue substantially smaller than the dimensions outlined on the scroll, the people of Rhodes would be severely disappointed.

He had in no way, shape, or form planned on his colossus being anything under a total of one hundred cubits with his name attached to it. He searched through the materials he'd brought with him, looking for options to lower the cost. He felt confident that once the construction began, the funding would eventually come. Whether it be from His Magistrate, the people of the island, or neighboring cities along the mainland. Fifteen years, after all, is quite a long time.

"I have an idea," said Chares, raising his cup.

Leonidas opened his eyes and fixed his gaze on him.

"If we use a thirty-cubit pedestal, that would be plenty high enough to clear the old wall, but the new wall being built is much taller. If we leave the wall lower on the west side, none of the statue would be blocked from approaching vessels." He shrugged. "You would save a little labor and cost keeping the wall lower in that section. Also, the original idea called for white marble. Instead, we could mine the Rhodian blue marble right here in Rhodes and use a white marble plinth. That would boost our economy, having the mines running at maximum capacity."

Leonidas stroked his beard and glanced at the councilman. "We could sell the siege engines left here by Demetrius after we remove the bronze plating."

The councilmen nodded in agreement.

"All but the helepolis," said Chares. "We need that for scaffolding and lifting the stones. However, you can certainly sell the armaments inside it."

"What else can we do, Chares?" Hermes asked, taking a handful of grapes from a large bowl on the table.

"Being the statue will be a little shorter, we could use a smaller, three tier pedestal. Instead of sixty cubits square at the base, possibly forty would suffice. Also, instead of building a separate pedestal for the spear, we will attach it to the same pedestal the statue stands upon."

"Does it need three tiers?" asked Ares.

"Yes, the middle stones will be without mortar to protect the statue from potential earthquakes," replied Chares. He glanced back at Leonidas. "We can make *The Colossus* a functioning lighthouse. Not only to aid our merchant ships but others visiting the island. Surely this feature will be of value to many, possibly raising the potential of other city-states helping to fund the statue?" he explained.

"Perhaps," replied Leonidas, rubbing his chin. "Anything else?"

Chares bit on his lower lip, tilting his head. "Not that I can think of," he replied.

"Fine. With all we've discussed, can we build *The Colossus* for three hundred talents?" asked Leonidas.

"Yes," replied a smiling Chares.

The men laughed and touched their cups.

"Now we need to figure out how to build this colossus of yours a bit sooner," said Leonidas. "I like to see it completed before I die."

Chares snickered, raising his glass to the man. "The sooner we start, the sooner it will be done."

"We do have the issue of payment yet to discuss," said the councilman.

"That's right," said Leonidas. "We are prepared to pay you two thousand drachmas a year, and you can stay here at the palace during its construction." The magistrate fixed his gaze on Chares. "You will have full use of the courtyard and the servants as well."

Chares raised his brow, quite happy with their offer, although he tried to conceal his excitement. He nodded slightly and rubbed his chin. "How about—"

"Forget it," interrupted Leonidas. "That's more than most of us here make in two years." He folded his hands in his lap.

Chares chuckled. "It's a deal," he replied, leaning back in his chair.

"Now, we just have to figure out *where* to build it," said Leonidas, raising his hand and gaining the attention of the servant.

The next morning, Chares, Leonidas, Hermes, and the councilmen surveyed the area southwest of the capital. Still stuck in the ground stood the three siege towers left by Demetrius. Soon the slaves would be ordered to begin removing the bronze plating from them. This would lighten each tower significantly, making removing the weapons from the sunken ground much easier.

His Magistrate expressed his wish to have the statue built upon the heights of the acropolis, putting the tip of the spear close to three hundred cubits above the Aegean. Chares, on the other hand, wanted to build it closer to the square, no more than a hundred cubits from the massive siege tower, and he realized moving the helepolis to the high ground would take thousands of men several weeks. The additional cost of manpower seemed unnecessary, and Chares also considered the helepolis the height of the battle. He felt the statue should be placed near the spot the Rhodians were ultimately triumphant in stopping the siege weapon.

"Chares, if we build the statue in the plain, it will be obstructed from view by the acropolis," insisted Leonidas.

"Perhaps, but only for the ships sailing from the east to the capital."

"What good is a light house if the ships can't see it?" asked Takis, crossing his arms.

"I understand your concern, but the statue should be placed near the point of victory and near the heart of the city, close to the people," replied Chares, rubbing his neck. "Think of the manpower we would save building it here, compared to the acropolis," he added, raising his palms.

Leonidas and the others continued walking as the magistrate pointed in the direction they headed. "It's going up there, Chares, and that's final," he insisted.

Chares exhaled forcefully as he followed close behind. The three men talked amongst themselves as Chares thought heavily about the additional cost of labor to place *The Colossus* on the acropolis. Not only would they have to move the helepolis up there, but every block, chunk of limestone, and slab of marble.

Chares sighed. "Haven't even started and we're already over budget," he muttered, picking up his pace to catch up to the men.

CHAPTER 19

OVER THE NEXT FEW WEEKS, Chares spent half of his time in Lindos and the other half at the palace. He selected a crew of foremen and overseers to keep preparations moving. Leonidas traded heavily with Cyprus, who controlled the largest ore mines in the Mediterranean. With the resources of the island already under demand for rebuilding the capital, a good portion of the bronze would have to be purchased.

As the first phase of *The Colossus* took shape, Chares decided the time had come to leave Lindos and stay at the palace for good. Later that evening, he took a horse cart to his home and packed up his few remaining items. He purposely departed at night so he would not have to say goodbye to many folks or be harassed by the crowds still approaching him from time to time. He figured it was the price of being famous.

He did say his goodbyes to his neighbor Medeia. Even though the old woman at times annoyed him, he would still miss her. He failed to mention the home would be taken over by Pythia and Zotikos, figuring the woman would find out on her own.

As he rode back through town, he passed Alyna's home

and glanced over at it. As fate would have it, she emerged from the home carrying a pot of waste matter to be picked up by the slaves. He brought the cart to a stop and called out for her.

She smiled and walked toward him. "Hello, Chares," she said as he climbed down from the cart. The two embraced, then she glanced at his items piled inside. "Are you leaving us?"

Chares nodded. "Yes, construction has begun, and I have to be available at all times," he replied.

"I heard you've been staying at the palace?"

"Yes, it's quite nice there. It comes highly recommended," he replied with a grin.

"Well, maybe I could come visit you sometime?"

"Absolutely, I would enjoy that very much," replied Chares, raising his brow.

Alyna winked before looking toward the ground and swiping her foot across the dirt.

Chares's brows drew close together as he studied the woman. "Are you okay?" he asked.

She looked up and smiled. "Yes, I've just been thinking a lot about what you said to me a while back."

Chares moved his eyes side to side, trying to think of the time she might be referring to. "Yeah, that battle on the mole was something," he said, eyes widening.

She giggled and punched him in the arm. "No, silly man, about me being beautiful and amazing…"

Chares chuckled, playing like he'd known what she meant from the beginning. "Well, it's the truth, Alyna. I have always thought that about you," he said, locking eyes with the woman.

A young girl emerged from the house and called for her. "Mama, where are you?" she said, peering into the darkness.

"I have to go," Alyna said, kissing Chares on the cheek. "I

will see you soon." She spun on her heel and raced toward her home.

Chares watched the woman until she closed the door behind her. A smile on his face, he climbed up onto the cart and rode toward the capital. While riding along, his mind stayed fixed on the woman. His newfound fame might not only bring him financial security, but also the woman he had dreamed about for many years.

Later in the night, as a naked Chares climbed into his kline, he still had Alyna heavily on his mind. He became excited thinking of the woman and rubbed his phallus, envisioning her naked and touching her body. As he stroked himself, a servant passed through his room carrying linens.

Chares instantly sat up and glanced across the room. "Excuse me," he said.

"I was just cleaning the wash," she replied. It was none other than the woman he'd first seen in the courtyard while discussing *The Colossus* with Leonidas and the others.

"Thanks," replied Chares, clenching his jaw and feeling embarrassed the woman had walked in on him.

She smiled and walked to the door but stopped before leaving. "Would you like me to help you with that?" she asked.

Chares's eyes grew wide, then he nodded.

"Of course," she replied. "Let me take care of the linens, and I will return shortly."

Chares leaned back, closing his eyes. "Please hurry," he said with a snicker.

As she reached the door, Chares sat up quickly. "Wait, what's your name?" he asked.

"Selene," she replied.

Chares leaned back in his kline. "Selene," he whispered, closing his eyes.

The next morning, Chares rode to the plain where the helepolis was being stripped of its bronze plating. He instructed the slaves to dismantle the ballista but leave the pulley and ropes for raising the boulders. Between the steep grade and heavy weight, moving the helepolis would certainly prove difficult.

He surveyed the ground in the surrounding area. The climb to the top of the acropolis would have to be smooth and as gradual as possible. To his dismay, he knew he would have to put hundreds of men on extending and smoothing the road. He also ordered the construction of a large casting pit and several smelting furnaces to be placed along sloping ground to maximize oxygen to the flames.

He rode to the quarry where the stonecutters separated huge slabs of limestone. The men cut the stone larger than needed, just in case they were damaged during the move to the acropolis. The early preparations needed to build *The Colossus* were in motion. Chares knew it would be a few years before the pedestal would be complete and the first piece of steel frame put in place, upon which the bronze skin would be fastened.

Over the next two weeks, Chares and Selene became extremely close. They regularly dined together and spent countless hours in the courtyard. Chares figured the other servants, and probably Leonidas, didn't like him around the woman, interfering with her duties and his own. Chares had already made his mind up to pay for her freedom. He would ask her to be relieved of her servitude and work with him as an assistant.

On a typical early afternoon, Chares returned from the acropolis, pulled off his tunic, and stepped into the bath to wash his face. After cleaning up, he heard the door open and in walked Selene. The two quickly embraced and kissed several times. He ran his hand up and down her side, lifting her chiton.

"Not now. I only came by to say hello," she said, stepping back from him.

He reached for her hand and pulled her close. "Please, it will only take a minute," he said with a chuckle. He raised her chiton, exposing her near perfect backside and ran his finger along her crevice.

"Okay, but we must hurry. I have to finish cleaning the courtyard," she explained, bending over the kline.

He rubbed his hands up along her back, under her garment, and caressed her breasts. Chares heard a squeak of the door and glanced over his shoulder in the direction of the sound. He saw a guard standing there with Alyna beside him. The woman covered her mouth and stepped back.

"Sorry, the door was open," said the guard, now backing away and pulling it closed.

Selene and Chares locked eyes as she broke out laughing. Chares rubbed his head, backing away from the woman and finding a seat in a chair. Selene sat in his lap and kissed his cheek.

"What's wrong? Who is that woman?" she asked.

"A friend of mine," he replied, rubbing the back of his neck.

"Don't worry, I am sure she has done it before. It's too bad she didn't join us," she said, placing her finger to her chin.

Chares smiled halfheartedly and gently smacked her butt. "Hop up."

She kissed his cheek, then rose from his lap and fixed her chiton.

Chares left his seat and grabbed a fresh tunic, then walked toward the door. After opening it, he noticed the guard and Alyna were gone. "I'll see you later," he said, stepping out of the room and walking briskly to descend the steps leading to the entrance.

Once outside he saw her horse cart riding away. He wanted to call for her but decided not to make a spectacle. The guard who'd walked in with Alyna stepped toward Chares.

"Sorry, about that," the man said.

"What did she say?"

"Just that she will come see you another time," the guard replied.

"I won't hold my breath," said Chares, turning on his heel and heading back into the palace.

⟵━━━━━━━►

After returning home, Alyna walked to her neighbors to get her children. She had informed them she would most likely not be back until the morning, only to return a couple hours later.

"That was quick," said the neighbor.

Alyna smiled. "Yes, he was busy… Thanks," she said, leading her children home.

A short time later, there was a knock at the door. Alyna opened it to find Pythia and Zotikos standing there.

"Hello, Alyna," said Pythia.

Alyna smiled and opened the door farther. "Please, come in," she said.

The two entered, then strolled out to the courtyard and found their seats.

"Would you like some wine?" asked Alyna.

"Yes, that would be nice," replied Pythia.

Alyna walked to a nearby table and filled two cups and handed them to the couple. She poured a glass for herself and found a seat. "To what do I owe the pleasure?" she asked.

"We haven't seen you at the meetings lately and wanted to make sure you are doing okay," replied Pythia, fiddling with her bracelets.

"Yes, I'm fine. I've been busy is all."

"To call on the gods, then abandon them is dangerous. Through our ceremonies, the gods surely heard your pleas for your husbands return," said Zotikos. "Now that he has returned to you, we should thank the gods. Even if he has crossed the Styx, he still returned."

Alyna nodded, and Zotikos stood from his chair and stepped toward her. He stroked himself as he placed his hand to the back of her head.

Alyna pulled back. "Not now. My daughters are home," she said.

Zotikos turned toward Pythia, his eyes widened as he sat back down.

Pythia squinted and sucked her teeth as she stared at her. "Fine, we can meet in the morning on the beach and pay homage," she insisted.

Zotikos gazed at Alyna for several moments, running his

hand over his beard. "I think I know what bothers you," he said. "It's that statue Chares is building."

Alyna stared at the ground. "Why would that bother me?" she asked.

Zotikos smirked. "You know why," he said confidently. "Your husband was the designer of the statue, and Chares took it. Now he lives at the palace and is the most famous man on the island. They have given him fine clothes and ample allowance, but what did you get?" he asked, tilting his head and widening his eyes.

Alyna bit her lip, thinking about the man's words.

Pythia reached out and placed her hand on her knee. "I am sorry he used you like that. He has always been a liar and a swindler," she explained, before leaning back in her chair.

Alyna gazed at the floor. She considered telling them about her recent visit to the capital to see him. However, she wasn't sure how Pythia would react knowing she'd visited her ex-husband. Alyna remained confident that Pythia didn't have any feelings left for the man, but she knew the woman would be greatly disappointed, knowing Alyna's feelings toward him.

"What are you thinking, Alyna?" asked Pythia.

"Oh, I don't know," she said, shaking her head. "It wasn't my husband who designed the statue. He merely drew himself holding a spear and a bowl of olives," she said, shrugging.

"No, my dear, do not play into his hands on this," said Pythia through her teeth, glaring at her. "He should pay you for the idea."

"What am I supposed to do?" asked Alyna, running her hand through her hair. "Demand that he pays me?"

Zotikos nodded. "Yes, tell him if he doesn't, you will let the good people of Rhodes know who the real creator of *The*

Colossus was." He stood from his chair and approached her, then knelt beside her and rubbed her thigh.

Alyna cocked her head at the man as he smiled.

"C'mon, let's step over there, out of sight, where we can reward the gods for opening our eyes to that man's evil ways," he insisted.

Alyna drew a deep breath and rose from her seat. She reached for his hand. "Pythia, will you keep an eye out for my daughters?"

"Of course," she replied, lifting her cup to her lips.

Alyna led the man to the other side of the courtyard and bent over a nearby table.

Moments later, Pythia came over and slipped off her chiton. "There's no one coming. Except us," she said with a snicker.

CHAPTER 20

AFTER THE FIRST YEAR OF construction, the limestone and blue marble mines ran at full capacity. Furnaces, molds, and scaffolding were nearing completion. Much to Chares satisfaction, the onerous job of moving the helepolis was also finished. He additionally had the slaves assemble lifting mechanisms to help position the massive stones used for the pedestal. He also requested the white marble for the plinth. The money allocated to build *The Colossus* dwindled and not a single stone was set or piece of bronze cast.

When Chares met with Leonidas and the councilmen, he could see the animosity written across their faces. They demanded the pedestal completed by years end. To help speed up production, Leonidas convinced Ptolemy to provide four hundred slaves for two years. This much welcome surprise not only supplied the badly needed workers, but Ptolemy graciously offered the men at little cost.

On any given day, there was close to one thousand men working on the acropolis, quarries, and furnaces, not including the many ships designated to delivering bronze, copper, iron ore, coal, clay, and marble. To his relief, they were only days from setting the first layer of the pedestal. Chares would place orthostatic stone upon it to protect the statue from earthquakes, followed by the final tier to which the white marble would be fastened. The Rhodian blue marble would be attached to the sides of the pedestal, not only to give a much more aesthetically pleasing finish but to protect the feebler limestone from corroding. With the new men sent by Ptolemy, his confidence grew that he could have the pedestal completed by years end.

Much had changed for Selene in the last few months. The woman originally taken from Sidon, located on the eastern shore of the Mediterranean Sea, then later sold to Rhodes was now free. Chares had paid the full amount needed, releasing her from servitude. She frequented the building site, bringing Chares food, water, and wine. She enjoyed the man's company and his newfound wealth, taking advantage of his generosity by visiting many clothing and jewelry shops at the agora.

After running into the woman, Alyna, at the square near the capital, the two women talked for hours. They developed a close friendship, and she would often visit the woman at her home in Lindos.

Although she largely felt pleased, her desire to return home constantly pulled at her heart. As the months passed, she saved every drachma she could. She rounded up the costs of her purchases and pocketed the rest, frequently buying items and returning it soon after. Once she had enough money saved, she decided to ask Chares about returning home, at least for a while.

"What?" said Chares. "I just paid to free you. I thought

you were going to stay here with me, and we would eventually get married."

Selene raised her palms. "I'm not saying I won't return. I'd just like to see my family again."

"Well, how long would you be gone for?" he asked.

She shrugged. "Two years, maximum."

Chares shook his head. "Two years?" he said through clenched teeth.

"At most," she replied.

"I don't understand it. I should have left you a servant," he said, raising his hands and pacing the room. He stopped and glared at her. "I won't pay for this jaunt to Sidon," he insisted.

Selene bowed her head. "Don't you want me to see my family again?" she asked.

"Why can't you wait until the statue's complete and we can go together?"

Selene cocked her head. "When will that be?"

"I don't know…ten or eleven years," he replied.

Selene chuckled, stepping toward the man. "Don't I make you happy? Haven't I always pleased you?" she asked.

"Of course. That's why I am so upset."

"Then let me have this time to see my family. When I return, you will still be nine years from completing your statue and you will still be mine," she explained.

Chares stared aimlessly at the floor, then glanced up at her. "Seems strange, when you put it that way," he said, scratching his chin. "But my answer is still no." He walked toward the washroom.

Selene hung her head and found a seat on the kline.

"I am not punishing you, Selene," he yelled from the other room. "I am doing this because I love you."

Selene smirked. "Lucky me," she muttered, as he stepped back into the room.

"What was that?" he asked, as he stopped walking and glared at her.

"Lucky me," she exclaimed.

"Don't get cheeky with me, woman. You would be wise to remember, you were nothing but a slave getting your ass grabbed by old men in the courtyard when I found you."

"You were the only old man grabbing my ass, Chares," she replied with a chuckle.

He stepped close and found a seat beside her, reaching for her hand. "I love you, Selene. Can we discuss this next year?" he asked.

She faced the man, her brows drawing close. "What would be the difference a year from now?" she asked.

"Well, if you play your jacks right, maybe I'll be sick of you by then," he replied with a laugh.

She leaned her head to his chest and closed her eyes as he rubbed his hand along her hair.

He placed his lips to her head and kissed. "I love you," he said.

Selene sighed. "I love you too."

<hr>

Two days later after returning home from another long, hot day, Chares entered his room and found it surprisingly clean. After a closer inspection, he found Selene's clothes were gone. He noticed a figurine and a piece of papyrus lying on the kline. He lifted the figurine of a spearman in full armor, rubbing his thumb across the tiny soldier's chest. He reached for the letter and bowed his head.

It read, "Best wishes, Selene."

Moments later, the door opened and in walked Alyna. A wide-eyed Chares set the note to the bed and stood as she approached.

"I'm sorry, Chares," she stated.

His lips pressed into a line. "You knew she was leaving?" he asked.

"Yes, I did. Her and I spent the morning together, and I helped her pack," she explained, embracing him.

"Why wouldn't you tell me she was going to leave?" he asked.

"It's for the best, Chares. She deeply desired to return home," she explained.

Alyna kissed his cheek. "I have to go, but I will return to-morrow, and you and I will have a nice dinner and talk about everything," she said, stepping away.

"Everything?" he asked, scratching his cheek.

She smiled at him and closed the door behind her.

CHAPTER 21

Pythia seethed at the mere thought of Chares living at the palace with fame and fortune while she struggled in her meager existence, hardly fit for a peasant rather than living as a woman of her standing and social network should.

Zotikos pleased her in every way except financially. The man lived on donations from what the people gave, and these days, it was very little. The couple had taken the house she once shared with Chares, a big step up from the hovel Zotikos owned, but hardly enough to appease the woman.

She and Zotikos sat in the courtyard drinking wine as she stared at the floor in deep thought.

"What are you thinking about?" asked Zotikos.

Her eyes squinted. "It's hardly right that Chares has all this fame and fortune, but we struggle. I am his ex-wife, and he should have some responsibility to my wellbeing." She rubbed her belly. "We have a little one coming, and we need money to provide for the child."

"We have plenty. Our membership only grows, and many know that's because of me," he said, raising his brow. "Including Tanis," he added.

"We have taken about all they are willing to give. You saw the last donation we received. Pathetic," she said, glancing up and locking eyes with the man. She tapped her finger on the arm of the chair as her eyes widened and her grin spread wider. "I have an idea."

Zotikos cocked his head. "Let's hear it."

"I am sure he never helped Alyna a bit, even though he stole her husband's idea to make himself rich," she explained. "What we need is for her to get the man out at night by himself."

"And do what?" asked Zotikos.

"We kidnap him. And hold him for ransom," she insisted.

Zotikos drew his chin to his chest. "For ransom? Who would pay for him?" he asked, snickering.

"The magistrate, of course. He needs Chares to finish that hunk of junk," she replied.

"This is a small island. Where would we hide him?" he asked.

Pythia placed her hand to her chin, thinking. "What about those tunnels southwest of the capital?"

Zotikos shook his head. "No way I am staying in a tunnel, waiting for a ransom to be paid."

"Well, you tell me then. I thought you were the thinker in our relationship?" she said, raising her palms.

Zotikos squinted, biting his lip. "Here," he said, lifting his limp appendage. "It will help me think."

Pythia rolled her eyes and got to her knees in front of him, taking him in her mouth.

"Yes, it's coming to me now," he said, followed by a moan.

Her eyes glared up at the man.

"Nope, that's not going to work," he said, followed by another moan.

For a moment, an irritated Pythia became tempted to bite the man's phallus, but she quickly changed her mind with it being her favorite part of him.

"I got it," he exclaimed.

She made a smack sound, releasing his shaft from her mouth, and pushed herself up using his knees.

"Where are you going?" he asked.

"I want to hear your idea before I continue," she said, sitting beside him and wiping her mouth.

He closed his eyes and shook his head slightly. "No, that's not how—"

"Just tell me," she insisted, reaching over and grasping his penis.

"Okay, we have Alyna lure him out at night to a private spot where no one will be," he whispered, raising a finger. "Then we take him and hold him for ransom." He grabbed at the air quickly with his hand.

"Uh, huh," said Pythia, cocking her head.

The man looked at her. "Yeah," he said, nodding.

Pythia blinked repeatedly. "You do realize that's exactly what I said from the beginning?"

"It was?" he asked.

She nodded.

"Well, you have to let me finish." He bit his lip and looked toward the sky. "After we abduct him, we have someone take him to the mainland and drop him off. By the time he returns, we will already be paid," he said, raising his hands.

Pythia bobbed her had back and forth a few times. "Yes, that would work, but who will take him to the mainland?"

"Well, it certainly cannot be either of us. We need to pay someone to do it," he explained.

"What about Alyna?" she asked.

"Nope, it can't be her either," he replied.

Pythia looked up, then sighed. "No, that's not what I mean. Chares will know she's involved."

Zotikos scratched his head. "Not if she plays along with it. She simply needs to act surprised when it happens." He shrugged. "Maybe scream and cry a bit?" He rubbed the back of his neck. "That would make it more convincing."

Pythia smiled. "How much should we ask for? And how much would we give Alyna?"

Zotikos stroked his beard. "We ask for twenty thousand drachmas and give her five of it."

"No, we ask for thirty thousand," insisted Pythia, leaning back in her chair and lifting her undergarment. She pointed toward her private. "Now, come over here while I think about how to convince Alyna."

Zotikos knelt in front of her.

A few moments later, Pythia leaned her head forward. "I got it!" she exclaimed.

Zotikos moved his head back and looked up at her.

"Nope, that's not going to work," she said, pressing his head back between her legs with a smile fixed on her face.

CHAPTER 22

O N A WARM AFTERNOON, CHARES had just finished setting the last orthostatic stone of the second tier of the pedestal. The men were tired, and it was time to call it a day. He walked to his cart and lifted a vase, filling his cup with water. As the men put tools away and cleaned up, he spotted a lady walking in his direction. As hundreds of men descended from the acropolis, many turned and gazed at the woman. She waved to him, and he quickly waved back, stepping toward her.

"Alyna, what a surprise," he said, widening his eyes.

"Hello, Chares," she replied, stopping just cubits from the man.

"What possessed you to come all the way up here?" he asked.

"Well, I wanted to see you," she replied, smiling.

"You could have waited until later and come by the palace."

"I don't think I will show up there unexpected anytime soon," she said, then chuckled.

Chares grinned. "I figured you forgot about…"

"I am kidding with you. I was there for a few hours and got tired of waiting," she said, with a grin.

Chares chuckled. "Here, climb on up," he said, motioning toward the cart and extending his hand to assist her.

She glanced over at the pedestal being constructed in the distance. "Don't you want to show me what you have done so far?" she asked.

Chares exhaled forcefully. "I been looking at that pile of rocks for months," he replied. "I'd rather ride around the city and talk."

"Okay, but next time I want a tour," she replied.

The two rode down the long rocky slope until reaching the bottom of the acropolis.

Chares steered the cart toward the water. "How about we go for a swim?" he asked.

Alyna smiled, raising a brow. "That's a great idea."

The cart came to a stop on the western shore of the island directly below the acropolis. Chares climbed off, circled to Alyna's side, and helped the woman down. Holding hands, they strolled toward the cool sea. A few cubits from its edge, she released his hand, then removed her chiton and under garment.

Chares's eyes widened at the sight of the naked woman. He kicked off his sandals as she raced to the water, his pulse quickening at the sight of her backside before it disappeared into the waves. Removing his tunic, he stood rubbing his hands together.

"Hey, put on some clothes or—"

Chares turned toward the man yelling down from the acropolis. "Will you shut up, you dirty bastard?!" he shouted.

"You shut up!" the man replied.

"You better pray to Helios this swim lasts long after you're gone. I am gonna ride up there and—"

"Chares?" said Alyna. "Who are you talking to?"

Chares turned his gaze on the woman, then pointed behind him. "Some asshole who keeps telling me to put my clothes on."

Alyna creased her brow, moving her eyes side to side in confusion.

Chares smiled, then laughed. He rushed toward her in great anticipation. The two swam about thirty cubits from shore, diving under the water several times. They splashed each other until they came in close contact, and Chares drew her to him. They gazed into each other's eyes at length. He leaned toward her, and just as their lips met, a splash in the water a few cubits away drew their attention. They swam for shore, then sat in the shallow water together, laughing.

"What was that?" asked Alyna.

Chares grimaced. "Not sure, but it interrupted a beautiful kiss," he replied.

She smiled, then leaned toward him and let her soft lips press against his as the waves lapped in around them.

Chares had spent years desiring Alyna. He could almost pinch himself, as he reached a state of euphoria from merely kissing the lovely woman. Basking in every moment, the two held hands and watched a magnificent sunset. Before the last of its rays disappeared, they climbed on the wagon and rode toward the capital.

"Would you like to come to the palace and have a bite in the courtyard?" he asked.

"I would love too," she replied, then bowed her head.

"I don't have much time though. I left the girls with the neighbor."

Chares cracked the rein to get the horse moving a bit quicker. Once reaching the palace, the two walked up several steps and down a long hall to reach the courtyard. There the servants brought fresh fruit, olives, nuts, and bread. Chares and Alyna also enjoyed a glass of wine and talked extensively about *The Colossus*. He shared stories about his time as a young man in Argos, studying the art of sculpting under a famous Greek artist.

"Lysippus… Who's that?" asked Alyna.

Chares drew his chin toward his chest. "You never heard of him?"

"No, what has he done?" she asked, raising the wine glass to her lips.

"What has he *done?*" laughed Chares. "How about *The Horses of Saint Mark*, or the statues of *Zeus* and *Hercules* of Taras?" He smiled, reaching for a hand full of grapes. "What has he done…" He snickered, wagging his finger at her. "Not to mention he was the personal sculptor of Alexander," he added, raising his brows.

"Whoop-de-doo," replied Alyna with a chuckle. "He sure didn't build anything as grand as *The Colossus*, or I would have heard of him for sure," she added with a wink.

Chares's smile widened. "Well, *The Colossus* is not yet finished. So until then, Lysippus will remain the most famous sculptor in the land." He reached across the table, bringing the oil lantern closer to them. He could see the smile of Alyna reflecting in the light of the flame. She was beautiful, and he found himself drifting farther into her magnetic allure.

"Chares?" said Alyna, cocking her head and reaching across the table, pulling his sleeve.

"Huh?" he replied.

Alyna laughed. "What are you doing?" she asked. "Did you hear what I said?"

Chares grinned and shrugged. "I am sorry. I was just…"

"C'mon, we should get going," she said, standing from her seat.

Chares popped a few more grapes in his mouth, then stood. He waived to the servants, signaling they were finished, then reached for Alyna's hand. She accepted, and the two walked down the hall and steps to the waiting horse cart.

Before leaving, he hurried to his room and grabbed a leather satchel from his chest before racing down the steps to the entrance where the woman waited. He climbed on the cart and the two rode along the street, heading for Lindos.

"I have a little something for you," said Chares along the way.

Alyna glanced over at him as he held out the sack. She tilted her head and reached for it. "It's heavy. What is it?" she asked.

The sound of coins inside rattled as she opened it.

"Just some money to help get you by."

"Oh, Chares, no, I couldn't," she said, handing it back.

"No, I insist," he replied, holding up his hand.

He had given her three hundred drachmas, enough to support a family for an entire year.

"I know it's been hard," he said, biting his lip. "Besides, if it weren't for you, *The Colossus* may have never happened."

"If it weren't *The Colossus*, you would have certainly done something just as grand," she replied. She turned and looked out at the dark night, sitting silently for several moments.

Chares glanced over at her a few times, then placed his hand to hers resting on her lap.

She faced him, placing her hand to his cheek, and kissed him. "How about we just go back to your place tonight?" she asked.

"Really? What about your children?"

"They are fine. I told the neighbor there's a good chance I wouldn't return until tomorrow," she said, smiling.

Chares brought the horse to a stop. "Well, how can I say no to that?" he asked, turning the cart around.

As soon as the two reached his room, they began dropping their clothes to the floor. They passionately kissed and fell into the kline. Exhilarated by the prospect of making love to the woman, Chares could hardly contain his desire. Thinking he might be dreaming, he pinched the side of his own leg several times. Although he'd never cheated on Pythia physically throughout their marriage, his mind had a thousand times whenever Alyna was near.

Two days later, Alyna climbed up on a horse cart she'd rented to get much-needed supplies. She cracked the rein and the horse moved forward until she heard a woman call her name and stopped to glance behind her.

Pythia approached with her hand in the air. "Wait for me," she exclaimed.

Alyna waved, then faced the road ahead with a grimace as the woman approached.

Pythia climbed up and sat beside her on the narrow seat. "Where we going?" she asked.

"To the agora," replied Alyna.

"Great, I need a few things myself," said Pythia, straightening her chiton.

Alyna lifted the rein and clicked her tongue. As the wagon moved, she could feel the glare of the woman beside her.

"So, where did you get this cart?" Pythia asked.

"I rented it."

"Wow, must be nice to afford renting a cart just to go shopping," said Pythia with sarcasm in her voice.

"I haven't been to the market in several weeks, so I need many items," replied Alyna.

Pythia reached over and touched her hair as Alyna leaned the opposite way, before turning and facing the woman.

"What's on your mind, Pythia?"

"There is plenty on my mind, Alyna," she replied. "Why haven't you followed through with the deal we had?"

"We never had a deal," replied Alyna, glaring at the woman.

"You realize the farther he gets on that ridiculous statue, the less he is worth?"

"Will you leave me out of your schemes?"

Pythia pulled a ribbon from around her wrist and put her hair up. "I know you have been seeing him, Alyna," she said, raising a brow.

"You don't know anything," replied Alyna.

"If you are getting money from him, you have to share it with me. I am his ex-wife," she explained.

Alyna clenched her jaw, bringing the cart to a stop. "Get out of my cart," she insisted.

Pythia glanced at the satchel on her lap. "Let me see how much money you have in there?"

"That's none of your business, now get out!" hollered Alyna.

Pythia reached over to take the satchel, but Alyna quickly grabbed it. The two women wrestled over the leather sack until Alyna smacked Pythia across the face. The woman placed her hand to her cheek, mouth hanging open. Her face turned red as she drew deep breaths. She grabbed Alyna by the back of her head, pulling her hair with great force, and forced the woman's head to the bench, pressing her face firmly against it.

"Let go of me, bitch!" said Alyna, digging her nails into the woman's leg.

Pythia grimaced, lifting Alyna's head before slamming it back into the board. "Listen to me, whore. You ever touch me again, I will cut your tits off. Then we'll see how much money Chares would be willing to provide," Pythia seethed.

Alyna squirmed, trying to free herself from the pregnant woman's grasp, but she could not move.

Pythia leaned toward her, placing her mouth a handsbreadth from her ear. "You will split every dollar you receive from that man or you will be the one missing." She pushed out her lower lip and tilted her head. "Then who would take care of your precious daughters?" She ran her tongue across the woman's ear as Alyna flinched, struggling to get free. "They already lost their father. It would be a shame if something happened to their mother," she said, releasing the woman's head.

Alyna moved to the far side of the seat, rubbing her face.

"You have a week. I suggest you get to the palace and siphon him dry, and I don't mean his cock," said Pythia, stepping from the cart.

An old man and woman stared at her from just a few cubits away.

Pythia faced the couple. "Fuck off," she said, walking away as she placed her hands in front of her belly.

The couple gasped, then looked over at Alyna, "Are you okay, ma'am?" the man asked. "You want us to get the guards?"

Alyna shook her head. "No, I just had a disagreement with a friend. Well, a former friend."

The man blinked rapidly in disbelief, then the couple walked away.

Alyna reached for the rein, then looked around the cart for her satchel. She clenched her jaw while looking behind her for Pythia. "Bitch," she muttered, as she turned the cart around and headed back the way she'd come.

Lucky for Alyna, she'd had only five drachmas in the pouch and the rest safely hidden in her home.

Later that week, Alyna returned to visit Chares at the palace. She informed him of her run in with Pythia, but she did not tell him about the money or Pythia's crazy idea of abducting him. She felt Pythia's threats were baseless, like the one she made to her about the money. She explained jealousy had encouraged the confrontation.

He seemed surprised his ex-wife would care about who he is seeing, especially since she was the one who'd left him.

Alyna asked Chares to be careful. She had a feeling not everyone on the island approved of *The Colossus* and its constant financial drain. She told him there could be people wanting to abduct him and advised him not to travel alone after dark.

The man only chuckled, stating, "You worry too much."

CHAPTER 23

After two years of having the additional manpower, it unfortunately came to an end. The slaves sent by Ptolemy returned to Egypt, but their contributions for completing the first phase were invaluable. The pedestal was now complete and had turned out magnificent. Standing near forty cubits, it was constructed with three tiers, blue marble sides, and a white marble plinth. The cost to complete the pedestal surpassed expectation. The smaller pedestal, for the bottom of the spear, was also complete too.

Leonidas expressed his wish for no pedestal for the spear at all to save money, but Chares did not want to compromise. He explained the pedestal was as important as the statue itself. With the platform complete, he turned his attention to the statue's feet. Each foot of *The Colossus* would be cast in solid bronze, measuring twelve cubits.

Chares knew their stockpiles of copper ore and the bronze taken from the siege weapons would quickly dissipate once casting began, likely causing panic among the council. Having enough raw material to keep his smelting pots going for many months, he figured in total he had enough to reach the waist of his creation before more was needed. He also knew only one-third of the allocated funds remained. Leonidas had been trading and purchasing bronze now for many months, and the constant demand on the market had made prices soar. If they were to keep purchasing bronze while prices were high, just paying the workers over the next few years would be tight. Even though much more copper would be needed to complete the statue, he asked Leonidas to refrain from buying anymore until the market settled.

Chares also realized more money than the estimated three hundred talents would eventually be needed to keep the project moving. He figured it was a matter of time before Leonidas and the councilmen caught on to it themselves. With his newfound fame growing throughout the region, he planned on making busts again and selling them for high dollar.

Who wouldn't want a bust from a man who made the greatest statue ever?

However, making busts took an enormous amount of time. Something he had far less of than money. Chares did save a decent chunk of the allowance paid to him each month. Since his housing, food, drink, and clothing were supplied to him, it made saving easy. However, he did his best to conceal his wealth, fearing the council would want him to use his own money toward the statue, something he would avoid unless it was completely necessary. He was convinced if Leonidas put pressure on the neighboring towns along the mainland, they would certainly contribute.

Chares's biggest expense was Alyna, as his financial support of her continued to grow with each passing month. He freely helped the woman, believing it was her that had played the biggest role in his new wealth and fame. Their relationship also continued to grow and deepen. Feeling her daughters were now old enough to be left alone, Alyna stayed with him two or three nights a week.

She did bring the girls with her once, and they enjoyed a ride in Chares's new skiff, a much nicer boat than the one he'd left behind at his home in Lindos. He loved the water, and the island was surrounded by tranquil inlets. With almost every day sunny and warm, Rhodes was a paradise for anyone who enjoyed the water, beaches, and sunshine.

As much as he relished his stay at the palace though, he frequently missed his little mountain village of Lindos. The cove at the foot of town held a special place in his heart. During their better years, he and Pythia had fished and cooked on the beach, drinking wine until they fell asleep. Chares figured he must have made love to the woman a hundred times on that stretch of beach.

Since starting *The Colossus*, he'd had little time for recreation, and it wore on him. He decided to start taking a couple days off a week for a much-needed break. On those days, he would take his skiff to the bay at the foot of the acropolis and anchor there. He could look up at the plateau and envision the mighty statue towering over it. With the helepolis resting near the worksite, it made it easy to visualize since they would be similar in height.

With the impending completion of the statue, many homes were constructed on each side of the acropolis. Everyone wanted to be near the statue honoring Helios, the god who had blessed the island with beauty and sunshine and protected the inhabitants from all enemies.

CHAPTER 24

RETURNING TO THE PALACE AFTER spending much of the afternoon on the water, Chares journeyed to the courtyard after being summoned. Entering the courtyard, he was handed a cup of wine by a servant. Chares strolled toward the several men gathered there, finding a seat in an adjacent chair.

"Hello, Chares," said Leonidas.

Chares raised his cup to the man. "Your Magistrate," he replied, nodding to the councilmen and Hermes also seated nearby.

"Chares, we've been going over the finances and it appears we are way off budget," he said, handing Chares a piece of papyrus. "Here is a breakdown of what we have spent so far, and the second portion is a projection of when the allocated funds will be exhausted."

Chares looked over the sheet for a few moments before glancing up at the man. "The high cost of bronze has certainly had an effect," he replied. "However, we have a good portion of the material required to finish the statue."

Councilman Cadmus cleared his throat. "Chares, even if

we didn't purchase one more talent of copper or a single cubit of marble, we only have enough to pay the men for two more years," he said, raising his palms.

Chares sucked his teeth, focusing on the spreadsheet. "I see," he said, handing it back to Leonidas. "We could ask neighboring towns on the mainland who we deliver goods for to help?"

"Already have," said Hermes, tapping his fingers on the armrest.

"What about Ptolemy? Maybe he can send more slaves?" asked Chares.

"Ptolemy is in the middle of a war against Antigonus. I hardly think he would entertain the idea until the war is over," said Leonidas, shrugging his shoulders.

"Ugh. The price of bronze really hurt us," said Chares, drawing a deep breath. "Well, we just have to keep going for now and see where we are in a year or so."

Councilman Takis snickered. "No, we can do more than that, Chares."

"We have planned a two-phase deal that will help ease the financial strain on the island," stated Leonidas. "Phase one will include a tax on our shipments. It won't be popular, but we can pitch the idea as being temporary," he said. "Also, and this will impinge on us seated here, is an immediate pay cut."

Chares looked toward the ground, then to Leonidas. "A pay cut?"

"Yes, Chares. Starting next month, your allowance will be cut in half. We will also be taking a pay cut, as will every government employed person on the island."

Chares sighed. "In half?" he asked.

"Yes, in half," replied Leonidas, fixing his gaze on the man.

"This will secure the funds we need for the manpower, but we still will be short for the materials," said Hermes.

"That's right," replied Leonidas. "Phase two will be another pay cut for all of us and shutting down our festivals for two years."

Chares rubbed his head while drawing a deep breath through his nose. "What about tourism from the mainland? More and more people are coming to the island to see *The Colossus*," he said, his chin raised.

"To see a pedestal, you mean?" said Takis.

Chares glared at the man, then refocused on Leonidas. "These cuts will make the statue very unpopular, Your Magistrate. The people would believe it's the statue causing the financial hardship and not the war."

"Well, if that's the case…then so be it," said Takis with a smirk. "You promised us *The Colossus* at three hundred talents. Here we are, over two hundred talents later, and don't even have a foot or a single toe completed."

"The feet and pillars will be started next. Soon you will have your toe," replied Chares, clenching his jaw but wanting to kick his own foot up the man's ass.

Leonidas raised his hand and said calmly, "Let's not bicker about this. It's unfortunate for everyone here. Let's just find a sensible way to resolve it." He looked over at Chares. "It may be necessary for you to use your own money for essentials like chisels, hammers, nails…things of that nature."

"I have been," replied Chares.

"Also, you will have to supply the water to the men on the acropolis," explained Leonidas.

"Really?" asked Chares, squinting.

"Yes, really. The charge for delivery is outrageous and

there's no reason you or a foreman can't use one of your wagons to fill the casks," said Takis.

"I will literally be at the fountain all day to keep up with the men's thirst," replied Chares, closing his eyes and placing his fingers to his temples.

"Sorry, Chares. This is the way it must be for now," said Leonidas, raising his brow.

"I heard you got a new skiff?" asked Hermes, tilting his head.

Chares removed his fingers from his temples and opened his eyes. "What? Do I have to sell that too?" he asked.

"No, but you should probably use it sparingly," replied the man.

"I can do what I want, when I want, with *my* boat, sir," said Chares, his eyes narrowing.

"Okay, suit yourself. But if the good folks of the island lose their annual festivals and take pay cuts while the man building the statue is out sailing the shores in his new boat, it might not go over too well," Hermes stated with a shrug.

Chares leaned back in his chair, rubbing the back of his neck and focusing on the ground. He realized the effect the statue had already taken on him, and now the people would feel it too. As much as what Hermes had said about the skiff bothered him, he acknowledged the accuracy of the city manager's assessment. He knew once the new details went public, he would no longer be surrounded by people who wanted to shake his hand and give him bread and wine. Instead, it would be a mob throwing rocks and rotten eggs at him. *What a mess,* he thought, tapping his fingers on the arm rest.

"Chares?" said Leonidas.

Chares glanced up at the man. "Sorry, just thinking. Is there anything else?" he asked.

Leonidas shook his head. "Not unless you have a few ideas about how to lower the costs?" he asked, raising his palms.

Chares sighed, then rose to his feet. "Goodnight, gentlemen," he grumbled. Turning and stepping toward the entrance, he handed his nearly full cup of wine to the servant standing nearby.

After returning to his room, Chares sat at his table for several hours going over the design of *The Colossus*. He searched for anything he could do to speed up production and lessen the need of material. He believed he could make the skin of *The Colossus* a little thinner and reduce framing by positioning them differently than originally designed. He felt confident the changes would lower material cost and labor without compromising the stability or durability of the statue.

Chares had done well saving money with his two thousand drachma salary. Now with his pay cut in half, he still would be comfortable. However, it surely would have an impact on his future purchases and generosity.

His thoughts shifted to Alyna and her advice about being careful. The favorability of the statue would certainly diminish, becoming increasingly unpopular as the construction continued. Surely when *The Colossus* was completed, the island would rejoice, forgetting all about the tougher times.

But until then, Chares would keep his guard up.

***

Pythia sat in a chair at the courthouse holding her daughter Zoe in her arms. She was there to meet Zotikos, who had recently been jailed for assault and disorderly conduct after punching a man who had accused him of having relations with his wife.

Zotikos had denied having anything to do with the woman, but Pythia knew his assertions were untrue, having sampled the woman herself several times. Since the war was over and the soldiers were safely home, membership following the deities of Cabeiri had fallen to half its size. The group, comprised of mostly women, were now at home taking care of their husbands and no longer needed the deities of the great mother. However, Pythia knew firsthand the power of the gods. They had granted her a child and delivered her from the immoral and intellectually boring man, Chares.

Zotikos, still practicing his philosophy, dreamed of fame and fortune. But over time, Pythia's faith in him had all but crumbled. She would much rather he get a job like the other men of the island. She at one point suggested for him to work in the mines. They were in desperate need of men to keep up with the constant demand placed on them from that tower of rust being constructed on the acropolis.

Zotikos took exception to the idea, saying, "I would rather die," and "I am working on a plan."

It was always Pythia's idea to leave the island after the war, but financially, it verged on impossible. She could only hope the man she loved with all her heart and soul would finally figure out how to provide for her and their daughter. After the recent run in with the man at the agora, Pythia also now worried about more fallout from their ceremonies.

Even though the rituals were to please the gods and bring the men home safely, she knew there would be consequences if more men found out about what had transpired behind closed doors. Every new member had sworn to never share the group's location, leaders, and practices, but many members had left the group and she wasn't sure who would keep their vow of silence.

A door opened and a guard led a shackled Zotikos toward her. She rose from her seat as the man released the irons. Zotikos rubbed his wrists while glaring at the guard, who glared right back at him before finally stepping away. Sliding off the tunic they had made him put on while incarcerated, Zotikos tossed it to the floor and then wrapped his arms around his wife and child.

"You look awful," said Pythia, turning her cheek as he puckered his lips to kiss her.

"Well, I have been incarcerated for two weeks, my love," he replied. "Besides, the man who is the most without will always be the man who is the most within," he exclaimed, putting his member in his palm and peeing on the floor.

Pythia chuckled.

Zotikos moved his penis side to side, covering the entrance way floor with urine. After a couple shakes, he stepped toward Pythia. "C'mon, my love, let's go home and make another baby," he said, placing his arm around her.

As they walked outside and stepped from the porch, she faced the man. "I liked what you said back there. I think you should follow that advice," she explained.

"About making another baby?" he asked.

Pythia sighed. "No, about the more a man does, the better off he is," she replied.

Zotikos drew his chin to his chest. "I said that?" he asked, scratching his head.

CHAPTER 25

A S THE MONTHS DASHED BY, so did his celebrity status. Chares became so unpopular among the people, he rarely traveled anywhere except from the palace to the acropolis. Luckily for him, the workers' pay had not been cut. They still appreciated the man, and he felt safe around them.

The solid bronze feet of *The Colossus* were complete and fastened to the pedestal. The two pillars that were to run up each leg to the shoulder were also under way. The metal framing would be fastened around the pillars and the bronze plates attached to the frame.

For the first time since construction began, the people of Rhodes got their first real glimpse of the sheer magnitude of *The Colossus*. With each block and piece of frame put in place, Chares could feel the immense anger toward him dissipate. His ideas to use less framing and thinner bronze were also paying off, and he now contemplated stopping the pillars at the waist to further speed up production without greatly compromising the stability.

After loading the water casks, he climbed on the wagon

and was about to crack the rein, when he spotted Lykus walking toward him.

Climbing down from the cart, Chares said, "Hello, Lykus."

The man waved, stepping closer. "Where you off to?" he asked.

"To fetch water for the workers."

Lykus glanced over at the statue. "Wow, you really made some progress since I was last here," he said, squinting from the bright sun.

Chares shrugged. "Yes, finally. It has been a rough six months though."

Lykus fixed his gaze at the man. "Yeah, I heard they cut your pay along with the rest of us." He pointed to *The Colossus*. "Mind me taking a closer look?" he asked.

"Of course not," replied Chares, leading the man toward the plinth.

Lykus and Chares stepped up on the pedestal as the man put his hand to a bronze foot. "Wow, this is really something, Chares," he said, looking up at the pillars and framework. "When will you start attaching the bronze plating?"

"By week's end," replied Chares. "Soon we will move the helepolis in position, once we get a little higher."

Lykus looked over at the massive siege tower now stripped and open on the side facing the statue. "That sure was something when we brought that tower to a stop on the battlefield," he said, placing his hands to his hips. "Doesn't seem so scary anymore."

Stepping from the pedestal, the two men walked toward the wagon.

"Lykus, you enjoy fishing?" asked Chares.

"Yeah, sure," he replied.

"I am taking the day off tomorrow, if you are interested?"

Lykus raised his brow in thought. "Yeah, I am free tomorrow," he replied.

"Great, meet me at the palace in the morning and we will head out," replied Chares. "Want a ride back to town?"

Lykus glanced around. "No, I think I'll take in the sights and watch the men work for a while," he replied.

Chares nodded, then climbed up on the wagon and cracked the rein. As he approached the fountain, he spotted Alyna riding by on a cart and called out for her.

"Chares," she replied, smiling.

Happy to see the woman, he brought his wagon to a stop, climbed down, and raced to her arms. The two embraced while she remained seated in the wagon.

"What are you doing here?" he asked.

"I thought I would come stay with you tonight and spend most of tomorrow with you."

"That's great," replied Chares, before he remembered the fishing plans he'd just made. He kicked at the dirt.

"What is it?"

"I made plans to go fishing with Lykus in the morning."

"Can you get out of it?" she asked.

"I don't know. I would feel bad," he replied.

She shrugged. "We can still spend the night together, and I will leave in the morning when you head out to go fishing."

He leaned toward her, stealing a quick kiss. "I have to fetch water before the men quit working," he said, stepping back. "I'll see you as soon as I can."

She cracked the rein and rode in the direction of the palace.

Pythia and Zotikos strolled out of the courtyard toward the beach. Still too young to walk any sizable distance, Zotikos carried the toddler. Halfway to the beach they stopped and rested, sitting on Chares's old skiff among the many weeds growing around it. They stared out at the water as the girl squirmed in his hands, reaching for her mama.

"Hand her to me," said Pythia, extending out her arms.

Zotikos gave her the child and picked up a handful of sand. "If each of these grains of sand were an hour, how old would you—"

"A million years," said Pythia in a frustrated tone.

Zotikos turned to her. "What's wrong with you?" he asked.

Pythia shook her head and kissed her daughter on the side of the face.

He stroked his beard, focusing on a bird walking along the shore. "I once met a bird who only had one wing. The creature asked me, if I cannot fly, how will I eat? I thought about it for a moment, and replied, you will eat the way you always have."

Pythia raised her hand. "Please, stop," she said with a sigh.

"What is bothering you, my love?"

"I don't want to hear your philosophies and riddles."

"But you always enjoyed them before?"

"Yes, that's true. But you know what I think of when you talk about a one-winged bird?"

"Tell me," he said, tilting his head.

"I think the flightless bird is you, and it's your way of saying you don't need to work to eat," she explained.

Zotikos rubbed his temples. "I told you I am working on a plan," he said, rising to his feet and placing a hand to his hip.

Pythia bit her lip, looking away from the man.

"What good is life if you don't live it?" he asked.

"What good are hands if you don't use them?" Pythia fired back, her brows drawing close together. "You could have been born a crippled bird and accomplished the same amount."

"Fine. You want money?" His face turned red. "I will get you some damn money," he said, storming away.

"Get some dinner while you are at it, even if it's a one-winged bird!" she hollered at the man as he walked away.

CHAPTER 26

CHARES WALKED INTO THE COURTYARD where Lykus, Ares, Leonidas, and the councilmen were already seated, waving as he approached. "Hello, gentlemen," he said, finding his seat. He glanced around before focusing on Lykus, who offered him a cup.

"Here, you can have mine," he said.

Chares took the cup. "Thank you," he said, lifting it to his mouth.

"The servant went to get fresh olives and figs," said Leonidas. "She will be back shortly."

"How's our colossus coming along?" asked Cadmus.

"Great," replied Chares. "We have the pillars complete and the framing to the shoulders. The bronze is being fastened into place, and the spear and the bowl are just days from completion."

"Fantastic," said Leonidas, raising his cup to Chares.

All the men followed His Magistrate's lead and raised their cups as well, except Lykus, who raised his bare hand, simulating having a cup.

"We still have financial worry," said Councilman Cadmus.

"And civil unrest," said Ares, peering at Chares.

"Civil unrest?" asked Chares.

"Yes, mainly in the town of Kameiros and Lalyssos. The cost of goods has soared with the new tax, and many have taken pay cuts or lost their jobs altogether," Ares replied.

"We have been putting off the announcement that all festivals are canceled, but we can't wait any longer," explained Cadmus.

"Ares and Lykus will each lead a battalion of soldiers to the cities to quell the disturbance," said Leonidas.

Chares rubbed the top of his head. "Oh, boy," he said.

"I know you have ramped up construction significantly, Chares, but I need you to pull all stops," said Leonidas.

"As we sit here today, what is your guess as to when it will be completed?" asked Cadmus.

"Well, the plating on the torso will go quick. But the cloak, arms, and head will take time. Maybe two years?"

Leonidas sighed.

Takis curled his lip, leaning forward. "And we don't have enough bronze for the arms or cloak, do we?" he asked through his teeth.

Chares shook his head.

"Well, gentlemen, phase two is officially in effect. That means all fairs and festivals are canceled and the second round of pay cuts will begin immediately," said Leonidas. "Men, we have come too far to turn back now. The completion of the statue is our best chance to restore harmony to our island. I personally call on each of you to give anything you can, so we can purchase the bronze we need in the coming months. We will make the announcement of phase two in a few days, to give Ares and Lykus time to reach Lalyssos and Kameiros."

The men sat in silence for several moments.

Lykus glanced over at a defeated Chares and shrugged. "It will be all right, we have the advantage," he said with his lips curling into a smile.

Chares bowed his head and closed his eyes.

An hour after dusk, Chares climbed into bed alongside Alyna, who had already fallen asleep. His heart ached, and his stomach turned. The broken man stared up at the ceiling, drawing quick short breaths. His eyes watered, and his hands trembled. His restless mind continually reminded him of the decade of tribulations *The Colossus* had brought upon the island. The people suffered, and livelihoods had been lost. The island, once a bustling paradise, was a bankrupt, desolate wasteland. The once proud island had defeated the most powerful empire on the planet only to be destroyed by a single man in his pursuit of glory.

What could I have done differently? he wondered.

He thought about his early attempt to build *The Colossus* near the south side of town. If he could have convinced the magistrate and council to build it there, it would have saved an enormous amount of labor and money while significantly increasing the possibility that the statue would be completed by now. When he'd agreed to take the job at three hundred talents, he knew it would be near impossible to finish it for that amount. However, he thought for sure neighboring towns on the mainland would have realized the statues importance and contributed to its completion. He blamed himself for this gross miscalculation. Although the statue was over halfway complete, the allocated monies were expended. He would now be paid a meager five hundred drachmas a year, about that of a skilled worker.

Chares became so emotional he wept.

Alyna awoke and rubbed his head as he placed it against her chest. He explained to her how he'd single-handedly destroyed the island's economy.

"Nothing is your fault, Chares. You did everything you could do to complete the statue for as little money as possible," she said, kissing the top of his head. "You have given this island so much pride and hope. The statue will be completed, and when it is, the people will never remember these challenging times," she insisted, kissing his head again.

"I feel like I am shackled to a sinking ship," he said, drawing a deep breath. "And my reputation, finances, and happiness are sinking with it."

"Don't forget, Chares, they are the ones who pushed it to be built way quicker than you originally projected. As Lykus told you, they'd agreed to build that statue *before talking to you first*. They have a tremendous amount of ownership in this situation," she replied.

"Yes, but I am the one who the people will blame."

"No one will blame you for giving the island a monument so great, people will come to see it for thousands of years."

"The statue will not stand a thousand years," he replied. "The lack of funds and a hastened completion requires many concessions, which in turn, compromises stability."

She rubbed his head, and he drew her close. Their discussions continued throughout the night until her words of a brighter future relaxed his mind and they fell asleep in each other's arms.

CHAPTER 27

PYTHIA SAT AT HOME ALONE as Zotikos was jailed yet again for another fight, this time against two men who accused him of sleeping with their wives. Once again, Pythia knew it was true. With what seemed like continuous confrontations, she recognized it was time for her and Zotikos to leave the island.

With Zotikos jailed for weeks on end, the membership had dropped significantly in recent months. Even Pythia rarely attended the meetings anymore, spending more time with her daughter. The timing of his arrest could not have been worse. The man had informed her he'd finally gotten his plan in order and the money would soon start pouring in. Although she only half believed him, she did her best to keep faith that he would eventually do his part to support them. Now she would have to wait a couple more weeks to see his idea come to fruition.

Like Pythia's, the morale of the people was low. As prices for goods soared, she desperately hung on day to day. She had borrowed money from Tanis a few weeks ago, and the woman had already come by several times asking for repayment. Pythia, however, had no money to give and none coming. She thought of Alyna and how the woman had never made good on the deal they had. As she stewed over the thought of it, Pythia rose from her chair and walked to the woman's home, Zoe walking beside her holding her hand. She banged on the door until the oldest daughter answered.

"Larysa, is your mother home?" asked Pythia.

The young girl shook her head. "No, she is at the capital."

"Of course, she is," Pythia said, now looking past the girl. "Your mother has money put aside for me and said you knew where to find it?" she explained.

Larysa rubbed Zoe's head and gently squeezed her cheek. "She is so cute."

Pythia rolled her eyes. "Thank you, but did your mother mention I would be coming by for the money?" she asked.

"No, she didn't."

"Well, I am sure you can help me. Do you know where she keeps it?"

Larysa smiled, playing with Zoe again.

About to lose it, Pythia gave an exasperated sigh.

The girl opened the door farther. "Yes, follow me," she said, leading the way to the kitchen. Larysa slid the table to the side and pulled on a board along the floor. She reached inside, pulling out a brown satchel. "How much does she owe you," she asked, opening the pouch.

"Two hundred," replied Pythia.

The girl's eyes grew wide. "You will have to count that out," she said, extending her arm with satchel in hand.

"Here, watch her for me," said Pythia, releasing Zoe's hand. She found a seat at the table and peered into the satchel filled with coins. She then looked at the hole the satchel came out of and noted another satchel lay below it.

Larysa played with Zoe as Pythia poured coins on the table and counted. As she counted, she let a coin drop to the floor.

"Oops," Pythia said, reaching down and grabbing the other pouch in the hole. She placed it under her chiton, trying to keep the coins inside from rattling. She counted again. By the time she finished taking her share, there would only be a handful of coins left. She closed the satchel and asked Larysa for a pouch to place her coins in.

When Larysa left the room, Pythia placed the other satchel over her shoulder but still hidden under her garment. The girl returned with a sack and handed it to Pythia, who she slid the coins from the table into it. She set the sack on the table and placed the near empty satchel back in the hole, lying the board over it.

Facing Larysa, Pythia trailed her hand along the side of the girl's face. "Thank you, pretty girl," she said. She reached for Zoe's hand, and they casually strolled toward the door and said their goodbyes. "Tell your mother I said hello," she said, stepping away from the door.

Pythia hurried back to her house and shut the door behind her. She placed the sack on the table and pulled the satchel from her shoulder, then opened it. Her eyes widened as a smile streaked across her face. She found her seat and began counting. Once reaching four hundred drachmas, she snickered and put the coins back inside.

With the near two hundred in the sack and four hundred in the satchel, the woman had scored an enormous plunder. She took out thirty coins, which was plenty enough to pay Tanis and spend a little on herself.

Turning toward Zoe, she said, "I'll be right back."

Stepping into the courtyard with sack and satchel in hand,

she walked out on the path leading to the beach and stepped off the trail. She walked a few cubits and grabbed a stick, then dug into the sandy ground. After raking out a little more than a cubit, she buried the sacks and covered them. She stuck a stick in the ground, marking its location.

Pythia raced back to her home, grabbing the thirty coins and Zoe before heading straight to Tanis's house. She repaid the woman the money she had borrowed and asked if she could stay with her until Zotikos was released, telling the woman she was frightened to be alone.

Tanis welcomed Pythia and Zoe into her home and showed her to a room upstairs. Later, Tanis prepared food and the two women stayed awake late into the night, drinking wine and laughing, among other things.

CHAPTER 28

IN THE EARLY MORNING, STILL a couple hours from day light, Chares dragged his skiff to the water. He'd planned on getting an early start, fearing a storm may roll in by early afternoon. He pulled the rope attached to the front, dragging the boat to deeper water. Waist deep, he dropped the anchor and splashed water to his face before climbing inside. He moved his pole and bait to the back of the skiff and raised the anchor. After placing figs on his lap, he reached for the oars.

Thirty minutes of nonstop rowing later, he stopped for a quick break. Chares was more than excited to be away from the workers and dust-covered acropolis. The water was calm, and only the slight sound of tiny waves striking the boat could be heard, much different than the constant clanking and banging of hammers at the acropolis.

Relaxing, he felt the enormous burdens on him dissipate as he chewed on a fig and stared out across the Aegean Sea, making out only the silhouette of the island. After finishing the fig, he raised his cup of water and washed it down. He reached for the oar and continued paddling, reaching his destination fifteen minutes later.

Still in Lalyssos, Lykus had his hands full as talk of the new cuts spread like wildfire across the island. His soldiers stood face to face with an unruly crowd shouting profanities at them most of the day.

Lykus had arrested over thirty citizens in the small village and realized many more could follow. He ordered a dusk to dawn curfew as they became more and more disorderly and destructive. Citizens of every village on the island were in an uproar, many marching to the capital. Lykus sent half his men back to fortify the gates around the palace, becoming increasingly worried about His Magistrate, council, town managers, and Chares's safety. If the people were to breach the gates and infiltrate, anyone inside would be in tremendous danger.

Someone in the unruly crowd threw a rock that bounced off Lykus's breast plate. He glanced up at a man standing on a nearby mound behind the crowd. Charging into the mob, he pushed through as he chased the man. It wasn't long until Lykus caught up, dragging him to the ground by his hair. The man fell to his knees as Lykus delivered a blow to his head. He dragged the man back toward the soldiers before being surrounded by the pedestrians.

"Release him!" they shouted.

"Stand back!" said Lykus, wielding his sword.

Several men closed in on him, and Lykus released the man, lifting his sword in front of him. The man Lykus had been dragging stumbled to his feet and fled the area holding his head. A bystander reached for the sword, and Lykus drew it back and struck him in the side. He collapsed to the ground amid the horrified gasps of the crowd. Seconds later, several other men attacked, viciously swinging their fists and sticks at him. His soldiers closed in to protect their commander, and a violent clash ensued. Soldiers wielding their swords hacked at the men, and within a few minutes, the citizens of Lalyssos retreated farther into the square.

Lykus had taken several hits but had no serious injury. He glanced at the ground around him, seeing eight civilians lying motionless. Two of his men climbed to their feet checking their own injuries as the crowd continued shouting from afar. Several women sat nearby weeping at the horrific scene. Lykus figured the dead men on the ground were their fathers, sons, or husbands.

Lykus raised his sword. "To the palace," he shouted to his men.

As the soldiers dispersed, the citizens surrounded their dead. Men and women alike shouted at the soldiers, promising retribution and calling it an unprovoked attack.

Lykus climbed onto his cart and raced back to the capital to inform the council of what had taken place. Upon his return, he would shut down the city and put all available guards along the walls and gates surrounding the palace.

***

Leonidas sat in the courtyard, surprised by the sight of Lykus rushing toward him covered in blood. "What happened?" he asked, mouth hanging open.

"The people of Lalyssos attacked me and my men. Sir, the civil unrest is spreading village to village, and now many are marching here to the capital," explained Lykus.

"My god," said Leonidas, rising to his feet and placing his hand to his forehead.

"Your Magistrate, we must barricade the palace until this settles down."

"Yes, begin your preparations. I will summon the council and town officials immediately."

Lykus nodded. "We should also send word to Chares. His safety is also in danger."

"Yes, and please have a group of men protect the statue."

"Right away," replied Lykus, stepping away from the man.

Leonidas summoned his servants, ordering them to find the council and city managers and bring them to the palace at once. He sat in his chair, pressing his fingers to his temples and bowing his head.

Lykus climbed onto his cart and rode swiftly to the gate as the guards opened it. "Close the gates, and I want fifty men at every entrance around the palace," he shouted as he passed.

Already, a crowd had gathered and Lykus rode right through them. "Move!" he shouted, as they jumped out of his path.

Lykus raced to the acropolis and jumped from the cart upon arriving. He glanced in all directions, looking for Chares but not seeing him anywhere.

He walked to the men gathered by the pedestal. "Have you seen Chares?" he asked.

The men shook their head.

"Where is the foreman?"

They pointed toward the helepolis, which had been moved alongside the statue.

"You men are relieved for the day. Return home and stay inside. There's a dusk to dawn curfew in effect until further notice." He walked to another large group of men running the furnaces, casting the large plates of bronze. "You men arm yourselves with whatever you can find and protect the statue," said Lykus.

"What's going on?" asked one of the men.

"Just do what you are told. I want a hundred men here at all times. Protect your work," he shouted, turning on his heel and stepping toward the helepolis.

As he neared, the foreman emerged from the giant tower with a puzzled look on his face. "Why have the men stopped working?" he asked.

"Work is finished for the day. We have civil unrest spreading across the island," explained Lykus, wiping his brow. "Where is Chares?"

The man shrugged. "He took yesterday off but never showed up this morning," he replied.

Lykus rubbed his hand across his head. "Okay, have a hundred of your men protect the statue and send the rest home. I will need you and them out here all night. Understand?"

"Yes," replied the foreman.

"In the morning, I will return and let you know what our plan is from there," said Lykus. "If you see Chares, have him return to the palace immediately."

Lykus returned to his cart and rode to the western edge of the acropolis to look out across the water for Chares's skiff. He gazed in the area the two had been fishing several times but saw no sign of Chares or his boat. He cracked the rein and rushed back to the capital. Once arriving, he hurried to the harbor where many vessels were docked and being unloaded.

He looked around at the many ships, seeing two about to leave port. He climbed from his cart and raced along the pier, calling to the helmsman.

"Halt!" shouted Lykus, drawing the attention of many along the busy port. "I need two vessels to circle the island. We are looking for the skiff of the sculptor, Chares of Lindos," he said. He pointed to a couple helmsmen ready to leave port. "You and you," he said, pointing to each of them. "Let's go!" he ordered, walking the wooden plank and then stepping on board the nearest ship.

The slaves removed the ramps and untied the vessels, and the helmsman gave the order to row. Once outside the harbor, Lykus directed the ship that followed them to head the opposite way. He stepped toward the bow and stood on a platform, looking across the blue waters of the Aegean.

A little over an hour later, Lykus spotted something floating in the distance. It was out quite a bit farther than Chares would have usually taken his tiny vessel, but he decided to investigate anyway. Lykus glanced to the helmsman and signaled to his right.

"Starboard," shouted the helmsman as the ship turned.

As they neared, Lykus squinted, then dropped his jaw. "Fuck me," he whispered. "Halt!"

"Drag your oars," shouted the helmsman.

As the vessel drifted closer, Lykus leaned over the bow to confirm it was Chares's capsized skiff. He pulled off his armor and tunic and leaped into the water. He swam alongside Chares's boat, then dove before emerging under the vessel. He popped his head up and looked around. He saw ropes and a fishing pole floating nearby, but no Chares. He submerged and came out alongside the vessel.

Many men watched from the railing of the merchant ship as Lykus shook his head and raised his hand. "Toss me a rope," he instructed.

Moments later, a sailor appeared at the bow and slung an end of rope into the water.

Lykus gave a few kicks and grabbed the rope. He kicked his feet again several times before reaching the ill-fated vessel. He reached under the water with rope in hand and tied it off. He turned and swam back to the awaiting vessel as the men lowered a ladder for him to climb aboard. Lykus reached for the lower rung and ascended to the deck of the ship, then glanced at the helmsman.

"Return to port," he instructed.

Lykus then sat on the deck, elbows on his knees and face in his palms.

CHAPTER 29

ALMOST A WEEK SINCE LYKUS found Chares's capsized skiff a half mile from shore and after an extensive
search over several days by much of the island's fleet, Chares
was still missing. As news of the man's disappearance spread
across the island, so did a somber calmness. The uprising had
been quelled and construction resumed on *The Colossus*, now
headed by the sculptor Priamus.

Even though the search had been called off a couple days
before, Lykus could not help but stare out across the water
from the heights of the acropolis, hoping to spot the man.
He'd also commandeered Chares's skiff, using it to search the
shallows in hopes of finding his remains.

All he found was one of Chares's fishing poles washed up
on shore.

After waiting a week, and all the while keeping hope the man
would return, Leonidas ordered the servants to clear out his
room and prepare it for Priamus. The servants packed his belongings in baskets and placed them in a cart. He had guards

accompany them while they cleared the room, making sure nothing was stolen.

Leonidas instructed the guards to bring any money or valuables directly to him. Alyna had stayed at the palace for a few days after his disappearance and then came by several times over the rest of the week in hopes that Chares would return. The woman had wept many times as Leonidas did his best to comfort her. He decided to have the man's items delivered to her, as she'd been the only one outside of Lykus and the council who'd expressed any concern for his safety.

Clearly convinced of foul play in Chares's disappearance, Alyna shared a story with Leonidas about Zotikos. She informed him of a time a few years ago when Zotikos had approached her about abducting the man and holding him for ransom. She claimed to have informed Chares of the event, and he hadn't taken the man's threats seriously. Her strong suspicions that Zotikos was involved were made known to all who would listen. She also informed Leonidas of the cult that Zotikos and Pythia belonged to.

Giving plenty of details about their sadistic rituals, including the orgies involving many wives of the soldiers, she told him she had witnessed firsthand Zotikos penetrating many women. He had convinced them it was the will of the gods and would guarantee their husbands safety during the siege. In light of this information, Leonidas ordered Zotikos be arrested immediately, only to find out that he was already being held.

<hr>

Pythia arrived with Zoe at the jailhouse to meet Zotikos who was scheduled to be released at any time. Upon entering, a guard asked her business there.

"I am here for my husband, Zotikos," she replied.

"Wait here," instructed the guard as he left the room.

Pythia sat and waited as Zoe ran about the room and spun in circles. She gazed at the girl and smiled.

The door opened and in walked several men. She glanced up at them, raising her palms. "My husband?" she asked.

"He is under investigation and will not be released today."

"Excuse me?" replied Pythia, rising to her feet. "Investigation for what?"

"You name it," the man replied.

Another man stepped toward her and placed his hand on her shoulder. "If you don't mind following us, we have questions for you as well," he said.

Pythia drew her head back. "I *do* mind," she replied, twisting her shoulder from the man's grip.

The other guard subdued the woman as Zoe cried. "Let go of me!" she shouted, reaching for a man's neck and choking him.

They slammed her to the wall. "Calm down, ma'am. We just want to talk to you."

"Mama," cried Zoe, wedging herself between the guard and her mother.

Pythia drew deep breaths and seethed at the men around her.

They released their grip, and she quickly comforted her daughter. After holding Zoe for a few moments, she smiled. "Have a seat, sweetie. I will be right back," she said, then kissed the top of her daughter's head.

The men escorted her to a room where a table and a few chairs were placed. She sat, as a man found a seat across from her, with a pen and papyrus resting in front of him.

"Name?" the man asked.

"Pythia Bouras Galanis."

"Age?"

"Thirty-seven."

"Home?"

"Lindos."

"Are you the wife of Zotikos Galanis?" he asked.

"I am," she replied.

"Are you a member of the cult following the Telchines gods?"

Pythia stared at the man, clenching her jaw.

"Ma'am?"

"I am," she replied, curling her lip.

"At these gatherings, did you witness acts of the sexual nature being performed by your husband and its members?"

"Never," she replied, stoically staring the man in the eyes.

"Ma'am, let me remind you, your honesty on this matter would be appreciated. You are not on trial here," he said, raising his hands from the table.

"I told you, I have not seen any acts of the sexual nature during our meetings," she insisted.

"What were the ceremonies performed at the gatherings by the members and its leaders?"

"There were many prayers to the gods for the safe return of our men during the siege and the occasional sacrifice of a lamb to pay homage," she replied.

The man continued writing for several moments as Pythia looked around the room, before returning her gaze on him.

"Do you know the sculptor, Chares of Lindos?" he asked.

Pythia rolled her eyes. "Of course I do. He is my ex-husband."

"Is or *was?*" the man asked.

"You tell me," she answered.

"Did you and your husband ever discuss abducting or bringing harm to that man in any way?" he asked, dipping his pen in the ink.

Pythia's hands shook, and her eyebrows drew close.

"Ma'am, you seem distressed by the question."

"Of course I am. I deeply cared for Chares and have been quite upset about his recent disappearance," she replied, blinking her eyes repeatedly against the tears.

"I'll ask again."

"The answer is no," said Pythia through clenched teeth. "That is an absurd question."

The man finished writing and set the pen to the table. "Okay, you are free to go," he said, standing from his chair.

"And my husband?" she asked.

"He will remain here a few more days for further questioning. We have several witnesses and members we will be interviewing during that time," he said, stepping toward the door.

Pythia shook her head and stood. She followed the man to the front room where she was quickly greeted by Zoe with a hug.

"Come back in a few days. We will know more then," the man said, turning and closing the door behind him.

Pythia held Zoe's hand as they walked outside to the porch, tears streaming down the woman's cheeks.

A few days later, she returned and learned that Zotikos would be charged with several crimes against the people, including the abduction and bodily harm to the island's famous sculptor,

Chares of Lindos. After much persistence, the guards allowed Pythia to see her husband and led her through a corridor to a holding cell.

Zotikos quickly rose to his feet when she approached. He stepped toward her as the chains securing him to the floor pulled tight. Pythia instantly wept at the sight of him filthy and thin.

"Can I have a minute with my husband, please?" she asked the guard standing just behind her.

The man took several steps back but stayed within eyesight of her and Zotikos.

"My love," he said, raising his iron-clasped wrists.

Tears streamed down her cheeks. Her lips trembled as she whispered, "I love you."

"I love you too," he replied.

She wiped her cheek and leaned toward the gate. "Zotikos, tell me. Did you have anything to do with Chares's disappearance?" she asked.

He shook his head.

"Please, be honest with me," she pleaded.

"I swear I didn't, my love."

"Then what was the plan you were working on?"

"A natural healing saloni," he replied.

Pythia cocked her head. "A what?" Then she waved her hand to stop him before he explained. "It's not important. What's important is that you were not involved with his disappearance." She bit her nail in deep thought.

"How is Zoe?" asked Zotikos.

Pythia lowered her hand and smiled. "She is fine. She really misses you."

He sighed and gazed into Pythia's eyes.

"Don't worry, my love, I will get you out of here. I don't know how, but I will," she insisted.

Zotikos raised a brow. "False accusations and false gods are extraordinarily similar. Although both are without substance, they somehow survive in the hearts and minds of men," he exclaimed.

Pythia lowered her chin. "I love you and that beautiful mind of yours," she said with a fresh set of tears rolling down her cheeks. "And I am sorry about what I said about you and the one-winged bird. What you said was brilliant, and I am truly sorry."

Zotikos laughed, then coughed. "It's okay, my love. I know your heart and I know you love me more than anyone ever has or ever will."

She smiled until she heard footsteps approaching.

"Time to go," the guard insisted.

Pythia blew her husband a kiss before being directed out of the holding cell. Once entering the corridor, she turned to the man. "Has he been fed since he's been here?" she asked.

He shrugged.

"If I gather him a basket, can I give it to him?" she asked.

The man shook his head.

"I will give you five drachmas."

He held out his hand.

"Well, how about we wait until I return with the basket?" she said, curling her lip.

"You come back with anything in that basket except food, and I am going to punch you right there," the man said, pressing his finger to her nose.

Pythia smiled, then quickly lifted her chin, locking his finger between her teeth.

"Ouch, you bitch," said the man, pulling away when she loosened her bite and released his finger. "I will have you arrested," he said.

"Oh, come on. I'm sure it's been a while since you had any part of you inside a woman's mouth," she said before stepping away.

"You can forget about that deal with the basket," he said as she reached the door.

Pythia stopped and fixed her gaze on the man. "We'll see about that," she said, pushing the door open.

An hour later, Zotikos sat in his cell next to a basket Pythia had brought for him. He dipped the bread in his cup of wine, smiled at his wife, then raised the bread and took a large bite. "I love you," he mumbled with his mouth full.

She giggled. "I love you too."

"Will you two be quiet?" said the guard, grabbing her hips and pulling her tight to him.

Reaching between her legs, Pythia asked, "Are you sure it's in? I don't feel anything," followed by a chuckle.

"Hold still! I can handle this," he grumbled.

Pythia leaned across the table, resting her head on her hand as she kept her gaze fixed on Zotikos.

The man behind her continued rocking back and forth, drawing deep breaths, and moaning. "Ahh, you feel good," he said, increasing his speed.

Pythia rolled her eyes. "Are you almost done?" she asked, turning her head and glancing behind her.

"Yes, but it would be a lot quicker if you two would shut up so I can concentrate."

She faced Zotikos and smiled as he swallowed the last bite of bread.

CHAPTER 30

THE MOST ANTICIPATED TRIAL IN recent years had finally arrived. The accusations against Zotikos included everything from greed, sex, and murder. It was held outdoors, in the capital's square because the crowds that had gathered were too large to house inside.

Tension between the victims and the accused, the civilians and the soldiers, ran high. In light of recent violence, the capital remained heavily guarded by soldiers and hired security. Although not completely convinced that bringing the masses together was a good idea, Leonidas certainly was happy the people were focusing on something other than *The Colossus*.

The jury had been selected, and the trial would be overseen by His Magistrate himself. He as much as anybody wanted an explanation as to the disappearance of Chares. He hoped by the end of the trial he would know what fate had befallen the sculptor. Even though Leonidas was often frustrated with Chares, he truly missed him.

As the trial began, each side had a chance for opening statements. Zotikos, who had few people there in his support, took this opportunity to share his disapproval of his treatment and the false accusations against him, followed by a long rambling about the end of man and an all-powerful god they were yet to meet.

He stated, "Creation of gods is misguided confidence. The truth is, we have created a god for everything man sees and desires, but not everything man desires has god created, or sees to be the truth."

A low grumble befell the crowd.

"Shall we perish from all annals of history, or shall we forge a symbol of man so great, even the gods shall bow to it?" He glared at the crowd and the jurors, fixing his gaze on His Magistrate. "You will soon have your answer!" he shouted, pointing at the man.

"Enough!" yelled Leonidas, rising from his seat. "Silence him!"

"He will punish all of you!" bellowed Zotikos to the horrified crowd. "He will destroy your false gods and that tower of treachery on the acropolis!"

The crowd gasped.

The guards subdued the man, gagging him with a stone in his mouth and wrapping a strip of cloth around his head, then between his teeth and drawing it tight.

The man gagged, lowering his head and trying to push the stone from his mouth. He glanced over at Pythia who shook her head, obviously not amused.

As the trial continued, forty-six women gave statements about the ceremonies and their own personal encounters with Zotikos. Although many felt deceived, they all agreed everything they had done as a group was entirely for the victory over Demetrius and the safe return of their husbands. A few women also spoke of the storm that had destroyed many of the enemy's ships, giving full credit to Zotikos.

Others, who had provided large sums of money to the group, explained it was at their own free will that the money was given. Not one of the women providing statements remembered a single instance when Zotikos mentioned harming the sculptor Chares. The men who had participated in the ceremonies were not asked to speak. Most wanted to keep their identities hidden, fearing repercussions from the women's husbands.

So far, the case against the man was weak. But the two key witnesses, Alyna and Tanis, still hadn't given their testimony.

Tanis spoke first and explained how Zotikos had humiliated her during his first time at the meeting. She described him forcing her on a table and defiling her. She recounted in detail, each of the four times she was sodomized by the man and explained that he had frequently taken the money given to the group for his own personal use. She finished out by saying that Zotikos blamed Helios for the Macedonian siege of the island.

Quoting the man verbatim, she said, "Just as the sun god put the enemy in the womb of their mothers, he led them to our shores."

Many in the crowd grumbled and shouted at Zotikos, as Leonidas struggled to regain order. After a few minutes, the crowd settled down and Alyna stood. As she began her statement, many in the crowd reacted. She was the whistle blower and many praised her bravery, but there were others who detested her. Mainly people still active in the deities of the mother goddess, Axeirus, felt betrayed by Alyna.

Although never popular among the people, now the group became condemned by the masses after being associated with

Zotikos. Alyna explained her participation at the ceremonies had been limited, but the man had violated her many times. She'd only agreed to the wicked acts because he used her missing husband as leverage over her. Her most damning testimony came when she recounted the time Zotikos asked her to lead Chares to a remote part of the island, under the cover of darkness. There he would beat the man, take him to a secret location, and make demands in exchange for his safe release. The woman wept as she recalled the encounter.

Leonidas asked for the specifics of the demands.

"He wanted thirty thousand drachmas and vowed five thousand to be given to me," she replied.

"Was his wife Pythia present at any of your discussions with Zotikos about his desire to abduct the man?" he asked.

The woman looked at Pythia and nodded. "She was."

The crowd moaned.

"And is Pythia present here today? If so, can you point to her?"

"Right there," said Alyna, pointing at the woman.

"Let it be known the witness identified the wife of the accused, Pythia Bouras Galanis," he said, making notes on his ledger.

The last to speak was Pythia, and the crowd berated her as she testified.

"Enough!" shouted Leonidas. "Anymore outbursts and I will have the guards disperse the crowd." He looked over at Pythia. "Please, continue," he said, lifting his pen.

"You are so quick to condemn my husband, and for what? While many of you were away fighting, he did nothing but inspire hope and love and participate in many sacrifices to the gods. He certainly did not *blame the gods* as Tanis likes to say.

The membership swelled while he was leading the group." She looked at the many women seated around her who had given testimony. "None of you ever told anyone about what took place during our ceremonies…and why?" Pythia scowled at the many spectators before refocusing on the group of witnesses. "I will tell you why. Because you enjoyed it and you believed in it!" said a fiery Pythia, pointing a finger at them. "Even after your husbands returned, many of you still frequented the meetings, and yes, embraced all aspects of the ceremony with open arms…and *legs*."

"That will be enough, young lady," said Leonidas. "You may sit down."

Pythia glanced at the man before focusing her gaze on the crowd. "Oh, and about adducting my ex-husband? Who would pay for such a fool? Half of you would kill him yourself if you had a chance for destroying our economy and bankrupting the island."

"Sit down, now!" shouted Leonidas. "One more word and I will have you restrained!" He pointed at the woman, the blood racing to his head. He rubbed his face with his hand. "This hearing is adjourned. We will resume tomorrow morning."

He stood and clutched his ledger, walking briskly toward the capital and wanting nothing more than to relax with a cup of wine in the courtyard.

The next morning, the trial continued. The proceedings were short, and it was just before noon when Leonidas gave his final instructions to the jury before deliberation. They were granted use of a room in the palace while they mulled over the testimony of the witnesses.

Leonidas, the council, and several others strolled to the courtyard and had some wine. The decision on whether the man was guilty or innocent could take from hours to days. He remained disappointed that there wasn't hard evidence linking Zotikos directly to the disappearance of Chares.

An hour passed and a man entered the courtyard. "They have reached a verdict," he stated.

Leonidas tilted his head, surprised their decision came so quick. He set his cup down and walked to the square, taking his seat among the council members. The crowd remained in great anticipation, as did everyone else, awaiting the verdict. All rose from their seats when the jury returned and found their chairs.

Leonidas quieted the crowd, then returned to his seat and focused on the panel. "Have you reached a decision?" he asked.

"Yes, Your Magistrate," replied a man.

"And what did the jury find?" he asked.

"Guilty on all charges."

The news was followed by a tremendous roar of the crowd.

Leonidas let the crowd have this moment without quieting them. Instead, he made notes in his journal as he glanced at Pythia hunched over with her hands to her face. He tapped his fingers on the table and stood, raising his hand. "Quiet," he said, as the sound of the crowd dissipated. He returned to his seat, making a few more notes in his journal and then glanced toward the panel. "Has the jury decided on the man's sentence?"

"We have, Your Magistrate."

"And what will be his punishment?"

"Crucifixion," the man replied.

The crowd cheered once more.

Leonidas looked to his right at the council sitting next to him. "Do you accept the panel's ruling and sentence?" he asked.

The men nodded. "Aye."

Leonidas calmed the crowd. "The council has accepted the verdict and the sentence." He focused his gaze on the accused. "Zotikos Galanis, you are hereby convicted of the following crimes. Sodomy, manslaughter, abduction, exploitation, disorderly conduct, soliciting, coercion, sacrilege, and adultery. Your sentence is death by crucifixion. Judgment will be carried out in accordance with Rhodian law, on the first day of the new month. That will be the first of Carnieos. This court is adjourned." He stood as the crowd cheered.

Zotikos was led away by guards, struggling in the irons clamped to his ankles and wrists.

As Leonidas walked toward the palace, he stopped near two guards. "Will you make sure the wife of the condemned man makes it home safely?" he asked.

"Yes, Your Magistrate," they said, stepping toward the crowd.

CHAPTER 31

A FEW DAYS AFTER THE TRIAL, a defeated and emotionally exhausted Pythia forced herself out of bed and into the kitchen. She poured a glass of water for herself and Zoe who stood beside her. The woman had not eaten in days, and she struggled to provide for her daughter.

In less than a week's time, her husband would be crucified, and the mere thought of it made her ill. There was nothing worse than the thought of sitting by the post with her husband enduring such a slow, agonizing death. She remained convinced it was Alyna's testimony that had doomed the innocent man. Without her statement, he might have been found guilty of the smaller crimes, but it was from her tearful testimony that the conviction of murder found its footing, ultimately leading him to his final path at the top of the acropolis.

No matter how hard Pythia tried to withdraw from the thought, she knew the money she'd taken from Alyna had played a huge role in the woman's decision to testify against Zotikos. It was an obvious and simple way for her to hurt Pythia, and the woman had played it perfectly.

Pythia curled her lip at the thought of Tanis's fake crying

episodes while giving her statement. She was certain Tanis's betrayal of their long-standing friendship had something to do with Alyna. Pythia believed the woman had paid Tanis for her teary-eyed statement, further condemning Zotikos. Although Alyna had out foxed her this time, Pythia smiled, vowing to make it her life's work to destroy the woman.

She handed the cup to Zoe, and the girl took a drink. Looking at her daughter, she regretted that the child had not been outside in days. "Would you like to go for a walk?" she asked.

The girl smiled up at her. "Yes, mama," she replied.

Pythia took the cup from her hand and placed it on the table, then led the child through the courtyard only to see the old hag Medeia sitting there. She walked right past the woman without saying a word.

The two walked along the beach, Zoe stepping into the water and retreating when small waves closed in on her, washing over her feet. After a good hour, they strolled back in the direction of their home. After walking another half hour in the loose sand, Pythia's legs grew tired. She looked for a place to sit upon reaching the trail leading to her house, but the skiff she regularly sat on was gone. She glanced up and down the trail, making sure she hadn't passed it.

"Do you see the boat anywhere, sweetie?" she asked, as the girl glanced around and shook her head.

"No, Mama," Zoe replied.

Pythia continued investigating, but soon decided it had been stolen. "Damn," she said.

She glanced around once more, biting her nail, before leading Zoe the rest of the way home. She walked into the courtyard, relieved to see the old hag was gone. Once entering her home, she poured some water into a cup and handed it to Zoe. The girl took a drink and handed it back to her. Pythia raised the cup, and as she held it to her mouth, her eyes widened. She slammed the cup to the table, shattering it in her hand.

"That dirty bastard!"

Zoe jumped. "What is it Mama?" she asked, eyes wide.

Pythia grabbed her daughter's hand and raced for the door. "C'mon, I have to get to the capital."

A man riding a horse cart was passing by as she emerged from her home, and she quickly waved to him. "Go that way," she said, climbing up and pointing as Zoe hopped into the seat beside her.

The man curled his lip. "Excuse me?"

"Move!" shouted Pythia.

With an indignant sigh, the man adjusted his position in the seat and cracked the rein.

After a few minutes, Pythia pointed to a home on the right. "Stop right there and wait for me," she instructed.

After the cart came to a stop, she led Zoe to the door and knocked. She glanced back at the man in the cart, then to the door as it opened. It was Nysa, one of the few remaining friends she could trust.

"Hello, Pythia."

"I need you to watch Zoe for me."

The woman shook her head. "I am exhausted."

"Here," said Pythia, pushing Zoe forward. "I will be back in the morning," she stated, kissing Zoe on the forehead.

"Pythia, please," said Nysa, dropping her shoulders.

"I will pay you," she said, turning on her heel only to find the man and his cart pulling away.

She ran full speed after him, as he cracked the rein several times. She ran alongside, yelling at him to stop. As the cart distanced itself, she fell to the ground and rolled, lying motionless.

The cart came to a halt and the man climbed down and hurried toward her. He knelt and rolled her over, asking, "Are you okay?"

Pythia smacked the man in the face. "I told you to wait," she said, clenching her jaw and climbing to her feet.

The man stood back from the woman with his hand to his cheek.

"Now, let's go," she insisted, walking toward the wagon.

"Go where?" he asked, following behind her.

"The palace."

"What?" he said, stopping and putting his hand to his hip.

Pythia faced the man, stepping toward him. He hurried to the wagon and into the seat as she climbed up, sitting beside him.

"My wife told me you were crazy," he said, cracking the rein.

"Egina said that?" asked Pythia, adjusting her chiton to wipe the dirt from it.

He nodded.

"Make sure you tell that lupa I said hello," she replied with a smirk.

The man exhaled, then focused on the road ahead. The two didn't say another word the rest of the way.

Upon reaching the capital, the man brought the wagon to a stop.

Pythia tilted her head and blinked repeatedly. "Thank you," she said, beaming at the man. She held out a drachma with a smile and said, "For your trouble." But the smile dissipated from her face before she climbed down.

The man smacked the rein and glanced over at her. "I am telling Egina," he said, raising his brow.

Pythia made a face of fear and began shaking her hands, then spit toward the man and marched toward the gate securing the palace.

A man staggering along the street in filthy clothes and obviously intoxicated gasped upon seeing her. "How much for a lick and a stick?" he asked.

"Excuse me?" replied Pythia, glaring at him.

"I heard all about those things your little group was doing," he insisted, slurring his words. "So how much?"

Pythia smirked. "You can't afford either," she said hastily. "Besides"—she stepped close to the man, putting her mouth to his ear—"I bet that little thing doesn't even work anymore."

She shoved the man, and he staggered backward and fell to the ground. She pointed and laughed, then continued toward the gate.

Two guards at the palace entrance glared at her.

"Instead of standing here twiddling your thumbs, why don't you arrest that drunk pervert?" she asked, walking past the men.

"What's your business?" asked a guard.

"It's my own," she replied, as she picked up her speed.

"Halt!" shouted the guards, both hurrying after her.

Pythia raced up the steps and thrust the door open. She followed a long corridor, running at full speed. The exhausted woman rounded a corner, opened a door, and stepped inside, quietly closing the door behind her. She heard the footsteps of the guards run by, then disappear.

She waited a moment, catching her breath, before slowly cracking the door open. Just as she thought the coast was clear, the door was abruptly pushed wide from the other side and a guard reached in and grabbed her by the arm. Pythia quit resisting and smiled at the men.

"I need to see His Magistrate. Can you take me to him?" she asked, raising her brows.

"Get out of there," said the man, pulling her arm. He led her down the hall from the direction she'd come.

"Are you taking me to him?" she asked.

The guard glanced at her and shook his head.

She sat on the floor, and they dragged her along as she hollered for help.

"Quiet," said the guard.

"What's going on here?" asked a man they encountered along the way.

"Don't know. She ran past us at the gate." The man knelt beside her and placed his hand to her chin, examining her face. "You are that fanatic's wife, Pythia. What are you doing causing all this commotion?" he asked.

"I need to talk to His Magistrate," she replied, still struggling to catch her breath.

"What about?"

"I have information that might be of interest to him," she answered, climbing to her feet.

"Why didn't you request his audience?"

"I don't have time to make an appointment," she replied.

"Well, he's in a meeting. You will have to come back," he said, fanning her away.

The guards reached for her arm, but she pulled away from their grip.

"It's about that bucket of rust on the acropolis."

The man's brow creased, and he stared at her momentarily, then exhaled forcefully. "Okay, I will take you to him. But if he declines to meet with you, you must leave immediately or be arrested," he explained, stepping away from the woman.

Pythia glanced at the guards with a smirk, correcting her chiton, then followed the man leading her to His Magistrate.

<hr>

Leonidas, Takis, Ares, Lykus, and Hermes, sat at a table discussing *The Colossus*. Priamus had taken over for Chares and seemed confident in his work, and the statue only required the arms and head to be attached. Even though Leonidas was happy with the speed of construction, it was still close to a year from completion.

The sculptor had assured them the best way to complete the head and arms would be on the ground and then raised into position. He was confident it would save on time and labor. As the men discussed the statue and the budget, there came a knock on the door.

"Yes," said Leonidas, still focused on his spreadsheet.

"Your Magistrate, there's a woman here to see you," the man said, cracking the door and peeking inside.

"Who?" asked Leonidas, raising a brow.

"Pythia, the wife of the condemned man, Zotikos."

Leonidas rolled his eyes. "We're busy," he said.

"I told her that, sir, but she has urgent information about *The Colossus*."

Leonidas sighed. "Okay, come in," he said.

All eyes turned to the door.

In walked the tall, dark-haired woman in a slow sensual

stride. Finding a seat next to Lykus, she smiled at the man before turning her attention to Leonidas.

"Can I help you?" asked His Magistrate, figuring the woman had come there to beg for her husband's life.

"No, we can help each other," she replied, reaching for a cup and filling it from a vase resting nearby. She looked around the room and to the papyrus on the table. "So, this is where all the big decisions are made, huh?" she asked, raising the cup to her mouth.

Leonidas crossed his arms. "Ma'am, either state your business or leave."

Pythia took a quick drink and set the cup on the table. "I want to make a deal with you. I will give you valuable information in exchange for my husband's freedom."

"No deal," replied Leonidas. "Lykus, will you escort her from the premises."

Lykus rose from his chair and placed his hand on the woman's shoulder.

She looked up at him, then back to Leonidas. "You fool," she said, curling her lip. "Can't you see you've been swindled?"

"C'mon, let's go," said Lykus, reaching for the woman's arm.

"It's Chares, you imbeciles. He's alive," she said, pulling her arm from the man's grasp.

"What are you talking about?" asked Leonidas.

"Don't you think it's a little coincidental that the man disappeared right before the completion of the statue?" she asked, raising her palms.

"What coincidence? Why would he want to disappear before seeing his finished work?"

"Because he knew he built a piece of crap," she replied.

Leonidas clenched his jaw and shook his head. "You know, I have honestly had enough of you and that maniac husband of yours."

"Hear me out," she insisted. "You found his boat floating in the Aegean, right?"

Leonidas creased his brow. "Lykus, please," he said, motioning to the door.

"Wait," she said, pulling away from the man again. "He had two boats. The man took both boats out to sea and abandoned one of them. Also, the day he went missing, there was a storm that afternoon. He waited for the perfect day and faked his own death." She then raised her palms. "Seriously, why in the world would he go fishing the day of a storm?"

"Okay, Pythia," said Leonidas. "I will entertain your non-sensical twaddle. Let's say the man faked his death. What would be the reason to do that? He wasn't running or hiding from someone. He's no criminal like Zotikos. He was quite the opposite. Hardworking, well off, with celebrity status around the island. I believe you are hatching these falsehoods to convince us Zotikos had nothing to do with Chares's disappearance." He chuckled. "I assure you, ma'am, it won't work."

"Woman, I suggest you go home and hope you're not arrested for your own contribution to the man's disappearance," said Takis, pointing at the door.

Pythia firmed her chin. "Are you convicting me prior to having my day before the jury?" she asked, glaring at the man.

Leonidas raised his hand. "Hold on now." He looked over at the woman. "We have heard what you have to say. Now please, leave us. We have urgent matters to discuss."

She shook her head. "Then explain the missing boat to me."

"Probably stolen," said Ares.

"Don't you see, there must have been a problem with the statue," she said, leaning over the table toward His Magistrate. "I imagine either he was way over budget, or you cut his wages, or both? Whatever it was, it had something to do with that statue," she insisted.

"Maybe he did it to get your husband arrested?" asked Takis, chuckling. "Maybe after Zotikos is dead, he will show up here on a ship and say he was stranded at sea for six months?"

Pythia placed her hand to her chin. "Yeah, that could be part of it as well," she said, nodding.

"I'm sorry, Pythia. As entertaining as this has been, it's time to go," said Leonidas, nodding to Lykus.

The woman sucked her teeth, fixing her gaze on Leonidas. "Your Magistrate, my husband was convicted of many crimes and will do his time for them, but a murderer he is not. If we prove Chares is alive, regardless of his motivations for faking his death, my husband's crucifixion will be rescinded." She smacked her hand to the table, before bowing her head.

"Even if what you are saying is true, where would we look for him?" asked Ares.

Pythia looked up at the man. "I know exactly where he will be," she replied.

"Where?" asked the councilman.

"Argos."

"Why Argos?" asked Lykus.

She looked up at the man standing beside her. "That's where he went to school to learn how to sculpt. He lived there for eight years."

Leonidas exhaled forcefully. "Will you stop feeding into

this woman's preposterous speculations?" he asked, glancing around the table, his brow creased.

"Let me ask you something, Your Magistrate," she said, facing him. "If you were hired to do a job and couldn't finish it because it was faulty or the funds were gone, but you had already been paid a fortune, what would you do? Would you continue working on it for little or no money? Or would you take the money and disappear?" she asked, then raised her finger. "Let me ask you something else. You know exactly how much you paid Chares the last ten years. How much money did you find in his room after he went missing?"

"C'mon, it's time to go," said Lykus, placing his hand on her arm.

Leonidas leaned back in his chair and rubbed his hand across his beard. Then he raised his hand to Lykus, still standing next to the woman. "If, and I mean *if*—he pointed to the woman—"I order a stay on his sentence while I send men looking for Chares around Argos, and *if* he is indeed found, we will consider your husband's time as *served*. But you and him will both be exiled and never allowed to return." He tilted his head. "If he is not found, your husbands crucifixion will be carried out immediately. And regardless of what the jury finds with your involvement, you will face your punishment and be exiled alone." He tapped his finger against his arm rest. "As for the rest of it, that's our business and nothing to do with you, understand?" He pointed at the woman again. "If I hear one person mentioning that Chares is alive and well, living in Argos, the deal is off and your husband dies. Understand?"

Pythia nodded. "I haven't told a single soul. No one even knows the boat is missing or the fact that he had another boat. The only persons that know about this are in this room." She placed her hand to her heart. "I promise you. Please, let us not allow an innocent man to die over another man's greed and betrayal of the generous people of Rhodes. The people have suffered greatly because of his scheming."

Leonidas raised his hand. "Okay, enough. It's agreed," he said, fanning her away.

Pythia clamped her hands in front of her chest, then covered her face with her hand, drawing deep breaths and moaning.

Lykus, who stood closest to her, glanced at the magistrate, who shrugged. He gently helped the woman out of her seat, and she wrapped her arms around him. Lykus patted her on the back.

"C'mon, we have to go," he said, slowly pulling away from her.

She looked at the man with tears rolling down her cheek. "You're handsome," she said, swiping her finger across the tip of his nose. She giggled, drawing sporadic breaths, and looked around at the men still seated at the table. "Thank you for your time, gentlemen. I'll show myself out." The woman left the room, closing the door behind her.

Leonidas shook his head. "My goodness, what can you say to all that?" he asked.

"I think she's just buying more time for her husband," said Takis.

Ares nodded. "Yeah, you are probably right."

Leonidas fixed his gaze on Lykus, who appeared in deep thought and still had not taken his seat. "What about you, handsome man?" he asked. "You spent more time with Chares than anyone."

Lykus looked to the floor, rubbing his chin. "I truly don't

know," he said, finding his seat. "There is a possibility that he couldn't handle the pressure placed on him. Not to mention the enormous pay cuts. The whole island plunged into chaos over his statue and its financial strain." Lykus shrugged. "I just don't know, Your Magistrate."

Ares cleared his throat. "The woman asked about the money left in his room after he disappeared. Was it what you would have expected from a man of his salary?" he asked.

Leonidas shook his head. "No, but he was extremely generous to the ladies. Let us not forget how much he paid for Selene's freedom." He reached for his cup of wine. "Well, gentlemen, I guess this means you are heading to Argos in the next few days," he stated, glancing at his commanders.

"I'll go," said Lykus.

"No, I'd rather you both went. You will cover more ground that way," replied the magistrate, leaning back in his chair. "Remember, no one knows about this secret mission."

"How will you explain to the people why Zotikos's sentence has been postponed?" asked the councilman.

Leonidas raised his cup. "I will think of something," he replied, looking toward the ceiling.

CHAPTER 32

A FTER TEN DAYS AT SEA on a merchant ship, Ares and Lykus arrived at the seaport town of Nauplia, one of the many ports Rhodian vessels frequented, three miles south of Argos. The men had brought two horses and carts for faster traveling once they reached land.

It had been agreed that Ares would search the heart of the city while Lykus searched the outskirts of town and surrounding villages. Traveling the short distance from Nauplia to Argos, they planned on meeting back at the port in ten days with their findings. After riding together for a half hour, the men shook hands and headed separate ways.

Lykus had spent a great deal of time thinking about his companion of war and friend the last few days. While the others didn't believe the man had faked his own death, he was not entirely convinced. He had spent enough time with Chares at the construction site and fishing trips to witness the enormous pressure placed upon him. When the funds had dried up and its effect not only hit Chares but the entire island, Lykus knew he had felt responsible.

The original price tag of five hundred talents for *The Colos-*

sus had been lowered to three hundred, Leonidas and the council giving him no real option. *How could it be effectively reduced so much?* thought Lykus. He wondered if what Pythia had said were true, and *The Colossus* was a scam from the beginning. If so, Chares had known from the minute he agreed to build the giant statue that he would eventually have to disappear.

Even the boat bothered Lykus. *Why would the man buy a boat when the entire island remained under such financial pressure?*

He certainly knew the finances were evaporating, and instead of using his own money to help fund *The Colossus*, he'd bought a boat. It would only make sense that the boat had played a significant part in his scheme.

Lykus stopped at an agora on the outskirts of Argos and climbed from the cart. He walked along the many shops, perusing the items for sale. Stopping at a booth, Lykus purchased a vine of grapes. He carried them in his hand, popping one in his mouth from time to time as he strolled along the busy street. He noticed a man and woman standing by a table with many figurines and small statues for sale. Lykus approached the merchants and nodded to them.

"Hello, good sir," said the merchant, motioning to the crammed table of clay and marble collectibles. "Please, take a look."

Lykus examined the figurines for several moments and picked one up of a skiff resembling Chares's boat.

"Ah, a fine choice," the man said. "Made of white marble."

Lykus looked over the four-inch figurine. "How much?"

"Six drachmas."

Lykus shook his head and placed it back on the table.

"Today, we have a special going on, so five drachmas," said the merchant.

Lykus rubbed his chin. "Three."

The man stepped back, raising a brow and tapped on the table. "Okay, I will let it go for four." He pointed at the tiny ship. "That is a fine piece of art you are looking at there," said the man.

"Okay, fine, I will give you four, but I have a favor to ask," said Lykus.

The merchant looked at him closely. "Favor? Those are hard to come by these days."

"Yeah, maybe so, but this one is easy," explained Lykus.

The man handed the figurine to the woman beside him, and she began wrapping it. "Okay, what is it?" he asked.

"I am looking for somebody in the sculpting business. A man in his late thirties. He has brown hair, clean shaven, a smaller frame, and is a few handsbreadths shorter than myself. He can do figurines, but primarily specializes in busts and larger statues," said Lykus, looking around him. "He would be relatively new to this area, maybe arriving here in the last six months."

The man stroked his beard several times. "A few come to mind," replied the merchant. "But I am pretty sure I know the man you are looking for."

"You know where I can find him?"

"Yes, he lives not far from here. Just follow this street and you will pass right by him. You will know when you arrive. He has a sign out front advertising his bust work," he explained.

"What's his name?"

"Taras," the man replied.

Lykus nodded. If Chares did fake his death, he would

certainly be using an alias. He handed the man four drachmas, and the woman gave him the figurine neatly wrapped in a piece of cloth. After getting information on two other men the merchant suspected could be a match, Lykus walked to his cart, still finishing off the grapes he'd purchased. He set the statue in the seat next to him, lifted the rein, and with a quick snap of the wrist, got the horse and cart moving down the street again.

As Lykus rode along, his anticipation grew. He thought about the man's reaction upon opening the door, seeing his old commander and friend standing on his porch. Lykus chuckled just thinking about it.

After ten minutes, he saw a sign by the side of the street that read *Statues and Busts*. He stopped in front of the home and climbed from his cart, then walked up the gravel path and onto the porch. He knocked, then listened and soon heard footsteps approaching. The door cracked open and stopped as Lykus peered into the small opening.

"Hello?" he said.

The door opened fully and there stood a man with a full beard who was taller than himself. "Can I help you?" he asked.

"Are you Taras?" asked Lykus.

"Yes, that's me. Do I know you?"

Lykus shook his head. "No, I am sorry. I am looking for someone and a fool at the agora thought it might be you."

"Who are you looking for?' asked the man.

"A sculptor about this high, late thirties, clean shaven, would have only been here for six months or so," replied Lykus.

"I know someone who fits that description," said the man.

After getting the whereabouts and name of the sculptor, Lykus shook the man's hand and thanked him for his help. He rode almost an hour before reaching his next destination, but much like his first stop, the man wasn't Chares. This pattern continued for several days, leading Lykus back and forth from one side of the region to the other. After ten days, an exhausted Lykus arrived back in Nauplia to find an equally exhausted Ares.

Both men were ready to return home. As they waited to catch the next ship heading to Rhodes, they discussed their journey and all the people they'd met over the last week and a half.

"Whatcha got there?" asked Ares.

Lykus looked at the figurine sitting next to him wrapped in cloth. "Oh, just something I picked up at the agora," he replied.

Ares nodded, then gazed out across the harbor. "Looks as if the councilman was right. Pythia was just buying time for her husband."

"Yeah, it appears that way," replied Lykus, rubbing the back of his neck.

Lykus's mind raced back to the meeting where the distraught woman barged in to explain her theory of the man's disappearance. He thought about the woman in a different way, finding her quite attractive. Her flirtatious attitude and the tap to his nose with her finger brought a smile to his face. He found it surprising that Chares had ever landed such a woman, but not because he thought Chares was ugly. He had an average appearance, but he was not very masculine. Zotikos, on the other hand, was quite muscular and tall, close to his own height. Although Lykus considered Zotikos a raving lunatic, he considered the man handsome and could see her attraction to him.

He chuckled thinking about all the women who had given statements during the trial. *That man has had a lot of fýlo.*

Ares faced him. "What's so funny?" he asked.

"Eh, nothing. Just thinking about everything," replied Lykus.

He thought about Pythia again, then shook his head to get the woman from his mind. Again, wondering how Chares landed the woman, he couldn't see it. However, Chares had gotten Selene, who was also quite beautiful.

"Selene," said Lykus under his breath.

"Did you say something?" asked Ares.

"No, just talking to myself," replied Lykus, placing his hand to his chin. *What's the name of the town that woman was from?* He turned to the man beside him. "There's one more place I'd like to search," he said.

"Where?" asked the man.

"Cyprus."

Ares drew a deep breath. "Lykus, I am exhausted by this search," he said, raising his hands from his lap.

"Fear not, old friend. I will go on my own. Advise His Magistrate to wait for my return before carrying out the man's sentence," said Lykus, placing his hand to the man's shoulder.

A couple of hours later, a ship leaving for Rhodes was boarded by Ares and his horse cart. Lykus stood on the dock and waved as the ship slowly faded into the distance.

Lykus had misled the man about his destination. He

planned on sailing for the port town of Sidon, on the eastern shore of the Mediterranean. The reason behind his deception wasn't exactly clear to him. However, before his journey ended, he felt sure it would make perfect sense.

CHAPTER 33

BY THREE MONTHS AFTER ARES returned without Lykus to the island of Rhodes, Leonidas had become rather impatient, as had the citizens wanting to see the condemned man's sentence carried out. He'd managed to buy more time, saying he received information of a man who had washed up on shore in Karpathos. With Ares and Lykus in route for Argos, the timeline worked near perfect. However, this extra stint by Lykus has pushed the timeline and the people's patience to the maximum. Now, he was questioned almost every day about who was found alive on the shore of the tiny island, just a mere thirty miles south of Rhodes.

Leonidas and Priamus sat in the courtyard discussing the progress of the statue. Priamus informed him that one arm was put in place that morning and the other would be raised the following week. The sculptor shared his ideas about the bowl to be used as a beacon for the many ships. He explained that changing the original design slightly would make cleaning and refilling mush easier. Leonidas agreed.

As they continued their discussion, Takis entered the courtyard in quite a hurry. "Your Magistrate, Lykus has returned," he said with great excitement.

"Excuse me, Priamus," said Leonidas, rising from his seat and walking toward the door.

Leonidas and the councilman approached the gate leading to the harbor, and the guards opened it as they neared. They continued through the gate following a path to the docks. Moments later, they spotted Lykus walking in their direction. The magistrate looked past the man for Chares but saw no one.

"Hello, Lykus. Good to see you have returned safely," said Leonidas, waving to the battalion leader.

"Good to be home, Your Magistrate," he replied.

"Well, any luck?" he asked.

The man sighed and shook his head. "Nothing."

Leonidas shrugged. "Well, that's it then," he said, and the group turned toward the palace.

"I knew the woman was lying to us," said Takis. "She was just buying more time for her husband."

Leonidas nodded. "Well, the time is up."

"We should have her reimburse us for our trouble," added Takis.

"It wasn't much trouble," said Lykus. "At least now we can safely say Chares is dead."

"Inform the council and prison guards that the sentence will be carried out on the first of the month," said Leonidas to Takis.

Lykus rubbed the back of his neck, catching the attention of Leonidas.

"What is it, Lykus?"

"Oh, nothing. Just feel a little bad for the woman," he replied with a shrug.

Leonidas smirked, looking at the man from the corner of his eye. "Your sympathies wouldn't have anything to do with her calling you handsome, would it?" he asked, followed by a chuckle.

Lykus laughed. "No, they are more sincere than that."

Leonidas raised his palms. "She has no one to blame but herself. She is the architect of this mess. After Zotikos is crucified, she will be banished from the island," he explained, looking over at the man. "As we agreed."

Commander Ares stood near the gate leading to the harbor and waved upon seeing Lykus. He stepped close and rested his hand on Lykus's shoulder. "How was your trip to Cyprus?" he asked.

Lykus grinned. "Hardly a trip. More like an unpleasant journey," he replied.

The men walked together through the gate, in the direction of the palace.

"Where's your figurine?" Ares asked.

"My what?" replied Lykus, drawing in his chin.

"The little statue you picked up in Argos?"

Lykus examined the man, then shrugged. "I got tired of carrying it, so I gave it away."

The man smiled at Lykus, then wiped his brow. "Yeah, I guess after a few months it would get rather annoying carrying that thing around." Ares then focused on His Magistrate. "Well, I suppose the sentence will be carried out after all."

Leonidas tilted his head. "Yes, and I suppose we will all be relieved when it's done," he stated, glancing over at Lykus. "I am sure you are exhausted. We will talk more about your unpleasant journey tomorrow," he said, stepping away as the three men followed him up the steps to the palace.

Early the next morning, Lykus went atop the acropolis to see the progress made on *The Colossus*. He remembered seeing the headless statue towering above the island while sailing home from Sidon. It brought a large smile to his face as the many men on the vessel stared in awe of its beauty and enormous size.

As he arrived on the plateau, the men made final preparations to the enormous head with the face of the sun god Helios and a crown of points representing the rays of the sun. Lykus looked up at the statue towering above him and wished his friend Chares were there to see it.

The spear *The Colossus* held was most impressive, being the highest point and reminding him of the day Chares first got his armor and spear. It always made Lykus smile thinking of the early days of the battle when Chares appeared unfit to be a soldier, yet the man stood alongside him during the most intense fighting and somehow survived. It was his character and part of his charm. Being the underdog but still coming out on top.

Lykus stared up at the statue for a few more moments before walking back to his cart. He climbed up and smacked the rein, heading down the long, rocky slope back to the capital. As he approached the gate, he swiftly turned his cart onto the road leading to Lindos.

An urge overcame him, and he decided to tell Pythia personally of his search for Chares.

Pythia sat at the table having prepared a plate for her and Zoe when a knock at the door startled her. She rose from her seat and stepped toward it. She'd had an argument with Alyna the days before about the missing money from her home and the payment required by the convicted to the informant. A custom of the Rhodians to get crimes reported to authorities. Pythia had condemned any possibility of payments, and Alyna threatened to report her. She assumed the knock at the door was something pertaining to the confrontation, but when she opened it, she saw the handsome soldier she'd met at the palace.

Her smile widened, confident the man brought information about her missing ex-husband. "Hello, please come in," she said, opening the door farther and motioning him inside.

"I apologize for coming over unannounced. I wanted to talk to you directly," he said, stepping inside the home.

"No trouble at all. We are just sitting down for lunch. Please join us," she said, leading him to the kitchen.

Lykus looked around the place, seemingly interested in her home. He found his seat as Pythia placed a bowl in front of him filled with grapes and a plate with a piece of fish and figs.

"Is the search still ongoing?" she asked.

Lykus bit his lip.

Pythia's breath subsided as she stared at the man.

"The search is over, Pythia," he said, raising his hand from the table.

She reached for her chair and found a seat next to him, staring aimlessly at the floor.

The man reached over and placed his hand to her shoulder. "I am sorry, but he was nowhere to be found," he said, bowing his head.

"Did you search the area thoroughly?" she asked.

"Yes, I even sailed to other nearby regions and searched there. I must have met a hundred sculptors during my campaign. Who would have thought there would be so many?"

She smiled slightly, a tear rolling down her cheek. "When is the sentence to be carried out?" she asked.

"Ten days," replied Lykus.

She tilted her head back and drew a deep breath. She leaned forward, pressing her hands against her face.

Lykus brushed his palm across her back several times.

"I am so stupid," she stated. She sat up and wiped tears from her face. "Now not only will my husband be crucified, but I have to leave the island."

Zoe came to her mother's side and wrapped her arms around her. Pythia held her close as they both wept. Lykus reached over and placed his hand on Pythia's shoulder, and she released her grip from her daughter. She wiped her cheek and smiled at the man, then extended her hand across the table, placing it upon his.

———————————➤

People from every village on the island lined the road leading up to the acropolis. The landscape around the plateau had changed substantially since the start of *The Colossus*. There were many new homes and shops constructed around the bottom of the acropolis on either side. Everyone wanted to be close to the massive statue.

The Colossus neared completion and the shining bronze statue brought tremendous pride to every man and woman of the island. However, today wasn't a celebration of the enormous statue.

The crucifixion of Zotikos was underway. The man would soon be walking this road, carrying his own stauros up the hill, to the northwestern portion of the acropolis. Dating back many centuries, they'd carried out their punishment for the condemned at this site, located a couple hundred yards from *The Colossus*.

Following the condemned man would be Lykus, Leonidas, Takis, and Ares, among several soldiers and guards. Also following close behind would be Pythia and several others who still cared for the man.

Pythia waited by the door of a holding cell as they opened the gate. She stood back as the guards unshackled him. He was clean this time, having been recently bathed. He was extremely thin and obviously weak as he struggled to walk.

"Take a few minutes, ma'am," said one of the guards.

Pythia raced to the man, wrapping her arms around him tightly.

"My love," he said, wrapping his arms around her.

They both wept and held each other close without saying a word.

After a few minutes, the guard tapped her shoulder. "It's time," he said.

Pythia placed her hands to her husband's face and kissed him passionately. The guard pulled her arm until she took a step back.

"I am sorry, my love. I did everything I could," she exclaimed through her sobs.

Zotikos placed his hand to her head. "Has there ever been a man who wanted nothing more than the love of his wife? I assure you, my love, I will die a happy man and wanting nothing more," he said as the guards pulled him along toward the front entrance.

The tears flowed down her face as she fell to the floor gripping the iron bars.

Lykus appeared beside her, extending his hand. "Come, Pythia," he said.

She pulled herself to her feet, and the two walked side by side out the front door to the street.

The guards fastened the stauros to the man using shackles around his wrists and neck. Zotikos grimaced in pain as they fastened them tight. The long wooden beam put tremendous weight on his weak legs, making them tremble.

"Move!" shouted the guard repeatedly as the caravan traveled down the street, through the square, and approached the road leading to the peak of the acropolis.

Zotikos hunched his back to keep the large pole from dragging behind him.

Pythia followed a good dozen cubits behind her husband, Lykus and Ares by her side. Positioned between her and Zotikos was the magistrate and Takis.

Once turning the corner out of town, a loud roar arose from the mass of people gathered on both sides. As they journeyed up the hill, many yelled at Zotikos while some threw stones. The guards moved closer to him to deter any further rock throwing. Women seethed at Pythia as she passed.

One woman yelled to her, "Helios be praised! Finally there is justice!"

Pythia glanced at the woman, and it was none other than her neighbor, Medeia. After a few more moments of walking, another woman emerged from the crowd. That time, she saw Egina.

"You're a filthy whore," the woman shouted, spitting at her. "Stay away from my husband!"

Pythia remained unmoved by the women and their words. She focused on her husband, who struggled with each step. The guards pushed and pulled him along until finally reaching the top of the acropolis. The crowd followed behind the caravan as they moved past *The Colossus* and toward the site where Zotikos would be crucified.

The shouting and cheering intensified. About thirty cubits in front of the site stood a line of guards who allowed the caravan through but kept the crowd at bay.

Zotikos walked another ten cubits past the line of guards and collapsed on his back, lying on top the mast. Pythia moved quickly to his side as he squirmed and grimaced. She kissed his face and rubbed his chest.

"Move it!" shouted a guard, pulling the woman away.

Several men pushed on the stauros, sliding the base of it to the hole. The man lay on his back, breathing heavily as blood ran from his wrists and neck. They hammered a small board to the base to rest his feet, shackling them to the stauros as well. The guards lifted the top of the mast as it raised the man in the air. They walked their arms down it as the man continued to rise. The post slid into the hole, and the large jerking motion caused Zotikos to cry out in pain. The crowd cheered. The guards took smaller pieces of wood and hammered them in around the base to sturdy the stauros.

Pythia raced to her husband, reaching up to him as he fixed his gaze upon her. "My love," she cried.

Zotikos peered at her, then smiled. "Look across the water," he said.

She wiped her cheeks and turned.

"You see that vessel on the horizon? That ship carries the best of man," he said, as she nodded. "You see the other ship?"

Pythia nodded again.

"That one carries the worst of man," he then sighed. "Let's see which one makes it to port first."

Pythia closed her eyes. "I love you," she said, resting her back against the post and focusing on the ships as he'd asked.

CHAPTER 34

I T HAD BEEN SEVERAL DAYS since Zotikos was crucified on the acropolis, yet the man somehow hung on for
dear life. Most of the crowd lost interest in the condemned,
their attention shifting to *The Colossus* now just days from
completion. The road to the acropolis remained closed as the
final touches were performed. Only the workers and family of
the condemned man could pass the guarded entrance.

Pythia spent every day on the acropolis with Zotikos. The
only time she left the man's side was when she descended the
western edge of the acropolis to bathe and cool herself in the
sea.

The days were hot and the sun bright. Her husband's skin
turned dark red under the relentless sun. The soldiers raised
wet rags on their spears to the man's mouth several times a
day, giving him a much welcome drink of water. His chest was
covered with a mixture of dried and fresh blood dripping from
his neck.

Pythia and Zotikos talked for hours each day as he continued his philosophies. His resilience and strength were impressive to her and the guards around them, all equally surprised
the man still survived.

A few times a day, the guards would ask the man, "Mercy?" Every time, Zotikos shook his head.

<hr>

"We are in the final day of construction, and the man still breathes!" said Takis to Leonidas. His Magistrate stroked his beard as the councilman continued. "We should have the soldiers run a spear through him."

"He is barely alive," said the magistrate. "Most likely will be dead by sunrise."

"The first festival we have in over two years, the unveiling of *The Colossus*, and we have a nearly dead man staked up beside it?" said Takis, shaking his head.

"Who would have known the man would live so long?" asked Lykus.

"Unless the man begs for mercy, all we can do is wait," said Leonidas, shrugging. "The heart of the festival surrounds *The Colossus* over two hundred yards from him. I don't think anyone will really care if he is there or not."

"I say we throw him over the edge of the acropolis and be done with it," said the councilman.

Lykus stood. "Now that you've got me thinking about it, I will go check on the man," he said, stepping away.

"Check on him, or Pythia?" asked Leonidas.

Lykus laughed. "Still not letting that one go, are you?" he replied from a distance.

<hr>

The day of the festival arrived to celebrate the completion of *The Colossus* and honor their sun god, Helios. The areas around the statue were packed with people eating fresh fruit, fish, and figs, drinking wine and playing games. There were also many merchants, dancers, musicians, and performers and continuous plays that depicted the siege of Rhodes with Lykus and Ares as the heroes. They had plays about building *The Colossus*, involving a young man named Chares and his extraordinary dream leading him to build something so great, the entire world would be inspired by it.

It was a perfect day with the sun shining and a cool breeze rising off the Aegean. The citizens of Rhodes who had suffered a year-long siege followed by a ten-year recession had finally arrived on the other side. The constant demand of men and materials required during the construction of the statue was over. Now, thousands of people from every corner of the world would flock to their island to see the magnificent structure.

On the far side of the acropolis sat Pythia at the feet of her dying husband, and next to her, two guards and Lykus, who had brought the woman grapes, water, and wine from the festival still underway. A half hour from sunset, Pythia sat talking to her husband like she had every other day.

That day, his words came much slower and his responses much shorter. Zotikos spoke about the festival, doing his best to look in its direction. Pythia talked about their daughter who she hadn't seen in several weeks.

Zotikos said, "She is beautiful, like her mother."

Pythia smiled, glancing up at the man smiling down at her.

Over the next hour as their conversation continued, Zotikos responded less and less to her words, until finally, there was no response at all.

Lykus stood near as the woman rose from the ground, raising her hands to the man's feet. Tears rolled down her cheeks as she gazed up at her husband. Lykus turned the woman away as two guards approached, running their spears into his abdomen. They reached for the lower part of the mast as Lykus turned her away again. The men pulled up, and Zotikos's lifeless body tumbled to the ground with a loud thud.

Lykus glanced over at the man and his contorted arm making a gruesome sight. "C'mon," he said to Pythia. "He's gone."

Moments later, he felt a trembling below his feet. He stopped and glanced back at the guards, thinking they'd dropped the stauros to the ground. They looked back at him, equally puzzled. He felt it again and focused on the ground, then to Pythia. Another large shudder came as she reached for him.

"It's an earthquake," he said.

The guards moved closer and stood alongside them. Moments later, there came the largest tremor yet, and this one struck fear into the eyes of Pythia. They heard screams in the distance. Lykus turned toward the cries and saw the arm of *The Colossus* hanging and then falling to the ground, crashing into the stage and audience alike.

Lykus released Pythia and darted toward the chaos. The loud screeching of metal twisting and the cracks of stone rupturing could be heard echoing across the acropolis. The arm holding the spear detached from the structure and with a loud snap, barreled toward the ground. The long spear broke in two and tumbled down the side of the acropolis, into several homes. The statue rocked back and forth as the masses ran from it, trampling one another.

There was a long eerie silence as Lykus came to a stop a little over sixty cubits from the statue. He stared up at the neck and watched it separating at the shoulder. Within seconds, the enormous head of Helios detached and crashed to the ground with such force, it shook like an aftershock of the earthquake. The torso leaned, snapping the structure below the knees, then collided into several homes as the hordes of frightens civilians ran down the hillside. One of the thighs separated from the torso, descending the hill behind them and crushing many more citizens.

Lykus ran to the aid of the hundreds injured amid the constant screams carrying across the acropolis. The stages and many booths erected for the event had been ignited by the cook fires, making the situation even more chaotic under a thick blanket of smoke. Lykus lifted a crying girl with a streak of blood running down her face and carried her to Pythia, still standing back a safe distance. She consoled the girl as best she could while Lykus ran back into the fray to find others.

Over the next hour, Lykus would help carry over fifty men, women, and children to safety, away from the raging fire. However, there were many lives lost, and it would take several days to gather all the bodies buried under the fallen giant.

On the third day of searching for the dead, Lykus and the men moved the bronze arm and hand that held the bowl. Crushed underneath it was his old friend, Leonidas.

CHAPTER 35

ON THE ONE-YEAR ANNIVERSARY OF the devastating collapse of *The Colossus*, the people of Rhodes gathered on the acropolis. The pieces of the statue had been gathered and placed alongside the pedestal. Even though the massive statue had collapsed, its story carried throughout the Mediterranean, bringing many visitors to the island. While earning a new name for the crumpled structure. *Collapsus*.

The people of Rhoades gathered, reminiscing on that tragic day. It was a somber affair, and many cried and lay flowers upon the pedestal. However, on the western side of the acropolis, another group gathered.

To the dissent of those mourning, this other group did not grieve the collapse of *The Colossus*. They celebrated. The group of Zotiacs, nearly three hundred in all, had spent eight days and nights on the acropolis, the same duration their leader had spent.

This conflict in ceremonies made the mourners uneasy, and several squabbles broke out between them. Many had asked the new magistrate to force the Zotiacs off the acropolis, but he refused. However, he did send guards to keep the groups separated.

After many months of planning, Alyna packed her bags to leave the island and its memories behind. She'd endured a year of ridicule from the followers of the cult she once belonged to. Even the women who gave statements condemning the crazed man, Zotikos, would no longer speak to her. Now deemed a martyr, his many followers were known as Zotiacs.

Of all her planning and preparations, this recent rise of the man's popularity among the people was most unexpected. His teaching on precipitates, circle of animals, and the celestial path of the sun were embraced across the region. Beloved by Helios, his crucifixion had angered the sun god so extensively that he brought down *The Colossus* in retribution. Eventually, there would be twelve signs accredited to him, each representing his strengths and wisdom, becoming known as the signs of the Zodiac.

Standing firm by their convictions when Ptolemy offered to rebuild the statue at no cost, the new magistrate declined, saying, "No god, empire, or statue will stand the test of time. All will be destroyed by the same principles on which they were created."

This was a verse well known among the followers of Zotikism. The same verse was later placed upon a statue the sculptor Priamus raised to honor the man. A pillar of marble with a man's torso, head, and arms. The man's face was that of Zotikos, and it depicted him extending his hands and reaching for the sun god Helios himself.

To make matters worse, Pythia married the new magistrate and war hero, Lykus. The man quickly pardoned Pythia for her part in Chares's disappearance, obstruction of justice, burglary, and her newest charge, public defecation after she sat near the edge of the public bath and relieved herself. Many women who had been bathing at the time were those who had testified against Zotikos.

Alayna did finally receive her retribution as a whistle blower of two hundred drachmas, less than half of what Pythia had stolen. It was no secret that Pythia blamed her for Zotikos's death. Now that Pythia was the wife of the most powerful man in Rhodes, Alyna's presence on the island was a dangerous endeavor.

After packing her last few items, she carried them outside and placed them in the wagon. Her daughters had both recently married and relocated to the island of Cyprus, making her decision to leave even easier. She climbed up, found her seat, and cracked the rein. Alyna planned on reaching her destination on the birthday of Apollo, seventh of Dalios.

Her excitement built as she reached the harbor in Lindos. She carried her few items to the docks and waited for her ship to finish preparing for its departure. An hour later, she climbed on board and the ship set sail for Cyprus. Arriving a week later, she thanked the helmsman and several sailors she'd gotten to know quite well during her travels.

After eating a quick bite, the woman took a cart to her oldest daughter's home just as nighttime fell over the city. She stayed with her daughters for a couple days and left early the following morning, keeping her hooded chiton raised as she journeyed back to the harbor. Sailing east for another three days, she finally reached the western region of Syria, gathered her things, and stepped off the ship. She arrived in Sidon on the seventh of Dalios, exactly as planned.

Walking along the dock, she carried the few items she'd brought with her. There were many people at the busy port, including slaves loading countless ships and groups of passengers waiting to board. She looked in all directions until her eyes lay upon a man sitting on a bench by the receiving dock.

Their eyes locked, and he raced toward her. She hardly recognized him with his thick beard. Once in his arms, he picked her up and spun her in circles. They kissed several times, celebrating her arrival.

After a few minutes of rejoicing, she complained briefly about the long trip, before asking, "Did you hear about *The Colossus?*"

"It's all they talked about here. Everywhere I went they asked, 'Did you hear about *The Colossus?*' " replied Chares, rolling his eyes.

"You always said it would fall."

"Yes, but I didn't think it would be that soon," he replied, scratching his beard. "C'mon, your new home is waiting." He wrapped his arm around her.

She laughed, knowing darn well what the man wanted.

His home sat a couple hundred yards from the harbor, and with Chares leading the woman at a quick pace, they were there in minutes. He opened the door, and she stepped inside.

"Wow, this is really nice," she said, feeling the back of her chiton raise up. She turned and faced the man. "What are you doing?" she asked, raising a brow.

"You know what I'm doing."

Suddenly the front door opened.

Startled, Alyna and Chares looked to the front door.

Alyna smiled widely upon seeing Selene, and the woman

rushed to her side. The two embraced and then retreated to the kline, holding hands, where they began a long conversation led by a series of questions from Selene about the island, Pythia, and Alyna's children. Chares tried to jump in the conversation several times but with little success.

Chares pressed his lips together, especially eager to be alone with Alyna, considering it had been well over a year since he'd been intimate with the woman. As the minutes passed, he realized the women would take their sweet time.

He sighed, glancing at a nearby table. He reached for the small soldier statue given to him by Selene during his time at the palace. He looked over the tiny statue before returning it to the table. Sitting next to it was a white marble figurine of a skiff given to him by his battalion leader and friend, Lykus. It was a near perfect replica of the boat he'd bought in Rhodes before that fateful morning...

THE END

If you have enjoyed reading this novel, please return to your favorite online retailer and leave a review. The author appreciates any and all feedback from readers.

From the blue waters of the Aegean arose the Colossus of Rhodes, constructed in honor of the island's creator and protector, Helios. The bronze crown upon the sun god's head towered above the island at seventy-six cubits high, becoming the tallest statue in the world while indubitably earning its place among the seven wonders. The sculptor who gained tremendous fame during its construction failed to see the enormous statue from the perspective of those who lay below it."

–Xenos Odious

HISTORICAL FUN FACTS REVEALED

ANCIENT GREECE PRODUCED POTTERY[1] OF many different styles and uses. The most common vessel was the *amphora*. This larger vase was often used for mixing wine and water. Another large vase used for storing fruits and grains was the *pithos*. A *kylix* was a broad, two-handled shallow cup used for drinking, often decorated with scenes of celebration. The *lekanis*, the gift Chares gave Alyna, was a lidded bowl typically decorated with flowers and used for ceremonies such as weddings. Typically between 8 to 10 inches in diameter, the *lekanis* was used for storing jewelry, perfume, and cosmetics.

From 900 BC to the end of the classical period of 400 BC, Athens produced some of the finest and most sought-after pottery around the Mediterranean Sea. These highly decorated vases and vessels often depicted their gods, athletes, and ceremonies such as weddings and funerals. The crafting style known as black-figure, red-figure, and white ground was left behind during the time of Alexander the Great[2]. As a result,

1   https://www.worldhistory.org/Greek_Pottery/
2   https://en.wikipedia.org/wiki/Alexander_the_great

Ancient Greece lost its role as the largest producer of pottery after adopting the far less popular West Slope ware[3].

Gods of ancient Greece were as stupendous as they were numerous. The Telchines gods[4] referred to in *Chares and the Colossus* originated on the island of Rhodes. In Greek mythology, these gods were nine children of the sea-god Pontos and the great mother Gaia. The Telchines were sea-god magicians and gifted craftsman responsible for constructing the sickle of Kronos and the trident of Poseidon. After their rituals began killing the sea animals and aquatic plants, Apollo, Zeus, and Poseidon destroyed them during the 10-year battle known as the Titan Wars[5].

Ancient Macedonian weapons during the time of Alexander the Great were far superior to any neighboring force. Before then, cities were easily defended behind the surrounding walls. Alexander's array of ballistae[6] and siege towers[7] gave the Macedonians a huge advantage as their enemies could no longer safely hide behind these barriers. Alexander was also the first to use ballistae on open battlefields. Along with his archer and cavalry corps, enemies were easily overrun. Following Alexander's lead, Demetrius and his massive helepolis[8] used during the battle of Rhodes earned him the namesake of "the besieger[9]."

Rhodes was a democratic city-state, and the origins of democracy have been traced back to Athens during the classical

3   https://en.wikipedia.org/wiki/West_Slope_Ware
4   https://en.wikipedia.org/wiki/Telchines
5   https://en.wikipedia.org/wiki/Titanomachy
6   https://en.wikipedia.org/wiki/Ballista
7   https://en.wikipedia.org/wiki/Siege_tower
8   https://en.wikipedia.org/wiki/Helepolis
9   https://en.wikipedia.org/wiki/Demetrius_I_of_Macedon

period of 500 BC. Their democracy existed for roughly 180 years until being abolished by Alexander.

During the battle of Rhodes, the most common warships were the bireme, trireme, and quadrireme. However, an ancient arms race soon ensued that prompted the making of even bigger warships, including the quinquereme, which required 300 rowers. The largest vessel of the time was an octareme ship known as the *Leontophoros* (Lion-Bearer)[10]. It's believed the ship was constructed for Demetrius but later fell into the hands of Ptolemy II. This massive vessel of over 300 feet in length was described by the Greek historian Memnon[11] when he wrote:

"There was one eight (octareme), which was called *Leontophoros*, remarkable for its size and beauty. In this ship while there were a hundred men rowing each file so that there were eight hundred men from each side, from both sides there were one thousand six hundred oarsmen. Those who fought from the deck were one thousand two hundred. And there were two helmsmen."[12]

Was Alexander the Great Greek or Macedonian? There is still plenty of debate on this subject. Pella, the capital of Macedonia[13] and the city of Alexander's birth, is in the northern region of ancient Greece and, in these modern times, still sits within its borders. In the book *Chares and the Colossus*, it refers to the attacking army as Macedonian and rightly so. Even though Alexander the Great is often classified as Greek, the Greeks and Macedonians were certainly two different peoples. Also, Greece was viewed as a conquered neighbor

10   https://en.wikipedia.org/wiki/Leontophoros
11   https://en.wikipedia.org/wiki/Memnon_of_Heraclea
12   http://www.attalus.org/translate/memnon1.html
13   https://en.wikipedia.org/wiki/Macedon

of Macedonia, although treated favorably compared to other defeated nations. With that said, the Macedonian armies were comprised of many different forces gathered across the Aegean, which included soldiers of city-states or barbarian tribes allied with Macedonia and many hired forces such as mercenaries and soldiers of Greek origins. In some battles conducted by Alexander, only half of his army would be from within the borders of Macedonia. Even the protection of the name Macedonia carried forward into recent times. In 1991, the country of Macedonia gained independence, creating instant outrage from Greece. So much so the country vehemently opposed the new republic from joining NATO or the European Union. It wasn't until 2019 and the passage of the Prespa Agreement[14] that the two nations finally settled their dispute, resulting in the country's name being changed from *Macedonia* to the *Republic of North Macedonia*.[15]

Alexander was a pupil of the philosopher Aristotle[16], hired by his father as his private tutor. It was during his three-year studies with Aristotle that Alexander found his passion for science, medicine, and botany. Alexander not only had a love for power and military might, but he also enjoyed music and often played the lyre[17].

Although much of *Chares and the Colossus* is fiction, the Seige of Rhodes battle depicted herein is historically accurate. For a short documentary covering this battle, I would encourage the reader to visit https://youtu.be/IVxIJBshYM0 and watch the short video titled *Diadochi Wars: The Siege of Rhodes*.

---

14   https://en.wikipedia.org/wiki/Prespa_agreement
15   https://en.wikipedia.org/wiki/North_Macedonia
16   https://en.wikipedia.org/wiki/Aristotle
17   https://en.wikipedia.org/wiki/Lyre

ABOUT THE AUTHOR

Xenos Odious resides in the state of Michigan not far from the great Gitchi-Gami. Odious is a firm believer that any book that covers the history of the human race is most important. Not only for second guessing our every step, but also so we are not horrified by the next dreadful chapter.